ALSO BY

RAPHAËL JERUSALMY

Saving Mozart

THE BROTHERHOOD
OF BOOK HUNTERS

Raphaël Jerusalmy

THE BROTHERHOOD
OF BOOK HUNTERS

*Translated from the French
by Howard Curtis*

Europa
editions

Europa Editions
214 West 29th Street
New York, N.Y. 10001
www.europaeditions.com
info@europaeditions.com

Translation by Howard Curtis
Original title: *La confrérie des chasseurs de livres*
Translation copyright © 2014 by Europa Editions

Library of Congress Cataloging in Publication Data is available
ISBN 978-1-60945-230-8

Jerusalmy, Raphaël
The Brotherhood of Book Hunters

Book design by Emanuele Ragnisco
www.mekkanografici.com

Prepress by Grafica Punto Print – Rome

Printed in the USA

For Sharon, my desert rose . . .

. . . written poetry is merely a milestone,
a way station, in the huge field
of activity encompassed
by the life of the poet.
—TRISTAN TZARA,
Introduction to *The Testament*
by François Villon (Audun, 1949).

THE BROTHERHOOD
OF BOOK HUNTERS

Born at the end of the Middle Ages, François Villon is the first modern poet. He is the author of the famous *Ballad of the Hanged* and *Ballad of Dead Ladies*. But Villon was also a notorious brigand. In 1462, at the age of thirty-one, he was arrested, tortured, and sentenced "to be hanged and strangled." On January 6, 1463, the Parliament quashed the sentence and banished him from Paris. Nobody knows what happened to him subsequently . . .

The guard's red face appeared through the barred window, eyes squinting into the darkness, the clink of his keys echoing. François held his breath. The door opened abruptly, and the beam of a torch blinded him. He immediately shrank back against the oozing wall, but the guard remained motionless in the doorway, his back stooped, his whip hanging limply from his belt. Two liveried footmen entered the dungeon and set up a little table with cabled feet. As one of them set about sweeping away the straw and the excrement with a disgusted air on his face, the other brought in two padded chairs and a large embroidered tablecloth. With affected gestures, he placed two brass candlesticks, a crystal carafe, a stoneware pitcher, baskets of biscuits and fruit, porcelain saucers and plates, and some neatly arranged silverware on the table. Neither of the two footmen deigned to cast so much as a glance at the prisoner, who followed their movements with alarm. Their work over, they withdrew without a word. The prison was again shrouded in the silence of the night. Even the rats hiding in the cracks of the wall were noiseless.

A figure draped in a white linen alb suddenly appeared in the doorway, holding a boxwood rosary in one hand and in the other a lantern whose rays illumined a scarlet cross sewed on his chest.

"Guillaume Chartier, Bishop of Paris," said the visitor, and ordered the guard to free François from his chains.

The bishop sat down and poured drinks. Seeming in no way repelled by the filth and the stench, he civilly invited his guest to join him. François got laboriously to his feet, pulled his shirt down to conceal his wounds, clumsily arranged his hair, threw back his shoulders, and even managed a slight smile. The bishop handed him a chicken thigh. François seized it and tore it to pieces with his teeth, gnawing it to the bone, while Guillaume Chartier explained the purpose of his visit.

He articulated every word with the unflappable calm peculiar to men of the Church, his smooth voice floating like mild incense in the rank air of the cell. François found it hard to listen to the man's words. The fumes of wine tickled his nostrils. Between big mouthfuls of meat and greedy gulps of Burgundy, he caught only the odd scrap. He would have to pay more attention, though, since Chartier, after insisting that he was here as an envoy of the king, was speaking of a way to escape the gallows.

As he reached for a wild boar cutlet, François knocked over a full sauceboat of truffle juice. Laughing stupidly at his own clumsiness, he looked at the dignitary out of the corner of his eye. It would have been easy to plunge a fork straight into his heart.

Guillaume Chartier had expected a warmer welcome, imagining an enthralled listener hanging on every syllable. Instead, he was faced with a horny-handed lout bent low over his bowl, greedily devouring his food. The task with which Louis XI had entrusted him demanded tact. The slightest blunder could well spark a terrible political crisis, even an armed conflict. Unfortunately, the prisoner he had before him was not known for his obedience. He was a rebel. But it was on that very spirit of insubordination that the Bishop of Paris was counting.

As François snatched a big portion of mountain cheese, Chartier took a book from beneath his cloak. It had a crude pigskin binding, devoid of any decoration. The title was handwritten on the cover in thick characters: *ResPublica*.

"The Holy See wants to ban this publication at all costs."

Chartier noted with satisfaction that François had immediately stopped eating. The flickering light of the candles now gave an impression of complicity between the two men. It was not the gloom of the dungeon that suggested this intimacy but the invisible bond of a shared passion, a strong, intense passion that reminded the bishop why he was condescending to dine with a man under sentence of death: the passion for everything to do with books.

François sat up straight, wiped his hands, and took the book from the table, on which Chartier had placed it. He first stroked the cover like a blind man, feeling the texture, smoothing the edges, following the folds of the leather with his finger. When he opened it, his eyes lit up. He leafed through it cautiously. The lout he had been earlier had vanished as if by magic, giving way to a man with a confident bearing and expert gestures.

Forgetting the presence of his distinguished visitor, François carefully examined the quality of the paper and the ink. A Latin text, interspersed here and there with Greek words, filled the pages with densely-packed lines, almost entirely devoid of punctuation, the paragraphs separated only by narrow spaces. It was an ungainly, almost slapdash piece of work. This was not a copyist's manuscript, full of languid strokes and rounded calligraphy, but a jumble of awkwardly aligned characters struck brutally into the paper. François had already seen a few volumes like this in university libraries. He found these machine-made books somewhat repellent in appearance.

The bishop coughed to rouse François from his contemplation. "This copy is being sold clandestinely. It was printed in Mayence by a man named Johann Fust."

François put the book down on the table and picked up a green apple. He could hardly hear Chartier's monotonous voice over the cracking sounds his jaws made as they crushed the pulp. The acidic juice of the fruit stung the abscesses caused by the prison's strict diet. He spat everything out on the ground in disgust. Chartier was sorry to see that the lout had returned. François seemed now to be listening only with half an ear, and was looking frankly bored. The bishop reluctantly resumed his exposition, less and less convinced of the validity of his visit. But he could not return empty-handed. The king stubbornly considered François Villon the ideal candidate, in spite of the opposing views of his advisers.

The way Johann Fust managed his affairs greatly intrigued the court. This German printer had opened several workshops in small isolated towns in Bavaria, Flanders, and the north of Italy. He seemed to draw no material advantage from these branches. On the map, though, their distribution suggested a military deployment. What was their purpose? According to information obtained, Fust was losing money every day. In Mayence, he published Bibles and pious works to order, but elsewhere his traditional presses printed volumes of quite another kind: ancient Greek and Roman writings and recent treatises on medicine and astronomy that he alone seemed capable of acquiring, without anyone being able to discover their provenance. Who was supplying him? In the copy of *The Republic* that François had just held in his hands, Plato propounded how a nation should be ruled. This text confirmed Louis XI in his political ambitions. It also strengthened the status of the Church of France, which wished to free itself of the Papal yoke. Hence the opposition of Rome. Why did Fust persist in publishing this kind of work, at the risk of bringing the wrath of the Inquisition down on his head?

François bent over the book with an intent air, estimating that it was sufficiently heavy to knock the bishop out cold. He pointed ostentatiously at the damp walls of his dungeon, then at the feast. "Is there such a shortage of informers?"

"I am not asking you to inform on this printer, Master Villon, but to become friends with him."

François smiled, reassured. It would have been somewhat ridiculous to hire him as an informer. Imprisoned and tortured more than once, he had never betrayed any of his accomplices. He had many vices and shortcomings, but informing was not one of them. Chartier refrained from insulting him in such a way, and magnanimously poured him a full glass of marc.

The King of France was trying to weaken the power of the Vatican in order to consolidate his own. As it happened, a growing industry had begun to undermine Papal supremacy. Unlike the copyist monks, printing was not subject to the Church. Cleverly used, it might confer a lot of power on those who were able to control it. It was therefore regrettable that there was as yet no printing press in France.

The bishop looked François straight in the eyes, trying to get his full attention. He was almost whispering. Bandits and booksellers used the same clandestine channels to circulate their merchandise without the knowledge of the censors and the men at arms. That was why it was to a member of the band of brigands known as the Coquillards, a man named Colin de Cayeux, that the mission to follow Johann Fust's every move had been entrusted. He had been watching him for months. Fust had opened several printing works in lands neighboring the kingdom but still none here. Colin de Cayeux had recommended his good friend François Villon, a fellow Coquillard, as the man most likely to persuade the German printer to set up shop in Paris.

"In other words, monsignor, you need a scoundrel."

"Yes, but one who is also a man of letters."

François accepted the compliment with a nod. He handed the copy of the *ResPublica* back to Chartier, omitting to tell the bishop that he already knew the text quite well and understood its political significance just as much as Louis XI. In it, Plato described a nation ruled by a monarch whose authority, held on behalf of the "common good," outshone that of the priests and the feudal lords.

François reflected for a moment. The ambitions of a young king eager to strengthen his rule were easy to understand. But what design was this Fust, a mere bookseller, pursuing?

The bishop started tapping the table with his fingertips, an exasperated expression on his face. The wicks of the candles floated in the melted wax. Their faint reflections danced on the crystal of the carafe. François raised his head, with a curl of the lips whose deliberate silliness was close to insolence.

"Tell Louis the Prudent that his loyal subject Villon, although otherwise engaged, will forego all other commitments with the sole intention of being agreeable to him."

The tapping of the fingers stopped immediately. Chartier's impatient expression gave way to a priestly smile. "Fust and his son-in-law will have a stall at the great fair in Lyons. Your friend Colin won't let them out of his sight. As soon as your sentence has been officially commuted, you will join him there. My diocese will provide you with bait for this printer. Some more wine?"

François held out his glass. The drink, as it flowed, hummed a pleasant refrain. Exchanging knowing looks, the bishop and the prisoner clinked glasses.

Although already quite drunk, François refrained from leaping out of his chair and dancing a bourrée around the table. He lowered his eyes, feigning gratitude and humility, aware only of the embroidered tablecloth, the food getting cold on the plates, the bishop's chest swelling the scarlet cross with each breath. He knew how much Guillaume Chartier hated him. And envied him. For of the two of them in this jail, it was François who was truly free, with no ties, and always had been.

Chartier put down his glass and abruptly took his leave. His alb floated for a moment in the doorway before vanishing into the gloom. It seemed to François that he must have been dreaming. Was he really going to cheat the gallows? Could he trust the word of a scheming churchman? He had to stay on his guard. But that copious meal had been worth making a pact with the devil himself for.

What remained of the stew swam at the bottom of the meat terrine, already lukewarm. The candles were gradually going out. François grabbed the opportunity to filch the bread knife and two silver spoons, which he hid beneath his rags. Still standing in the doorway, the jailer yawned. Outside, a lazy fog rose above the ramparts. The crenellations, freed of their veil of frost, stood out clearly. The first crows could be heard cawing on the roof of the keep. In the distance, bells pealed for matins.

François Villon had not yet written his last ballad.

2

The door of the tavern opened suddenly, blown inwards by a gust of wind. Spray and hail crashed onto the flagstones, sprinkling the sawdust and the straw. The dogs growled, the drinkers bellowed, the cats threw themselves under the tables. Their shadows swayed in the red light of the newly fanned flames of the hearth. Threats and curses rang out. Framed in the doorway, dripping with rain, a man stood, silhouetted against the whiteness of the hail. He was motionless for a moment, ignoring the tumult. A black velvet cloak floated around his shoulders like beating wings. Only two things were visible on this untimely specter: a wan smile and, below it, the milky reflection of a knife.

At the far end of the room, his back turned, another man smiled and seized a pitcher and a glass. An ink-dark, sharp-smelling wine gushed from the porcelain spout.

"Good evening, Master Colin."

Colin de Cayeux sat down opposite his friend. Icy water dripped from his greatcoat. He seized the glass, drained it in one go, then sat back to take stock. François let himself be examined at leisure. After all these months of solitude, it warmed him to be scrutinized in this way by his companion. Putting his glass down gently on the table, François savored this moment of friendship in silence. His gaze moved along the grain of the wood, sailing down the rivers it traced on the map of an unknown country. On it he made out the roads where Colin and he had lain in ambush, the forests where they had hidden when the mounted constabulary was hot on their heels, the villages with their dark hovels where Marion, Margot, and Cunégonde had waited for them. Every grease stain was an island, every drop of wine a lake beside a manor house. Tavern tables like this had accompanied François on all his wanderings. They had comforted and inspired him, welcoming his joys and sorrows, listening to his grievances, unflinchingly accepting the cuts he loved to make in them with his knife. Their cracks spoke a mysterious language. They breathed words and phrases in your ear. All it then took was the music of a few rhymes to reveal their secret. Not to mention the fact that their solid texture made them excellent desks.

Colin looked at his friend without saying a word. He was used to these silences, these moments when François left him, lost in a strange conversation with the angels. Or with his own demon. He did not hold it against him. François had a wandering soul.

Outside, the storm had subsided. Work resumed, even though it was the middle of the night. Colin heard the dull thuds of the mallets, the creak and rasp of the pulleys, the muffled yells of the foremen, the wailing of the donkeys as they were unloaded, the clerks screaming orders in Venetian, in Low German, in Arabic. The Fair of Lyons would open at dawn, come what may.

"You worry me, François. I thought you were going to regale everyone with a well-turned lament. The students are surprised at your silence. They were expecting fine words from your prison cell, a few rebellious verses. But you haven't stirred, haven't complained . . . "

"The students already have new songs. The booksellers have wiped my name from their inventories."

"You're wrong, François. The taverns echo to your verses. Your poetry is sold everywhere on the sly. It is whispered in the corridors at court. It is recited in literary circles. Even the judges delight in it!"

Colin opened his pouch, took out a piece of dry sausage, and cut it into thin slices with his knife. François chewed on it, all the while following the comings and goings of a serving-woman, dreaming of a companion for his night. A wrinkled breast hung over the woman's filthy apron.

"I'm well past thirty-two, my dear Colin. All that remains of my loves and my duels are the scars. Of the money I robbed, not even a crown is left . . . "

Colin knew his friend too well to fall for this declaration.

"But now I have this!"

François held out the list of works chosen by Chartier to arouse the envy of Johann Fust and persuade him to put his presses at the service of the French court. These volumes came from the royal archives as well as the secret collections of the diocese of Paris. The descriptions of them were deliberately succinct, so that only the initiated could spot their inestimable value. Colin skimmed through the tedious inventory, seeing nothing in it to justify such excitement.

"Another swig?"

François filled the glasses then lifted his high in triumph, like a chalice. Colin threw an embarrassed glance at the neigh-boring tables. It was easy to spot the foreigners who had come for the Fair, dressed in thickly stitched doublets or woolen cloaks, wearing hoods and hats with preposterous shapes. Whether they came from Flanders or Saragossa, whether they were highwaymen, clerics or merchants, each had a club or a knife, in full view, at their sides. Other weapons were barely concealed beneath their cloaks or inside the legs of their boots. Ill at ease, the locals shrank away, whispering in patois, looking at these strangers out of the corners of their eyes. Only the innkeeper was affable, jovially pocketing the coin of different realms. A maid swayed her hips between the tables, trying to tempt the customers. Colin drank without much conviction, again looking closely at the sheet of parchment. François hit the table with his fist and pointed to the crowded room.

"It's their future you hold in your hands, brigand!"

The two men spent the night drinking. François tried to make Colin understand what was truly at stake in this mission, but in vain. Colin could not see how this list of books could change the fate of all these people, these peasants and shop-keepers and soldiers of fortune. Much as he examined the inventory and deciphered the titles, it was no good. What con-fused him all the more was that François kept telling him that it was not the texts that mattered. They had been chosen by Chartier, and by the king, to assuage their ambitions of the moment. No, it was the books themselves, as objects of paper or animal hide, that constituted an extraordinary arsenal. But for what war?

The tavern gradually emptied. Colin meekly received his final instructions from François, then went out to face the rain. As he closed the door behind him, he glimpsed his crony busily making eyes at the servingwoman, who was laughing crazily.

The market square was waking up, warmly wrapped in the thick mist of morning. Sounds, sparse and timid at first, pierced the silence: little bells dancing on the necks of animals, gravel crunching beneath the wheels of the carts, baubles and canvases shaken by the wind. The men, still numb, did not speak, staring with heavy eyes at the few patches of color: red ribbon, green hat, purple cloth. Hawkers and merchants strode in dozens down the alleys leading to the fairground. Soon, they roused workers and mules, mercenaries and body-guards. Soon, the whine of haggling and the clink of coins echoed on all sides. That morning, a new era began, an era in which everything would be negotiable.

The wooden trestles creaked beneath the weight of the crates and jars. The air was heavy with the scent of spices and perfume and dye and the fumes of wine. Colin was assailed by touts pulling his arm, in no way abashed by his huge frame. He hurried on, cutting through the stream of onlookers, slipping between the carpets and fabrics hanging from the awnings. In the central aisle, he spotted a stand whose sober tones were out of place in the gaily-colored swirl of silks. There, customers and sellers alike argued in low voices, heedless of the cries and laughter all around. A discreet sign announced in Gothic lettering: "Johann Fust and Pierre Schoeffer, printers and booksellers." Rolls of parchment and leather-bound volumes were heaped up willy-nilly on shelves of rough and hastily varnished wood.

At the back, behind the counter, a slender fellow wearing gentlemen's attire, although moth-eaten and patched, was putting down a box filled with books at the feet of an old man with a well-groomed beard. The old man immediately plunged his thin hands into the box, skillfully searching and sorting. Then, with a disillusioned expression, he stood up again and stated his price. The squire refused, visibly offended. The old man would not budge. To cut short the performance, he untied a velvet purse, knowing that a feudal lord in debt would not long resist the sight of a handful of silver coins. Crestfallen, the noble pocketed the sum without deigning to count it and quickly turned on his heels, trying to regain the haughty air proper to his station.

Colin went closer. It was the first time he had approached the man he had been watching for months. With a hesitant hand, he held out his list. The old merchant first glanced negligently at it. Then, genuinely taken aback, he looked at Colin for some time, incredulous.

With the few crowns allocated by Guillaume Chartier,

François bought new clothes: two pairs of britches, two shirts, and a pelisse lined with otter skin, all in a dull gray that would not show the dirt for a long time. Splendid hats hung from the ceiling, but much as the shopkeeper insisted, François would not abandon his old headgear. It was a piece of crumpled felt, of an undefined color that might once have been an elegant green, the brim of which was turned up in three sections. This curious tricorn had escaped many trials and tribulations. Each of its folds, like a familiar wrinkle, evoked a memory. François refused to part with it. It was the only possession that still tied him to his past. He clung to it like a rope.

Before going back, he paid for a neck-length haircut, a close shave, and a clumsy plastering of his dental cavities. The barber cursed the great fair, which was stealing his customers with all its sales patter. There were even quack doctors there who claimed to be able to patch up teeth better than he could!

Back at the tavern, François climbed the stairs to the attic, a small, meagerly furnished, musty-smelling room. Colin was waiting for him, sitting on a stool. François tapped him on the shoulder, then went and took his pouch from under the bed. The books were all there. Now all they could do was wait.

Toward noon, François heard heavy steps growing louder as they approached, interspersed now and again by imperious knocks with a cane. Colin stood up even before the pommel struck the mildewed wood of the door. Doing his best to appear polite, he gave a kind of bow and motioned the visitor to the only chair that had a back.

"Fust. Johann Fust. Silversmith and printer in Mayence."

François, sitting cross-legged on a straw mattress, was less welcoming. He studied the newcomer with a suspicious air. The old man's venerable countenance, his haughty German demeanor, his impeccably correct clothes did nothing to set his mind at rest. Fust stared back at him, momentarily thrown by his host's less than winning appearance. He even found him insolent and crafty. The fellow was clearly suffering from a terrible hangover. In any case, neither the imposing brute who was standing with his back to the door nor this none too clean vagabond intimidated the old printer. This wasn't the first time he had dealt with receivers of stolen goods. They were of all kinds: defrocked priests, sons of good families who had fallen into debt, soldiers returning from the wars. The best books often met with the saddest fate, abandoned by simpletons surprised that anyone should waste time reading them, let alone want to acquire them for cash. Thus it was that knowledge circulated and spread, through theft, bankruptcy, and inheritance. Much to the delight of booksellers.

François knew perfectly well that his guest sensed a great opportunity. Nevertheless, he played the game according to the rules, letting Fust believe that he was the craftier of the two or, at least, the more expert. François had never flaunted his knowledge, often taking judges and university masters by surprise. He had learned never to use his erudition as a foil, but to conceal it beneath the appearance of a fool, and use it only at the right moment, like a secret weapon. He would throw a judicious quotation at an eminent rival as you throw a knife at a straw target, casually but going straight for the middle. And always catching him unawares. It was not his reading that had taught him this technique, but the many street fights he had been in, against adversaries for whom, unlike courtiers and clerics, he felt respect.

Fust, though, would not let himself be overawed—which made François all the better disposed toward him. The old man took his seat with ease, nonchalantly placed his cane on the floor, and calmly removed his mittens. On his finger, as a counterpoint to his otherwise austere attire, he wore a glittering ring with a ruby set in it as a cabochon. The matte gold of the ring was inscribed with a dragon, its tiny rhinestone eyes glittering brightly, a thread of flashing enamel spurting from its open mouth. Its claws held the central gem in a tight grip.

Still crouching, François opened his pouch and took out a book. A gleam appeared in Fust's eyes, and his hollow cheeks and hooked nose suddenly perked up like those of a bird of prey. François barely held out his hand, forcing Fust to bend very low, at the risk of falling from his chair. Fust managed to seize the volume. Without hesitation, he placed his finger on the name stamped on the cover: Kyonghan.

"The author, I presume?"

François guessed that his interlocutor knew the answer. He nodded briefly.

Fust made an effort to keep calm. He turned the pages with a detached air. Tiny beads of sweat formed on his wrinkled forehead. He had feared at first that this edition of the *Jikji Simkyong* had been printed with the help of terra-cotta or porcelain characters. But no, this was indeed the 1377 edition, composed in Korea using movable metal fonts. He already had a copy, brought fifteen years earlier to Mayence by a Jew from the Holy Land. Fust had been surprised by the quality of the ink, the clarity of the touch, and above all the fineness of the letters. The Jew had wanted to know if Fust, being a silversmith, would be capable of reproducing that alloy of Korean fonts, and if his son-in-law, Pierre Schoeffer, and their associate Johannes Gensfleisch, known as Gutenberg, could make a machine that would allow the use of characters thus obtained. The original press would have been too fragile to print on rag paper, which was more resistant to ink than delicate China papers. The Jew had paid a deposit in cash and promised to supply rare unpublished texts for the first attempts.

Johann Fust put the book down and asked to see a manuscript whose description had intrigued him. François again searched in his pouch and took from it a roll of parchment much worn by time. The writing on it was heavy and full of mistakes. A botched job by an overworked copyist? No, the old bookseller was no fool. He took off his ring and, with one finger, pressed hard on the head of the carved dragon. The gold claws retracted immediately, freeing the cabochon. Fust removed the ruby from its setting and placed it flat on the parchment. Leaning forward, he slowly moved the precious mineral along the sheet, noting that the vellum had been scratched. François realized with astonishment that the big, highly-polished red stone enlarged every detail.

Fust was unable to suppress a start of surprise. Between the clumsily traced lines, he detected the vague outlines of Aramaic letters. So it was not to salvage the parchment that the copyist had scraped it with a knife but to camouflage the original characters, which had been engraved into the hide with a stylet and then concealed beneath the thick ink of an innocuous text. It was in this way that the Jews disguised the works they wanted to save from burning by the Inquisition. This laborious process was only used for Talmudic or kabbalistic writings of the highest importance. At the time of the Crusades, the knights unknowingly carried these works disguised as pious breviaries. They thought they were returning them from Jerusalem to Avignon or Frankfurt, not suspecting for a moment that they were serving as couriers to the rabbis of these same towns. It was then only necessary to dissolve the mask of ink to reveal the secret copy. Today, it was Fust's peddlers who ensured, in all innocence, the distribution of clandestine works cleverly disguised as psalters or other Catholic items.

Again examining the list with a wise air, Fust wondered if he had not been lured into a trap. Only someone powerful could have collected so many rarities. They were worth a fortune! Unless they were items confiscated by the censors. In which case, Villon was probably not a broker, but an agent of the law.

A merchant discusses the sum to be decided on, the methods of payment, delivery dates. But no price had yet been mentioned. The old man looked at the unusual character sitting on the floor opposite him. He was crouching in the middle of a heap of bound volumes and scrolls of parchment, as if selling vegetables at the market. But he was clearly familiar with beautiful books. He manipulated them with dexterity. His slovenly appearance belied the natural elegance of his demeanor, the discreet refinement of his gestures. The frankness of his gaze might have instilled confidence in Fust if it had not been for that impish gleam. A narrow grin, always there even when he spoke, displayed an effrontery that he made no attempt to conceal. This fellow was not one to let good manners and conventional expressions get in his way. He did not pretend. It was Fust who felt he was being sized up, put to the test. The other man was challenging him with that smile that wasn't a smile, inviting him to enter the joust without forcing him to do so completely. Curiosity finally won out over caution.

"May I make you an offer?"

"The seller does not want money."

Fust's whole body stiffened. He was ready to make a run for it, but François reassured him with a little tap on the arm. The corners of his mouth creased even more, accentuating the mischievous expression of his face.

"But he is ready to graciously give you all these volumes in return for your services."

Taken aback, the German stammered. François immediately explained Guillaume Chartier's wish to enrich his diocese with a printing works and a few banned books. In order not to scare off his prey, he avoided mention of the king.

Fust quickly did his sums, even though he was hesitant to close a deal that seemed too attractive to be without pitfalls. He asked for time to think, to consult his associates, to obtain guarantees, but it was clear that he now had only one idea in his head: to get his hands on the books heaped at François' feet.

Fust took his leave, promising to give his answer within a short period of time. As soon as he left the room, Colin leaped for joy. François remained sitting. He put the precious volumes back in his pouch, without saying a word. He did not have any sense of victory. He hated himself for being Guillaume Chartier's broker, for obeying that two-faced churchman so meekly. And above all, for betraying books.

3

The Bishop of Paris crossed the street, cursing and grumbling, hopping to avoid the puddles. Two hooded clerics trotted beside him, trying in vain to protect him from the rain beneath a canvas canopy that the wind twisted and shook in all directions. The gutters of Rue Saint-Jacques carried mire and refuse, which the disgusted prelate prodded away with his episcopal crozier. Johann Fust rushed to open the door of his new shop while his son-in-law, Pierre Schoeffer, a brush in his hand, held himself ready to clean the mud-spattered miter.

As soon as he entered, Chartier held his nose. A rough smell of ink and sweat made him retch. Fust stopped the banging of mallets and ordered his workers to be silent. François Villon stood with his elbows on a handpress, smiling wickedly as he observed the bishop's authoritarian expression, Fust's obsequious gestures, the distressed faces of the apprentices. It was as if each of these people were trying very hard to conform to the character they had been assigned.

Schoeffer kissed His Excellency's ring and, without further ado, proudly launched on a guided tour of the printing works. Guillaume Chartier resolved to follow his host amid the maze of machines and piles of paper, listening to the explanations with only half an ear. The printers stood stiffly, their caps held tight in their hands. Once the tour was over, the bishop blessed the premises with a hasty sign of the cross while one of his clerics energetically waved a big brass censer. Beaming with pride,

Schoeffer handed Chartier the very first book printed in Paris, in the Year of Grace 1463, by permission of the King. He declared pompously that this was the cornerstone of an edifice that would enlighten the world as much as the lighthouse of Alexandria, spreading the glory of France among the nations. Unmoved, Chartier put the book down negligently on a work-bench all sticky with birdlime.

François felt a certain bitterness at seeing the bishop dis-pose of the ceremony so casually. An event of such importance deserved a special effort of protocol. Angrily, he walked to the back of the room, where the presses were at rest. There were twelve in all, arranged in two parallel rows that François walked along slowly as if inspecting the troops. Massive, made of a heavy, robust wood, bristling with levers covered in grease, they exuded a disturbing power. They were solidly nailed to a platform to avoid any shifting during the printing process. This raised position made them as imposing as statues of Roman emperors. François sensed the hold they might have on men in the future. They were also a little like him, docile in appear-ance, giving the impression of being easy to handle. But also like him, they could not limit themselves to serving a Fust or a Chartier, to being merely the instrument of their ambitions, political or financial, their pitiful plans. There was too much strength in them for these people to keep them to themselves, to confine them in a prison or a shop. François suddenly saw in these presses a possible ally. For him, and for poetry. They reminded him of the horses he had stolen, opening their enclo-sure in the middle of the night, taming their spirit, disciplining their trembling muscles, riding them into the dark woods, ever faster, ever further. Were these machines also capable of kick-ing and snorting?

Fust signaled to his employees to resume work and invited his eminent visitor into his office. Schoeffer and François followed, taking care to close the door behind them. Fust told Chartier that he had rented all the vacant premises on Rue Saint-Jacques. Several German printers were ready to join him, apart from his former associate Gutenberg, who persisted in his refusal to open a branch in Paris because of an old quarrel. The poor man was in debt up to his neck. He was living on a mea-ger income allocated by the Archbishop of Nassau even though he too could have benefited from the generous patronage of Louis XI or Charles of Orléans, who were much shrewder when it came to letters than the curates of the Palatinate clergy.

Uninterested in Fust's report, François let his gaze wander over the rows of books lining the walls. In a dark corner, the flickering light of a candle made the surface of an emblazoned binding gleam. The coat of arms, struck in fine gold, was eas-ily recognizable. It was one of the most famous in Christendom: the coat of arms of the Medicis of Florence. Curiously, these resplendent arms were deprived of their motto. In its place, the escutcheon was interspersed with motifs in matte gold that had nothing Italian or heraldic about them. François looked closely at the sinuous border, thinking suddenly he could make out Semitic characters. Hebrew and Arab themes were often used to give a biblical or Eastern connotation to the holy books. Scenes from the life of Christ were strewn with Judaic letters, as were portraits of Satan. But here, the mixture of marks of nobility and Jewish figures seemed to bear witness to an unusual union, a kind of pact. The two symbols, the Italian and the Jewish, intertwined to form a single symbol.

Noticing François's surprise, Pierre Schoeffer got abruptly to his feet, came over to him, and stood there with his back turned for a moment, doing something. When he sat down again, the book had disappeared, hidden among the others. The volumes that had been lying about everywhere were now lined up in ser-ried ranks. The little candle had been extinguished.

The bishop was growing impatient. A mere manufacturing process could not be enough. The crown expected much more of Fust than merely to run a printing works. He had not been chosen for his skill at handling pots of ink but because, unlike his colleagues, he had first refusal on banned texts that might give Paris a head start over the other capitals. It was with the quality of the books published here on Rue Saint-Jacques that Louis XI intended to ensure the influence of France. Patronage of the arts was the surest sign of a monarch's prosperity, as well as the manifest expression of his power. That at least was what Chartier gave them to understand, taking care not to reveal the true purpose of this whole undertaking. He had not even said a word of it to François, who was surprised by this sudden infatuation of the king for the things of the mind.

The monarch's true motives were much more down-to-earth. It was a simple matter of finance. At this time, everything coming from Byzantium, Alexandria or the Levant had to pass through the valley of the Rhone. The Pope having sovereignty over Avignon and the Comtat, the papal legate reaped huge profits from imposing rights of passage and taxes on foodstuffs, which went to fill the coffers of Rome rather than those of Louis XI. The king wanted to force the Vatican to cede this source of revenue to him. It so happened that the works published by Fust greatly antagonized Rome, undermining the Church's hegemony over men's souls. The young monarch's plan was simple. After letting Fust flood the market with texts that corrupted believers, Louis XI would set himself up as defender of the faith and undertake to avert the danger. But, in order to stem this deadly tide of publications, it was essential that he gain control of Provence. Such blackmail could only work if the Holy See felt genuinely threatened by works of undeniable significance capable of shaking the foundations of the dogma. And it was up to Fust to supply the necessary ammunition. But all he had done so far was extol the virtues of his machines. No more than that.

His fist clenched over the handle of his crozier, Chartier frowned and glared at François, who immediately felt a tightness in his throat at the point where they placed the rope. Although Colin had been watching the German for months, he still had not been able to discover where Fust acquired the books the crown needed in order to achieve its ends. Chartier was within his rights to demand an explanation. The agreement reached with Fust clearly stipulated that the granting of patents and privileges to his printing works went hand in glove with the publication of rare and influential writings, to which he so mysteriously had access.

A fragile silence now hovered over the room. Fust knew perfectly well what the bishop was expecting of him but he had to follow his instructions to the letter. His superiors had not authorized him to negotiate further. Even though a possible alliance with the King of France was an unexpected godsend, they seemed reluctant to commit themselves. Paris had to remain unaware of what was truly at stake in their actions, or years of preparation would be put at risk.

The old printer turned his ring nervously. The golden dragon plunged beneath his finger in search of the ruby cabochon, then reappeared, its claws digging into the bright red stone, as if sucking its blood.

"I have informed my patrons of your demands," he said at last. "They are honored by the interest you have shown in them. And somewhat intimidated . . . "

Guillaume Chartier was surprised to discover that, like him, Fust was only an intermediary. But he forbade himself from uttering reassurances as to the intentions of the crown. Louis XI owed the deference shown him by Fust's mysterious masters to the fear he inspired in them, and that was all to the good.

"In order not to offend His Majesty, they are ready to receive an envoy."

"Where and when?"

"The date is up to you, monsignor. The place is not at all near."

"No matter. We will supply good mounts."

"I fear that will not be necessary. The Holy Land is a lot easier to reach by sea than by land."

The bishop gave a start, which he suppressed. Then, with ecclesiastical calm, he turned slowly to François. "Do you have sea legs, Villon?"

Chartier was obviously not expecting an answer from François. He ordered a prompt departure, dictated conditions, fixed dates, and demanded guarantees, especially as Fust stubbornly refused to reveal the identity of his patrons. Nor did he mention their place of residence. Jerusalem? Tiberias? Nazareth?

François was to travel to Genoa, accompanied by Colin. There, somebody would be waiting to give him further instructions. Only if the negotiations bore fruit would Fust's patrons break their anonymity. Chartier took offense at this, proclaiming that such secrecy was an insult to the crown of France, since it cast doubt on the probity of the king. But he had to face facts. Fust was far more afraid of attracting the disapproval of his superiors than of wounding the pride of Louis XI, even if it meant rotting in one of his jails. That of course made a great impression on the bishop.

Chartier brought the interview to an abrupt end and withdrew without even bidding François farewell. Fust and Schoeffer hastened to escort the bishop to the door of the works. Alone in the office, François threw a last glance at the shelves, trying to spot the emblazoned volume that Pierre Schoeffer had hurried to hide from him. The Medicis were the declared allies of Louis XI. He had persuaded them to trans-

fer to Lyons, at the very time when François had been meeting
Fust there, the branches they maintained in Geneva. In addition to these commercial relations, it was likely that they
advised the king in matters of erudition and letters. They were
great book lovers, and their library was one of the most presti-
gious in the West. But what was the meaning of the Hebrew
signs placed beside their emblem? Just like Louis XI, the
Medicis were famous for their scheming. If need be, they
would not hesitate to make a pact with the devil himself.

Schoeffer came striding back, seized François by the elbow,
and dragged him quickly toward the exit. Dumbfounded,
François found himself outside again. A gentle breeze caressed
his cheeks. He tried to recover his composure. What had he
gotten himself involved in? He had never been afraid of the
unknown. On the contrary, he hated predictable things, fore-
gone conclusions. But he didn't like to feel himself being
moved like a puppet, at the whim of fortune. He had always
tried hard to be master of his own fate, his own choices, even
the bad ones. So far, in fact, he had never made any good ones.
He could quite well run away, join a band of brigands in the
forest of Fontainebleau or Rambouillet, or go to ground in a
village in Savoy, far from Chartier and the Parisian judges, who
would lose all trace of him in the end. So why were all his
thoughts of that ship waiting for him in the port of Genoa,
white sails swelling in the wind, a prow cutting through the
waves and rending the horizon?

Schoeffer was still standing in the doorway of the printing
works, making sure that the intruder left the area. François
walked more quickly and turned the corner of Chaussée Saint-
Jacques. He had to inform Colin as soon as possible. They
would both have to present themselves at dawn at the police
conciergerie to receive the passes and money they would need
for the journey.

The streets were deserted. The rain had stopped. A pale

sunset could be glimpsed between the roofs. François pressed ahead, a curious shiver going through his body. To chase away this feeling of cold, he immersed himself in the warmth of familiar details: muddy cobblestones, milestones turned green with moss, signs swinging above the doors—the sign of the boar, of the pitcher, of the sundial. He had been banished, that was what it amounted to. He was leaving Paris, that noble city where jailers and torturers prized the antics of the poets they imprisoned and tortured. In any case, he no longer felt at ease here. Everything had become too refined and pedantic. Too complacent. He was hungry for something else, for vigor and boldness. For a place where every step counted, where every moment brought a new challenge, where neither body nor soul had the right to drop their guard. Did such a place exist on this earth? If it did, it was certainly a place filled with passion and torment . . .

4

The shrill prattling of the women, the hoarse cries of the men, and the rumble of the carts woke François at dawn. Genoa was a noisy, feverish city. People never stopped yelling, from one window to another, from within the carriage entrances, from the tops of terraces. A thousand untimely echoes whirled about the narrow streets, bounced off the stone, slipped in through the dormer windows and tickled your eardrums, without ever taking flight into a sky that was too calm, too blue, too distant.

François kicked Colin, who grunted, stretched, and dipped his hand in a bowl of water on the floor. With a grimace of disgust, he sprinkled his face and beard, then slowly opened his eyes to reveal his bleary morning-after look. François was already busy tying his bundle. With a moan, Colin turned his back on him.

"Our ship doesn't sail until tomorrow . . . "

Colin had not stopped cursing François since they had left Paris. He owed Chartier nothing. His mission was over. Fust had opened his printing works. He didn't see why he should go halfway across the world and throw himself into the jaws of the hydras and cyclopses that were surely awaiting him in those distant lands. He imagined those ancient monsters salivating with pleasure at the thought of devouring a nice pink Frenchman, all soaked in brandy and good wine. And besides, he hated the sea.

François would have been worried to see Colin enchanted by such a journey. Colin was a grouch who enjoyed his constant bad humor. He wallowed in it like a pig in shit. He swore and spat, stamped his feet and shrugged his shoulders, and was constantly looking for a fight. To comfort him, therefore, would have been a mistake. He was dying to meet those hydras and cyclopses and smash their jaws.

François tore down the stairs without further ado, his bundle on his back. He heard Colin groan, yell curses after him, and smash the shaving mug against the wall of the attic. In other words, he would be following him soon enough.

On the gangway, the stevedores bustled, some rolling big barrels, others hauling crates and equipment with the help of ropes, all gesticulating and yelling with that Latin good humor, that unbreakable spirit of the common people, who refused to be cowed by poverty and were philosophical in spite of everything. The sailors, who were less destitute, being fed and lodged onboard, observed these comings and goings with a false air of detachment.

By late in the afternoon, everything seemed properly stowed. Exhausted, the sailors lay down in the shade of the sails. The din of the loading gave way to a serene silence that gently cradled the ship. The warm hues of sunset slowly climbed the masts, staining the dark wood a deep red. Ropes stood out against the sky in straight, clear lines, as if drawn with a chisel. In the distance, a confused tangle of buildings and bell towers swayed in the dimming light. The storehouses and wharves dissolved into an orange-colored mirage. A solitary seagull addressed the sun with its overdramatic cries.

François turned his head to the open sea. He stared at the horizon as it faded, the vast expanse of sea and sky stretching as far as the eye could see, inviting, exciting. The daylight was lazily sinking, dragging the past down with it into the depths. Good and bad memories receded without a sound, slowly buried by the advancing night. François was distressed by the ease with which he was burning his bridges. However hard he tried to recall a street corner, a river bank, a cathedral square, all he saw were yellowing, shriveled images. However hard he tried to keep holding on for a while longer to the ghosts he had loved so much, Jeanne, Catherine, Aurélia, all those faces of women, suddenly aged, dissolved immediately, chased away by the mute promises of the wind. He hated himself for yielding so easily, like an innocent ship's boy, to the scent of adventure carried on the sea breeze.

Colin joined François on deck, chewing a piece of dry bread. He leaned over the rail and burst out laughing. Below, the captain was yelling at those of the sailors who had returned tipsy from the brothels, cheerfully kicking their backsides. The men, too drunk to protest, let themselves be pushed and prodded like cattle. Colin pointed at the shore. A shadowy figure had just come running onto the quay. A young monk, an overlarge cowl floating around his scrawny body, trotted in small, jerky steps toward the ship. Once he had nimbly climbed the gangway he came straight toward Colin and François and, without any preamble, began giving them whispered instructions. He had the self-confident demeanor of a novice from a good family. There was nothing humble about his attitude, on the contrary he was quite affected.

"The purpose of your visit to the Holy Land must remain a secret. You will travel as simple pilgrims. I see you already wear the shell of the pious penitents of Santiago de Compostela."

François and Colin merely exchanged smiles of complicity. The shells they wore around their necks on leather laces did not bear the sign of the cross. Their edges were of fine gold, and in the middle was carved the image of a dagger piercing a heart. This pendant did not commemorate any martyrdom or calvary. Only fearsome bandits and shrewd men-at-arms would unsheathe their weapons at the sight of this trinket, recognizing it, often too late, as the sign of the Coquillards.

The messenger held out a closed letter. François gave a start. The document bore the seal of Cosimo de' Medici entwined with a motto in Hebrew, just like on the bound volume he had glimpsed at the back of Fust's printing works. François immediately questioned the young monk about the meaning of the emblem. The novice seemed embarrassed. All he knew was that this seal came from Cosimo's personal library. It was used only for works from Palestine.

Colin crossed himself and muttered a pious blessing. The word "Palestine" awoke mixed feelings in him. It revived memories of the catechism. Not having the faintest idea what the land of the Bible looked like, he imagined it to be mysterious and splendid. In his mind, Carmel was a huge mountain, its peaks adorned with giant crosses piercing the clouds, and Samaria was a Garden of Eden filled with many-colored flowers, where white donkeys and curly-haired sheep frolicked. Not to mention hydras and cyclopses.

Once the monk had left, François hastened to break the seal. The wax crumbled into small red pieces that spread across the deck. He unfolded the letter. A simple penciled sketch indicated an itinerary leading from the port of Acre, not to the Mount of Olives, but to an isolated plateau in Lower Galilee. Disappointed, François contemplated the pieces of wax as they were blown toward the fore of the ship. He was angry with himself for destroying the seal so hastily. At his side, Colin cursed and moaned. Wasn't there even going to be a banquet to welcome the envoys of the King of France?

The vessel cast off at dawn. A leading seaman yelled orders. Half awake, the men let out a stream of curses before climbing to the yards. As soon as they had left port, the swell grew stronger, causing the sails to crack like whips. The captain remained in the shade of the foresail, making sure they avoided the reefs. Once he was certain they had reached the open sea, he yelled at the mate:

"Set sail for the Holy Land, Monsieur Martin!"

The captain's cry echoed in François's head: "Set sail for the Holy Land, Holy Land, Holy Land . . . " Just like Colin, he imagined great ocher-colored spaces strewn with palm trees and thick thorny plants, age-old olive groves, a blue sky from which the sun was never absent, a sky where only white doves flew, in silence, a rocky land with clear, sharp outlines, without moss or mud. It was a land of marvels, almost chimerical, which he had no difficulty in peopling with all kinds of angels, bearded prophets, bad genies, and Madonnas, but whose real inhabitants he could not imagine at all. Were they short and dark, or tall and slender? Muscular or skinny? Did they look like the Italians, the Moors, the Greeks? Were the women veiled, or did their curly hair fly in the wind? Not that it mattered. This land was much too fabulous to belong to anyone. And it was because it did not belong to anyone that everyone took turns seizing it. Even the gods fought over it. The current masters were the Mamluks, former mercenaries and slaves from Egypt, just like the Hebrews. They had replaced the Crusaders, who had replaced the Byzantines, who had replaced the Romans, the Greeks, the Persians, the Babylonians, and the Assyrians. And already the Ottomans were beating at the gates of Jerusalem, hoping to chase out the Mamluks. They were all only occupiers. Their presence was doomed to be precarious, transitory, quite simply because they had all made the same mistake, one after the other, for centuries: they constantly asked the wrong question. Who did the Holy Land belong to? To those who owned it? To those who occupied it? To those who loved it? If it was really as holy as they said, such a land could not be conquered by arms. It could not be a possession, a domain, a territory. And, in that case, shouldn't the question be inverted: What people belonged to it, then? For good. The Mamluks?

5

T here was nothing very Biblical about Acre. It was the kind of fortified town that could be found dotted all over France. Its crude ramparts, hastily hewn out of the rock, stood out against a clear sky filled with sparrows swooping in groups toward the refuse strewn over the quays. The harbor was small. Two ships swayed lazily in the heat, stirred by a light west wind. Sailors and soldiers strolled about, in search of the way to the taverns and the girls. Greasy barrels filled with olive oil, sacks of spices, and empty crates were heaped everywhere, abandoned to the rats. Neither François nor Colin felt the appropriate emotion. They did not prostrate themselves to kiss the sacred soil, buried as it was under all that detritus.

François simply bent one knee, for form's sake. He nevertheless felt a presence, or a breath, hovering above the roofs, stretching all the way to the slopes of Mount Carmel, covering the dunes that lined the coast. An invisible presence that was not necessarily God, but rather a kind of implacable radiance that made everything clearer, more established. Was it due to the dazzling light with its absence of shade? François had the impression that this harsh, arid land was challenging him. The gentleness of the banks of the Loire, the sad pallor of the northern plains, were conciliatory. They had always submitted docilely to rhyme. But how would he accommodate himself to the burning roughness of the stones, this harsh, uncompromising light? François rose to his full height, defying the brilliance of the sun, feeling the hot wind bake his cheeks. He was delighted with this challenge.

Colin set off in front, towering over Arabs, Genoese, and Persians by at least a head. He was like a peacock crossing a farmyard. He plunged at random into an alleyway filled with turbans and helmets. François picked up his pouch and ran to catch up with him. He found him already arguing over the price of two mares with an inflexible nomad who kept shaking his head in exasperated refusal. Colin gesticulated, seeking a movement of the arm that meant "discount." The nomad held out, stubbornly showing the sum required on his abacus. While François smiled affably and tried to turn on the charm, Colin scowled and rose to his full height, looming over the poor merchant. The price came down. Colin and François chose two saddles embroidered with richly colored patterns, woven and dyed by the women of the desert. Colin ordered the dealer to cut off the tufts of braided wool hanging from the harnesses. François nervously tried to hurry him along, advising him not to drag things out. A crowd had formed around the merchant, who was angry at these foreigners' lack of decorum. He had been prepared to yield the animals to them for a sum much lower than the one they had just paid. That was not the point. It was their way of bargaining! Custom required that you take your time, negotiate, laugh, cry, lose your temper then resign yourself. And the crowd agreed with him, growing just as indignant.

Colin and François leapt onto their mounts and, cutting through the angrily yelling throng, headed straight for the city gates. They paid the toll, passed the guards without any problem, and discovered an arid plain that stretched before them as far as the eye could see. François consulted the map that the Genoese novice had given him. The sun was still high. They could cover the distance before nightfall.

Galloping across dunes and scrub, the two men reached the first hills of Galilee. Colin rode in front, staying off the beaten track and avoiding villages, often turning to inspect the surrounding ridges. The mares were slavering with exhaustion. They had to stop and find a watering place. From deep inside an olive grove, an Arab peasant watched these horsemen as they made the silence whistle and flew off in a cloud of dust. He waited for the sandy powder to settle before plunging back into his manual labor. He tried not to think about them again. What was the point? And yet a small part of him continued to ride with them, on the quiet, as if swept away by the wind.

Colin suddenly gave the signal to stop. He placed a finger on his lips. A distant staccato murmur tickled his eardrums. A swirl of sand rose above the bushes lining the valley, and a troop of Mamluk soldiers appeared, their slender spears like the antennae of a swarm of bees. Light glittered on the coppery cones of their helmets. In spite of the distance, Colin and François noted that the detachment was following the furrow they themselves had just cut through the brambles. Without saying a word, the two men rode fast toward the hills.

Late that afternoon, they approached the point indicated on their map.

"It looks like Provence," cried Colin above the thudding of hooves.

"How right you are. Look up there!"

A cross rose in the sky.

"Good Lord, yes, rhymester, the noble cross of Christ!"

Colin immediately slowed. He rose high in the saddle and started dusting off his clothes. François did the same. In spite of the stifling heat, both assumed a dignified air and bravely set off up the steep path that seemed to lead straight to the clouds. When they reached the promontory, they saw a decaying building. At the entrance, arms folded, stood a tall man, surrounded by scrawny hens hopping, cackling, chattering, and pecking at each other. The man remained impassive. Colin and François dismounted. In spite of the arrival of twilight, they made out a monk's cowl and tonsure, rope sandals, and a boxwood rosary. Above, the great cross seemed to sway, its lines undulating in a hazy dew. A last ray of sunlight made the wrought iron flare like old brass then, sinking to the horizon, tinged it a darker, deeper red, like blood.

Colin crossed himself and muttered a few pious formulas. The monk, reassured by this evident veneration, uncrossed his arms, and bade them welcome in Latin. François detected a popular intonation: this was more dog Latin than book Latin. The monk's swollen paunch revealed the limits of his asceticism. This penitent enjoys his food, François told himself, and that means he's at peace with the world.

"Welcome, my lords. I am Paul de Tours, the prior. Let's take these poor animals to the trough."

The garden of the cloister looked like a farmyard. Bales of straw were heaped at the feet of a Virgin with crumbling fingers. Clusters of garlic hung from the arches. A strong smell of fermented milk lingered in this devout spot. Access to the chapel was obstructed by thorny bundles of firewood, crackling with dryness. François and Colin followed the fat monk, who pulled up his habit and stepped over it all with unexpected agility. Inside, quite a different scene awaited the visitors.

A dozen monks were standing at rudimentary lecterns cluttered with notebooks, ink bottles, and sheets of parchment. All around, on low shelves, bound books gleamed in the candlelight. In the middle, a candle illumined an old cat that lay curled up in a pool of white wax, dozing.

Like a lord stretching his arms over his lands, Brother Paul pointed proudly at the nave. "The library!"

Several bald craniums turned sternly to the intruders, examined them for a moment, then immediately plunged back into their reading. Their rough fingers scurried over the pages like insects, made their way between the paragraphs and the illuminations, foraged in the text, touched the commentaries, grazed the mysteries.

François peered into the gloom, looking for the altar, the confessional, the baptismal font. There was nothing here but books.

Six bells tolled, announcing mealtime. A cramped, windowless room served as a refectory. The prior blessed the vespers bread. The dinner guests noisily swallowed big mouthfuls of a thyme-flavored gruel, straight from the bowl. Once grace had been hastily recited, they hurried back to the chapel. The need to feed themselves seemed to be considered an exasperating waste of time.

Sacrificing himself for the sake of hospitality, Brother Paul remained for a few moments in the company of the two guests. Starved, Colin and François devoured the rest of the bread, scoured the bottom of the cauldron, knocked back glassfuls of goat's milk.

"We are not accustomed to receiving visitors. The cohorts of pilgrims rarely come this way. Sanctimonious fools with their cheap crosses! Better to tread the ways of the heart, to explore the solitude of the soul, than to beat a path to the gates of Jerusalem."

The fat monk stood up and walked to an oak chest to which he alone had the key. From it, he took two liters of wine. Drinking only a gulp himself, he was amused at the swiftness with which Colin and François drained the rest straight from the bottle.

François wiped his lips with his sleeve. "Will we be allowed to look at your precious books?"

"That depends on Brother Médard, who is rarely in a good

humor. He prays constantly for God's creatures but hates their company. Even ours. He scolds us endlessly, reproaching us for mishandling the books, and for misreading them, reading them too quickly or too slowly."

François wondered if this was the very place where the books he had come to find, the books that would break down the defenses of Rome, were stored.

Paul rose abruptly to his feet. He blessed the two men and smiled. "You can sleep here. There is straw over there in the corner."

The prior refused the crown offered by François as alms and left the refectory. A square of clear sky could briefly be glimpsed, then the door closed again on the stale smells and the stifling semidarkness. The banquet given in honor of the envoys of Louis XI had been frugal to say the least, their reception devoid of ceremony. Fust's suppliers were a sorry sight. It seemed strange that the German should get his stocks from these ragged monks, especially as the works with which they supplied him undermined the integrity of the Church. And yet Brother Paul appeared to be a good Christian.

Exhausted, Colin pushed his straw mattress against the wall and fell asleep, cursing his sad lot. François, though, was not offended at the frugality of this welcome. He had been dreading the idea of having to strut like a peacock at some dinner attended by diplomats or merchants. It little mattered if he went in through the main door or the back one, this was the threshold of a secret kingdom. He was sure of it.

Tantalized, he took a last swig of communion wine, toasting his own shadow on the wall, then blew out the candle. He placed his tricorn on the floor and lay down in his turn. He did not close his eyes. His hands crossed behind his head, he smiled up at the thousands of stars he imagined on the other side of the roof.

6

A pale sun freed itself from the morning mist. Fleeting shadows of monks bustled about the courtyard. The door of the chapel was ajar. Inside, the spent candles gave off a chilly smell. François could not resist the desire to go and stroke the bound books and parchments. He entered the nave, seized a volume at random, opened it without reading it, and turned the pages with the tips of his fingers, as if passing his hand beneath a waterfall. A flood of black letters poured from page to page. No punctuation slowed or stopped this rushed, apparently meaningless calligraphy. François quivered with pleasure. Was it not thus that the word became poetry?

"Get your filthy paws off that book, heathen!"

In the doorway, a dwarf was hopping and gesticulating frantically. His huge head swayed at the end of a puny, twisted body, like a loose rattle. His complexion was pale, the skin crumpled like badly-wrung linen.

"Brother Médard?"

"I'm nobody's brother!" he retorted, waving a stick as if about to strike the intruder. François looked at him for a moment with a nonchalant gaze then ran toward the dark nooks and crannies of the nave. Bursting with laughter, he made his way between the shelves that creaked beneath the weight of the clasped, studded and strapped volumes carelessly heaped on them.

The dwarf came after him, beating the air. At the far end, a colossal door with steel hinges blocked François's escape. It had only one lock, a massive one cast in one piece. Big nails hid the joints. To what was it guarding access? Unable to move, François leaned back against the imposing door, waiting resolutely for Médard, holding back his boyish giggles. In front of him, a thread of iridescent light pierced the stained glass window, lighting up a pedestal on which lay some books whose bindings were coated with beeswax, their edges gilded in fine gold. In this thin beam, he glimpsed, right at the top of the pile, the gold coat of arms of the Medici. It seemed to shine with its own light, like a talisman. The size of the book was impressive. It looked like an atlas. The other book, the one he had seen in Fust's printing works, although thicker, had only been a quarto. But the emblem was similar in size and encircled by kabbalistic signs, as if struck from the same seal.

Médard emerged at last and came and placed himself in front of François. He stood up on tiptoe, threateningly. A huge bronze key hung from his rope belt. Seeing its intricate surround, François, still with his back to the door, merely said, "You're protecting your secret well, little monk."

The dwarf held his club at arm's length, ready to strike. Brother Paul appeared. He advanced with measured steps and in a honeyed voice ordered François to leave the building. Outside, the brightness made him blink. François lowered his eyes to the ground. A shadow stood out on the fine gravel. François looked closely at it. It was that of a man crouching, perfectly motionless, as if lying in wait. François lifted his head. Blinded by the sun, he shielded his eyes with his hand. Perched on the roof of the barn, knees bent, an archer had him in his sights. François immediately rolled onto the ground to avoid the arrow. He took his knife from his boot, and rose to his full height to throw it. But the other man had not budged. And had not fired. His bow was still taut, aimed directly at François. If the knife hit him, he would release his grip and the arrow would go straight to its target. François hesitated, looking his adversary up and down. He was on the short side, although not a dwarf like Médard. He was too firm in his bearing. Impossible to see his face. A coat of mail hung from his pointed helmet, protecting his face. His chest was held in a tight leather doublet. He carried a sword at his side, curved and unsheathed, hanging from a knight's belt. François curled his lips in a clownish grin and did a little dance step to throw his rival. He might as well have been tickling a marble statue. How to trick him?

Brother Paul's booming voice put an end to this unusual encounter. The archer immediately lowered his weapon, but François remained on his guard, knife in hand.

The prior apologized. It was the commotion from the chapel that had alarmed the sentry. And Brother Médard's yells.

"A sentry?"

Brother Paul tried to reassure François. "And a monk. In his way. In his spare time, he helps our scribes to transcribe the teaching of a great sage he calls the Buddha. His forefathers fought beside our Crusaders. Even today, many of his countrymen can be found in Syria, Lebanon, and Persia. They are highly prized for their skill with horses."

François let his gaze wander around the perimeter walls. They were pierced with arrow slits. There was no doubt about it. This place, bucolic in appearance, was a disguised fort. And defended by Mongol mercenaries to boot!

Barely awake, Colin kicked his straw mattress away and cursed Villon, Guillaume Chartier, Louis XI, and God the Father. The bites of mosquitoes, the deafening song of the cicadas, and the ringing of bells had deprived him of a good night's sleep. He couldn't wait to leave this flea-ridden monastery, this cloister where the vapors of the summer heat fermented as if at the bottom of a vat of grapes. He felt trapped. Why should he rot here? What riled Colin most was his own stupidity. He had let himself be taken in by the magic of the words "Holy Land," "Galilee," "Jerusalem," by the mystery this land kept hidden beneath its stones, by the wind that blew differently here than elsewhere. Oh, yes, that wind was so hot, it roasted your ass! Colin hated the heat, the harsh, almost blinding light, the smell of burning sand that had been oppressing him since his arrival. Not to mention the food, which was too spicy, pickled in olive oil or dried in the sun.

Brother Paul burst into the refectory, followed by François, and took Colin's arm. He understood his irritation, his desire to bolt for it as soon as possible.

"A little patience, Master Colin. We are awaiting the arrival of a visitor who is very eager to make your acquaintance."

7

The Mamluk soldiers inspected the convoy. Three wagons pulled by mules. The first two overflowed with trinkets, glass jewelry, and wooden statuettes of saints. In the third, less heavily laden, were provisions, carters' tools, a few books and a religious painting. The young Florentine merchant who was leading the expedition wore impeccable, richly embroidered clothes. A plume of long colored feathers hung on the side of his hexagonal hat. A leather strap knotted around his neck kept this extravagant headgear aloft. Beneath it sheltered a haughty, impassive face, typical of a Latin gentlemen. From his hand, with its slender, well-tended fingers, covered with huge rings, he negligently dropped a small purse then, without waiting, saluted the soldiers and signaled to the muleteers to continue on their way. In spite of his courtier's attire, he nimbly remounted his horse with its glossy coat and bridle overloaded with pom-poms and bells. Astounded, the Mamluks followed the convoy with their eyes for a long time. They could still make out the flaming hues of the plume striping the austere ocher of the fields before disappearing into the groves lining the valley. It was only then that, out of sight beyond a bend in the road, the young merchant briefly dabbed the rivulets of sweat flooding his face and neck.

He felt a keen sense of relief when at last he sighted the welcoming hump of the hill, the blunt tip of the old bell tower, the great rusty cross rising into the sky. It had taken enormous stamina and determination to get here. The war between the

Venetians and the Turks had made the crossing more perilous than usual. On the Aegean Sea, the frail brigantine had somehow forced its way through fighting ships, Greek and Ottoman corsairs, Saracen pirates. Every time a sail was spotted in the distance, the captain would abruptly change course, and even threaten to turn back. But returning to Florence would have been just as hazardous, and the wind was unfavorable.

Cosimo de' Medici's instructions, even though uttered from his deathbed, were categorical. More than that, they were his last will, his testament: to save the painting and the clandestine manuscripts he had been hiding in the cellars of the Platonic Academy. The mission would not be at all easy, but fortune smiled on the young merchant when a decree from Lorenzo II, known as the Magnificent, made Florence a veritable protectorate for the Jews. Not only did Lorenzo lift all the humiliating prohibitions against the Jews of Florence but in addition, running counter to Papal censorship, he exhorted scholars to once again take up the study of Talmudic works, Judeo-Arab treatises on medicine, and even the kabbalah. The universities of Bologna and Parma openly ordered copies of the works of rabbis, exegeses composed in the Jewish quarters of Toledo and Prague or drawn up by the schools of Tiberias and Safed. Under the auspices of Lorenzo the Magnificent and with money from the faculties, including the Platonic Academy, as well as Cosimo de' Medici's secret funds, the young book hunter was able to fit out a ship for the Holy Land. Using as a pretext the purchase of Hebrew works of renown, he was in fact transporting, among the rare volumes bequeathed by Cosimo to the monastery, the final writings of the recalcitrant Cardinal de Cues, the secret notes of the philosopher Marsilio Ficino on the *Corpus Hermeticum*, an Eastern treatise on zero, and a painting by Filippo Brunelleschi, all banned by the apostolic censors.

In Cosimo de' Medici's library, the young man had feverishly noted down the information he was to provide Brother Médard's mysterious sponsors as to the immense significance of these clandestine works. "The moment has come," Cosimo had concluded laconically before dismissing him. "Tell them they can launch the offensive."

Cosimo had waited serenely for the end, surrounded by his collections, mixing his last breath with the smell of the books, going to join their authors in the world where the mind of man at last roams amid the spheres, talks with the angels, and smiles for no reason in the austere shadow of the gods. It was in death that he achieved his lifelong ideal, to be a *uomo universale.*

The news of another expected death has sent shock waves through Christendom: that of Pope Pius II, just after his final attempt to raise a crusade. The troops he had recruited in Mantua and Ancona had merely pillaged a few small towns and massacred some hundred infidels. In April, another abortive crusade left thirty bodies in the alleys of the ghetto of Krakow before breaking up in chaos. Had the Christians lost Jerusalem forever?

The Holy Land was now nothing but a confused jumble of outcasts and fallen adventurers. Educated priests preferred to obtain a small diocese in Anjou or the Rhineland rather than a bishopric in Palestine. European monarchs saw no interest in raising armies to conquer a devastated land infested with epidemics and noxious air. Even the Emir of Judea dreamed only of being relieved of his wretched post and returning to the luxury of Alexandria or Baghdad. He cursed the hordes of pilgrims endlessly landing on the coasts, the vast caravans crossing the country in the opposite direction, toward the ports, the relentless movements of nomads fleeing famine and drought. The penitents' donkeys, the merchants' camels, the peasants' goats had finally devoured what little green had still remained to cover the shame of the soil, the nakedness of the rock, the ugliness of the loose stones. This territory ruled over by a Mamluk governor was merely an inextricable intermingling of roads and tracks, a way station trapped between two worlds, East and West. Its epic battlefields had been abandoned to the weeds. The tombs of prophets and knights and Roman centurions were rotting in the sun. Only Jews and poets still turned toward Jerusalem, like the last remaining clients of a brothel who still pay their respects to the ageing madam. Most in fact had never even seen this city whose praises they sang so stoutly. And as the good whore that she was, she gave herself to all the symbols, all the rhymes, all the hopes, all the priests and all the soldiers, unflinchingly pocketing the wages of misfortune and poverty. And yet those few poets continued to venerate her with their convoluted odes and those few Jews predicted that she would be reborn from the ashes. For them, the destiny of Jerusalem was not carved in wars but in texts, in the Scriptures. She was a city not so much built of stone and bricks as fashioned out of words and dreams.

8

L eaning on the edge of the ramparts that protected the cloister, François and Colin watched the convoy arrive. They made out the bright colors of the plume crying amid the russet of the ripe corn, standing out against the brown of the carts, breaking the sobriety of the landscape with their city insolence.

At the foot of the hill, the monks unloaded the wagons then carried the packages on their backs up the steep path leading to the monastery. The Mongol sentries had taken up their positions on the roofs, the bell tower, and the turrets. The arrival of the book merchant seemed to have sharpened the Mamluks' vigilance. One of the guards thought he had seen a scout prowling around the cloister. Or was it only a poacher?

The dashing stranger emerged from the undergrowth, and reached the promontory. He walked confidently, barely out of breath, as if he were on his way to a ceremonial dinner. His laced boots slid over the rubble, but he did not stumble. He glanced rapidly in the direction of Colin and François, pretending not to see them, perhaps blinded by the light. When he reached the gate, he doffed his spectacular hat and bowed low to the prior. Then he took a keg from his bag, sprang the lid with his knife, emptied the contents—which smelled of brandy—and, from a false bottom, extracted a casket filled with gold and silver coins.

"For your books."

In the refectory, before sitting down, Brother Paul introduced the newcomer. For supper, the Italian had donned a fleece-lined housecoat in warm colors. The garment, artfully unbuttoned, gave a glimpse of a silk shirtfront as well as an area of muscular, hairy chest. Ostentatious as it was, this touch of vanity was nevertheless in good taste. The proud young peacock knew how to display his fabulous finery with a certain grace. As for his hats, each was more extravagant than the last. For the moment, he was wearing a broad black velvet cap such as master painters wore in their studios. To the rim of it, he had pinned a carnelian cameo showing the bust of a Roman lady. A genuine archeological find dating from the era of Marcus Aurelius, the hard stone was set amid baroque pearls, the work of a Viennese silversmith. From it ran a line of gold that intertwined with the ancient courtesan's hair. Finally, to emphasize his august attire, he wore high-heeled shoes that raised him at least ten inches off the ground, forcing François to crane his neck.

François, who did not normally bother overmuch with the dictates of etiquette, nevertheless put on a good show. Even though he feigned roughness and often behaved boorishly, a strange aura emanated from his hangdog face. Beneath his old tricorn there shone a mocking light, underlined by the discreet, wry smile that never left his lips. Nobody had ever known if this grin was natural or affected, sardonic, disenchanted, or a mere defect of birth.

The Italian quickly looked François up and down, trying immediately to decipher that fixed pout with its mixture of bravado and frankness, a good dose of suffering cut with a dash of goodness, whose secret depths he sensed at once. He had expected to find an arrogant, self-centered rebel. He discovered a man who was natural, who wore no mask—there were few such men in Florence these days. He bowed, gracefully held out his hand, and introduced himself.

"Federico Castaldi, Florentine merchant and agent of Master Cosimo de' Medici."

Now it was François's turn to examine the newcomer's features. He was surprised and incredulous. Were all these unexpected links with the Medicis merely the scattered ramifications of a great dynasty or else the meshes of a net that was gradually closing?

"What good wind brings you to the Holy Land, Master Villon?"

"Contrary winds. Zephyrs of escape and trade winds of fortune."

The two men exchanged almost conspiratorial glances. Federico, who hated dubious scholars and proud geniuses, found Villon remarkably pleasant for a fashionable author. And François, who could not stand pedants or the overprecious, sensed that the Florentine was a lot more perceptive than he pretended to be. Was he playing the powdered puppet as a mere merchant's trick or a deeper disguise?

Federico next observed Colin, who was noisily stuffing himself. His rough-hewn, imposing bulk, his bulging biceps, his heavily scarred face inspired fear at first. But his wide-open eyes, like those of a dim-witted little boy, soon won people over. Playing on this mixture of wildness and innocence, it was he who kept the guards occupied or cajoled the clerks while the Coquillards emptied church coffers and bailiffs' desks. Their finest coup dated from just before Christmas 1456. Five hundred gold crowns plucked as easily as a sheaf in a cornfield. Colin had stood by the entrance to the chapel of the Collège de Navarre, gesticulating, pontificating, joking, with the wardens looking on incredulously, while inside Tabarie and François had broken into the office.

At the end of the meal, the Florentine ceremoniously handed a book to François. The binding still smelled of alum.

The covers were studded with silvery flowers from the stalks of which emerged thin gilded threads applied with a trimmer. In the middle, embedded in the leather itself, a real butterfly spread its translucent wings. The back of the book, slightly marbled, was encrusted with plantlike patterns in mother-of-pearl. The threads were lined with salamander skin and the boards with lizard scales. The smooth waxed covers showed that nobody had ever looked inside the book. François carefully opened the lock with its finely chiseled arabesques. Inside, he found only empty pages, of an excellent texture, much softer than those obtained in a vat. He admired every detail. It was obvious that the talents of several master craftsmen had gone into the work.

"Allow me to give it to you. For the ballads you have not yet written."

Caught off guard, François stammered some formal words of gratitude, suspecting nevertheless that such a tribute was not disinterested. A shrewd merchant like Federico did not dispense such generous gifts without some ulterior motive. Had he himself had not done the same to lure Johann Fust? What was this Florentine merchant, whose acquaintance he had made only a few moments earlier, hoping to obtain from him?

Noticing François's embarrassment, Federico merely gave him a broad smile. He seized a bottle whose exaggerated curves, the red seals surrounding the neck, the small bubbles blown into the glass itself, promised a choice beverage. Expertly pulling the cork out with his teeth, he poured a few substantial glassfuls. As the connoisseur that he was, François breathed in the aroma, getting ready to praise the color, the body, the flavor. But the Italian abruptly withdrew, summoned by Brother Médard whose hairless chin had appeared suddenly amid the plates and pots.

On the table, the wings of the butterfly glittered in the light of the oil lamps. François again examined the immaculate binding, the embossing applied with both confidence and finesse. The unusual style of the ornamentation skilfully combined the sharp lines of the insect with the light curves of the gilt around it. Just like the Aramaic lettering he had seen around the Medici coat of arms.

9

A solitary chandelier hung from the ceiling. Brother Médard carefully laid out his inventory books and pencils. Federico took his seat on the other side of the desk, the precious packages at his feet. Although they were alone in the chapel, the two men spoke in low voices.

"You certainly know how to toady. Master Villon was genuinely touched. Have you read his works, then?"

"Not a line, my dear Médard. All I know is that—"

"One moment, please," the dwarf muttered as he started writing. "On this twelfth day of June, 1464 . . . various consignments . . . provenance . . . Federico . . . Castaldi . . . in his capacity as . . . articles . . . There. First entry?"

"Three manuscripts from the hand of Bishop Nicholas of Cusa, also known as Cusanum, concerning the composition of the universe. From algebraic deductions and observation of the skies, it has apparently been established that, and I quote, *terra non est centra mundi* . . . It seems there are thousands of stars and planets hovering in the ether. We are merely a grain of sand in the midst of that vastness."

Brother Médard gave a start, almost falling off his stool. "You can't solve the mystery of Creation with an abacus," he growled.

"My most Catholic lord Medici thinks the papacy has become trapped in the swamps of dogma. It persists in following Aristotle for fear of shaking beliefs that ensure it the blind submission of its flock. It even rejects zero, which both

Arabs and Jews use without in any way losing faith in their God."

"Zero? Neither Pythagoras nor Euclid needed that phantom number. They established the world on solid foundations, not on a fortune-teller's symbols!"

"How can an empty, worthless number threaten the Almighty?"

Federico took a painting from the rough cloths in which it was wrapped. He arranged the five wooden panels on the floor to reconstruct a fresco. Médard was reassured at first. He saw the pale hands of a Madonna, then the rosy-cheeked features of the child Jesus, his head duly crowned with a halo. Behind them, a stone colonnade stood out against the landscape in the background. You could see a blue river winding toward low hills. Trees, painted in astonishing detail, contrasted with a sky filled with hazy clouds. An ancient mausoleum stood on the summit of a plateau. In spite of the Madonna's gleaming robe and the strong colors of the central scene, your eyes plunged into the distance, abandoning the holy characters to wander amid hills and valleys. You felt a kind of dizziness. The Virgin and her child seemed to be sitting quite close to you, but it was the clouds and the trees, their hues at once smooth and deep, that led you into their strange world, and you stopped seeing the mother and son. You sensed them the way you would sense a presence, but your eyes were elsewhere, flowing with the river among the hills, engrossed in little brushstrokes that perfectly echoed the grain of the wood. The division of the panels added to the artifice, leaving it to the eye to weave the very texture of the space and the light. The religious scene was merely a pretext.

This work by the painter and architect Brunelleschi had briefly adorned the baptistery of Florence Cathedral. It had been hastily removed before its creator could suffer the wrath of his sponsors and remained for a long time hidden in the cellars of the Medicis. Only Master Verrocchio was able to see it and teach its secrets to his apprentices. At this very moment, one of his pupils, named Leonardo, had been given the task of mastering this new way of depicting the universe, this other way of seeing, known as perspective.

"Trompe-l'œil, that's all it is. Does it make the Madonna any holier?"

Federico put away his notes and concentrated on establishing the inventory. In any case, the monk's voice didn't count. The final decision was taken elsewhere, by his masters. They would only affix their mysterious mark to the Medici coat of arms if they approved Cosimo's choices. It was then up to them to decide whether they confined them to a library or disseminated the contents. Otherwise, Federico would have to take back the rejected books and paintings and sell them at the back of his shop as mere curiosities.

The consignment went on late into the night. The merchant opened the cases, held out the manuscripts one by one, without saying another word, yawning with exhaustion. The dwarf kept writing, looking offended but not daring to open his mouth. Author, title, date, author, title, date . . . Until the early hours of the morning.

10

E ven before the first light of dawn, the coachmen were busy, checking the horses' harnesses, inspecting the straps on the mules, kicking the wheels.

Brother Paul had received marching orders on behalf of the emissaries of the King of France. The date of their first interview with one of the Medicis' discreet allies had been fixed. They were expected in Safed. The way there was strewn with pitfalls. Saracens and Turkish brigands dispatched many a lost traveler to the other life, and diseases and noxious air took care of the rest. The hospitals set up by the various orders were overflowing with the dying and the wounded. Mamluk squads had been seen in the vicinity. Brother Paul did not know the reason for these patrols but such troop movements were common. Whether pale-faced knights or dark-complexioned mercenaries, the conquerors of this land were doomed to be constantly on the lookout.

The prior had decided to add François and Colin to Federico's convoy, which would be stopping at Safed and Tiberias to pick up supplies of Hebrew works for the Italian universities. It would not arouse suspicion. After all, it was carrying nothing but books. If it was stopped, the soldiers could easily be bribed.

François and Colin plunged their heads into the drinking trough, then shook their soaked hair like dogs. Colin donned a thin leather cabasset that flattened his skull. François put on his crumpled tricorn. They could already feel a burning wind on the backs of their necks. Federico appeared in the doorway of the refectory, lit by a first ray of sun. Clad in all his gleaming finery, he waddled like a court favorite on his way to a ball. Dazzled, the Mongol sentries stood aside to let him pass, unwittingly forming a comical guard of honor. Brother Paul, suddenly stern, whispered a few words in his ear. Federico nodded and half knelt to receive the prior's blessing. He dusted off his sleeves, and, with the help of a ribbon, tied his hair behind his neck. Throwing a satisfied look at the men and the horses, he gave the order to leave.

It was going to be a very hot day. A leaden light poured down on the arid plain, the motionless shrubs that no breeze stirred. In the distance, a solitary sparrow hawk soared. Distorted by heat haze, the countryside seemed to scowl. The bad-tempered shadow of a cloud splashed the line of the horizon then spread its grey stain over the ocher blanket of the fields. The riders went more quickly, abandoning the monks to their precinct of stone.

An air of freedom blew over their cheeks. The horses galloped, intoxicated by the light, tearing joyfully across the gilded brambles, cutting through the clouds of midges, shaking their loads from side to side as the terrain changed. The water lapped gaily in the gourds. François inhaled the scent of the scrub and let his eyes wander over the eroded curves of the plateaus, the winding roads, the paths trodden by the apostles, the valleys where the prophets were buried, at last discovering the Holy Land. He allowed it to permeate him. At first, he looked avidly for signs, inscriptions on the pediment of some temple. There was not even a milestone. Only stony tracks that seemed to lead nowhere. And yet this land was whispering a vague message in his ear, a secret from deep in the soul. He sensed intuitively that it had been waiting for him forever.

When night fell, Federico looked for a place to camp. Fabulous Galilee offered only the shelter of meager undergrowth. Emaciated pines, skeletal cypresses, and dwarf oaks barely concealed the horses. The moon was in its first quarter. Federico decided not to light a fire. The men sat down in the gloom, their whispers mingling with the mournful howling of jackals. François took his place on a flat rock, and grabbed a jug of Falernian wine and a smoked chicken thigh. Federico crouched in order not to soil his clothes.

"We'll get to Safed by tomorrow evening. A piece of oatcake?"

The Italian's pale smile glittered in the darkness. François passed him the jug then cleaned his hands with twigs moistened with dew.

"You are linked to the noble house of the Medicis. I thought I saw their arms on one of the volumes kept in the monastery."

"That may be so."

"They differ from the famous emblem by the addition of kabbalistic symbols whose meaning escapes me."

"I don't read Hebrew," the merchant replied curtly.

An owl hooted in the distance. Frightened, one of the horses gave a start. Federico stood up and went to calm it with a pat on the spine, making sure that its reins were firmly tied around a dead trunk. François followed him with his eyes, convinced that the Italian knew much more than he was prepared to admit. He had clearly been expecting to see François in the monastery, and had already planned to give him that splendid book with the butterfly. Brother Paul had nevertheless assured the two Frenchmen that the bookseller knew nothing of the mission that had brought them here. Federico's coming had been planned long before their arrival. He was a regular in the place and often came there for supplies. In any case, there was nothing to fear from a man in the pay of the Medicis. But

François felt a kind of anxiety around the Italian. The fellow was clearly playing a part. His unctuous merchant's gestures, the way he exaggerated his distinction to make its falseness clear, his showy attire, were so many layers beneath which to bury the person that François detected in spite of everything. There emanated from him the self-confident authority of a leader of men, the rigidity of a soldier, and an intransigence that was frightening. This was no courtly hypocrite, but rather someone who held a secret. Yet he did little to conceal his game. The aim of that half-open, half-closed mask he offered to people's gaze was not to disorientate, but to discourage any desire to remove it from him and discover his real face. It was a tactic that François knew well, one the Coquillards had used, to warn anyone who might pry too closely into their affairs that the result might be a knife in the gut. That was why François mistrusted Federico. And it was also why he respected him.

Colin took the first watch. François came to keep him company. He did not tell him about his suspicions, fearing that the fellow might relieve him of them in his way—by smashing the Florentine's head against a wagon wheel, or thrusting a bottle of wine down his throat, if not elsewhere. Colin seemed in a bad enough mood already. He stamped his feet and swore that Chartier would just have to wait. The Bishop hadn't even taken the trouble to write a letter of introduction. If things went badly, he would wash his hands of them. François mocked his friend. Since when did an honest bandit wager on the assurances of a clergyman? Colin shrugged. He crushed a mosquito in his hand, cursing all the saints in heaven, then went and leaned against a rock and began sharpening a branch with his knife to use as a toothpick. François took advantage of this brief lull to reassure his companion. He had absolutely no intention of following Chartier's orders. But it was too early to act. However much François claimed that he was concocting one of those brilliant coups only he seemed able to pull off, a really clever trick, Colin couldn't see anything good coming of this business. François stretched his hand toward the country-side as if the undergrowth and the sand agreed with him. It wasn't Chartier, or Fust, or anyone else who would tell him the way and guide his steps. It was this land. This country was call-ing to him. He felt it. And for quite another mission.

Colin, who was used to these lyrical flights, especially when François had been drinking, stood up without saying a word, his own response being to piss noisily on the undergrowth and the sand. And on this damned country.

11

T he afternoon was already well under way by the time the convoy began its climb toward Safed, roasting up there in the sun. The line of roofs shimmered slightly, giving the town a dreamlike appearance. The horses struggled up the last part of the ascent until their hooves struck the burning stones of the alleys. Here, there were no inns or taverns. No good Catholics either. The shadows of wretched-looking Muslims and Jews glided past the blue and green house fronts, thus painted to ward off the evil eye. There being little to pillage, the Mamluks were nowhere to be seen. Their detachments were content to patrol the outskirts and bivouac in open country, close to water sources and farms. Even the Church did not deign to favor this place with a monastery or a shrine. And yet this isolated town, devoid of the luxury that gave the cities of the East their reputation, was home to a number of important figures whose spiritual influence spread beyond the sea. Jews everywhere, hiding from the Inquisition or missing an appointment with their landlords, would hasten to their quarters in Seville or Prague to gather in a clandestine place of study. There, one of their people would be waiting for them impatiently in order to read aloud a missive, an instruction or a commentary newly arrived from Safed. Each word was drunk in like a comforting potion, each turn of phrase was applauded as if it were an exceptional acrobatic feat. It was as if the scholars of the Holy Land had come to recite them in person, their shoes still coated with sand, their eyes shining with the sun.

Could such a peaceful, isolated town really conceal such wisdom?

Women and children watched the riders pass by with a mixture of suspicion and curiosity. François smiled at them, but Colin sat stiff and erect, like a marshal inspecting his troops. Two old Jews with long beards were chatting on a stone bench beneath a palm tree whose branches were laden with dates and moths. They abruptly fell silent as the convoy approached. One of them seemed ready to leap to his feet and run away. The other, wrapped tightly in his caftan, ignored the strangers, muttered some psalm or other, and dozed off, his head propped on his chest.

At the end of the main street stood an imposing building that blazed white in the sun. Federico was the first to enter. Muleteers and carters waited outside, watering the animals. Inside the house, all was bright. The high walls were painted in bluish hues of a pastel lightness. The waiting room was lit with brass lamps from which hung brightly-colored amulets. On the floor, ceramic flagstones covered with arabesques vied with multicolored rugs. In the patio stood a sweet-smelling fig tree. The secretary led the visitors to a small room furnished with a table and four wooden chairs. He announced that the rabbi would be joining them shortly. Federico explained to François and Colin that Rabbi Gamliel Ben Sira was a highly respected figure, rather like a cardinal, and that it was a rare honor for them to be granted an audience with him. Rabbi Gamliel was a renowned scholar who corresponded with scientists in Nuremberg, professors in Turin, doctors in Amsterdam. He directed one of the most reputable academies in the Jewish world. In addition to that, every morning he dispensed cures and advice to the poor people of the region.

The rabbi made his entrance through a low door. As the door stood open, François glimpsed a study with a small inlaid

Damascus desk piled high with manuscripts and scrolls of parchment.

"*Shalom*, welcome."

Their host's easy demeanor surprised François. He had been expecting a bearded old man, a patriarch with a heavily lined face made pale by long nights of prayer, but here stood a tall, robust man in his thirties, entirely dressed in dazzling white, with tanned skin, a thick but meticulously groomed black beard, and a broad smile. It was evident that the rabbi had been expecting the two Frenchmen and that he knew the purpose of their visit. That was why his conduct took François aback. A Jew receiving a visit from emissaries of a king would have been expected to bow reverently, but this man remained straight-backed and simply held out his hand. He was almost six feet tall. François, who was shorter, and still dirty from the ride, felt somewhat intimidated. As for Colin, he was openly offended.

The secretary put some tea down on the table, then returned a few moments later with a thick volume under his arm. He looked quickly through the list of orders handed to him by Federico, ticked certain titles, then consulted a big register. Even though Rabbi Gamliel owned a well-stocked library, he never let the books he had read out of his sight, but was constantly scribbling notes and references in them. His phenomenal memory allowed him to cross-check different texts studied over a period of several years. He remembered the exact place to find such and such a passage. The inventory held by his secretary did not therefore list the Rabbi's personal copies. It comprised works that were not all kept in Safed, or even in the Holy Land. It was a kind of bookseller's catalogue, listing hundreds of manuscripts and printed books, with their dates and places of publication as well as the various places where they could be acquired. As soon as news arrived that a synagogue had been pillaged or a house of study razed to the ground, Rabbi Gamliel's secretary would consult his lists. If a Babylonian Talmud was burned in Cologne, it was quickly replaced with another copy from Orléans or Barcelona. If a scholar in York asked a difficult question about the dietary laws, he was referred to a commentary dealing with that same law, written in Smyrna a few years earlier. Whenever a sage was summoned to debate the Trinity with the inquisitors, he was provided with documents from several churches to help him to juggle skillfully with the often conflicting, even contradictory opinions of the various clergies.

When you came down to it, it was the tragic dispersal of the Jews that saved them. No tyranny, however widely it extended its net, could reach them all. No epidemic could wipe them out. For that to happen, it would have to spread immediately to the four corners of the earth. But it was to their books above all that the Jews owed their survival. For it was the same Talmud that was read—in Hebrew—in Peking, Samarkand, Tripoli, or Damascus. And as long as it was read, out loud or in hiding, by a whole congregation or a solitary hermit, they would be able to sail through any storm.

Being forbidden everywhere to raise troops, to bear arms, or even to ride horses, the Jews had been forced to create an invisible army, an army without a garrison or an arsenal, which operated under the noses of the censors. Thanks to their common language and this network of communication, they had for centuries maintained a nation without a king or a land. Louis XI had always been fascinated by the way the rabbis spread their teachings beyond borders, thus weaving the invisible links that united their people. Like them, he was trying to impose French as the official language of the kingdom and had just ordered the creation of a letter post. The young monarch reigned over a confused jumble of constantly squabbling provinces. Bretons, Burgundians, Savoyards, and Gascons did not speak the same language. How could they come to an understanding? Would Gamliel supply the books on which the King of France was counting to assert his power from Picardy to Lorraine, from the Languedoc to Normandy, and counter the hold the Roman Church had over his subjects?

François listened to the rabbi's explanations with redoubled interest. He was starting to glimpse the true extent of this Gamliel's activities, the influence he exerted from here, sitting at his desk, the significance of the texts he propagated. Was he the Medicis' mysterious accomplice? Johann Fust's patron? And the future accomplice of Louis XI?

François nevertheless remained puzzled. He could not see a practicing Jew in a white skullcap and caftan concerning himself with the humanities, opening clandestine print shops, publishing previously unpublished works by Lucretius and Demosthenes, gathering together treatises on algebra or astronomy, some of which contradicted the teachings of his own religion. Nor could François see any reason why a sage from the Holy Land would want to work hand in hand with gentiles from Florence, let alone a man of the Church like Chartier. Unless he was pursuing an aim quite different than that of his eminent allies, and without their knowing it. Just like François, who did not believe that any of them were well intentioned and was waiting for the moment to carry off his own victory.

While his secretary prepared the orders, Rabbi Gamliel conversed calmly with Federico. The Italian spoke of the Earth, which was no longer at the center of the universe, and of Florence, which was now where everything important was happening. The rabbi listened to all this with a somewhat condescending politeness. Once the packages were ready, Gamliel asked the two Frenchmen to excuse him. He would only be a moment. He stood up and motioned to Federico to follow him into the adjoining room.

Through the half-open door, François saw the rabbi hand a wide scroll to the merchant, who quickly looked through it. The edges were uneven and fraying everywhere into long yellow strands of a texture like straw or rushes. The body of the scroll was crisscrossed with stripes and plantlike veins. It was neither paper nor parchment. Sitting too far away to clearly make out every detail, François saw only a confused network of ocher patches on a blue background crossed with lines and arrows. The colors had so faded with time that he could barely make out the design, but the whole seemed to be like a sea chart. It could not however be a map of the world. There were far too many patches to be taken for islands or continents. Perhaps it was an ancient chart of a fabulous world.

Noticing a sudden change in intonation in the voices of the two men, François pricked up his ears. Until now, the conversation between Gamliel and Federico had been held in Spanish, the only Latin language the rabbi knew. Although he couldn't quite hear what was being said, François was certain that the dialogue was now continuing in a different language, a kind of guttural dialect that, in spite of its Semitic accents, sounded like neither Hebrew nor Arabic.

Federico came out, holding the mysterious scroll under his arm, and immediately took his leave. He apologized politely, announcing that he had to set off again early in the morning for Nazareth where he hoped to acquire a rare Syriac manuscript. The brevity of this farewell took François by surprise. The Italian had not even inquired about the two pilgrims' intentions.

12

Once Federico had left, the rabbi invited François and Colin to join him in his study. They sat for a while in awkward silence, while he stared insistently at the two men, as if trying to read a message in the lines of their faces. His knitted brows and fixed gaze seemed to be trying to penetrate their very souls, to probe the darkest recesses. He seemed unaware of the embarrassment caused by this prolonged examination. Even though the two strangers corresponded faithfully to the description that Fust had given of them in his letters, Gamliel was somewhat disconcerted by the wretched appearance of the King of France's emissaries. That vagabond with his crumpled hat and his falsely stupid smile really didn't look as he had expected. And the caustic, ever wary gaze of the brute who was with him was frankly discourteous. Were these the heralds so eagerly awaited by Jerusalem? Was their criminal appearance a disguise? Fust had suggested as much when he talked of Villon's surprising erudition and his passion for books. As for Colin, who thought himself so clever, Fust noted with amusement how he had let this brigand spy on him for months, letting him see only what would lead the Bishop of Paris to deal with him rather than with anyone else. Fust was convinced that there was much to be gained from a secret alliance with Louis XI: an opinion not shared by Brother Paul, who considered it too much of a risk to associate with a scheming bishop and an unscrupulous king. Jeopardizing thirty years of preparations struck him as inadvisable. They already had the Italians on their side, and that ought to be enough. What Brother Paul did not know was that it was his own sponsors, the Medicis, who advocated joining forces with the French monarch, their longtime ally in other matters. The offensive was going well, but an agreement with Paris could give it a magnitude they had not hoped for, inflicting far more damage on the enemy. It was now up to Rabbi Gamliel to decide. His colleagues in Jerusalem trusted in his good judgment.

Emerging from his reflections, he smiled with perfectly rabbinical bonhomie, mixed with a hint of mischief. Not won over, Colin scowled, but François appreciated this mark of cordiality. He was far from suspecting that, depending on the outcome of this interview, Jerusalem would either open wide its gates to him or shut them in his face forever.

"Instilling new ideas takes time. Often longer than one man's reign lasts."

"Any reign is likely to be short-lived if it is maintained only with the sword," retorted François. "Religion shows every day how to rule by the force of the written word alone."

"And by the force of faith. Hence the hints we have been giving the Christian monarchs. Our recent publications are there to remind them that David, Solomon and Alexander owed their power not to priests, but to God Himself. We've been waiting for the right moment to exhume a number of ancient works devoted to the theme."

"Is the fate of our rulers of such concern to you, then?"

"No more than it is to you."

"And that of the Jews?"

"That is my concern, yes, but it depends on those very rulers." Gamliel pointed to a vase filled with scrolls of parchment. "These manuscripts are from Athens. They are transcripts made by one of our people during the lifetime of Socrates. When he was sentenced to drink hemlock, who do you think made sure his words were preserved?"

"Wasn't it Plato?"

"Plato was no scribe. He manipulated ideas as he pleased. But it so happens that, well before him, an agent had been sent by Jerusalem with a mission to follow Socrates and be present at the public debates he conducted on the streets. The notes he made are preserved by us in a safe place. Nobody apart from us knows the contents."

"Why don't you publish them? What are you waiting for?"

"A sign. Cosimo de' Medici's friendship toward us, for example. Or even your coming here. That may be an omen, and not mere chance. Socrates was excluded from public life, just like the Jews. Out of ignorance. But those who control public life can learn. They just have to be taught a good lesson."

The rabbi did nothing to conceal the insolence of his smile. His suddenly arrogant expression embarrassed François. In it, he recognized his own, mischievous and rebellious. Shifting his gaze to the window, François looked out at the fig tree in the courtyard, its thick top ringed by a ray of moonlight. Rivers of silvery light flowed down the dark branches, making their way between the leaves and fruits, crawling as far as the roots, like reptiles. François thought of the snake in the Tree of Knowledge. Was he being lured into a pact with Satan? Rumors abounded that the Jews were plotting to take over the world, and there was no smoke without fire. They had killed Jesus. They drank the blood of babies. These accusations, so often whispered in the ear or proclaimed out loud in the public square, beat at his temples like waves crashing against a rock. The rabbi's sibylline attitude seemed to confirm all the hearsay. Colin, for his part, was certain that this Jew's motives were a lot more treacherous than he claimed.

In the subdued light of the brass candelabra, the rabbi's self-satisfied face beamed placidly. On the wall behind him was a silver plaque carved with kabbalistic signs like those that

François had seen on the Medicis' coat of arms. Gamliel noticed the direction of François's gaze.

"That's the seal of my academy. You'll find it on all the books coming out of Safed."

"And in the secret library of the most powerful dynasty in Italy!"

"It's a classification mark, nothing more."

Colin leapt to his feet. "By which one of the noblest families in Christendom forms a solemn union with a rabbi?"

"Union is a big word, Master Colin. I'd say rather an exchange of goodwill. Think. In both Florence and Safed, Jewish writings and those considered heretical are threatened. Where can they be most safely hidden?" Rabbi Gamliel was amused at Colin's stunned expression. "Yes, in a Catholic monastery in the heart of Galilee."

"The Bishop of Paris would never tolerate—"

"Guillaume Chartier tolerates whatever profits him. He'll use any means at his disposal. If you fail, he'll ally himself with the Pope again."

"And if we succeed?"

Gamliel looked first Colin, then François, straight in the eyes. "A fatal blow will be struck against the forces that have been ruling your lives for centuries."

François found it hard to believe in the rabbi's prophetic statement. Socrates's ideas had not convinced Athens. How could they threaten Rome? The renewed infatuation with the wisdom of the ancients was merely a passing fashion, whereas dogma was unshakable. A few seditious old manuscripts wouldn't change the situation. Yet Gamliel seemed sure of what he was saying. "This isn't the first time Jerusalem has conducted an operation on this scale . . . "

However François racked his brains, he could not see to what great feat Rabbi Gamliel was referring. What other large-scale plot hatched in Judea had struck at Rome? In any case, the rabbi seemed to be implying that the Medicis were pursuing an aim that went beyond their immediate financial or political interests, some more distant ideal. Their secret collaboration with Jerusalem was not limited to undermining the authority of the Holy See. Not that the unadmitted plans of the great and the good bothered François all that much. The rabbi's intentions intrigued him rather more, as did the risks he was taking if he agreed to ally himself with Louis XI. Since the mass expulsions ordered by Philippe the Fair, there were practically no Jews left in France. Just a few hundred in Alsace and in the Dauphiné. In the Comtat and throughout Provence, though, a prosperous, flourishing community enjoyed the protection of the Papal legate. Any action against Rome would expose the Pope's Jews to severe reprisals. Gamliel, though, did not seem too concerned with the fate of his coreligionists. It was the Christians he claimed to want to free from the yoke of the Church—whatever the cost. Even though he had little chance of succeeding, several Western rulers were already dealing with him. What this Talmudist from a small town in Galilee hoped to obtain from them in return remained a mystery.

Realizing suddenly that he had no idea of the true purpose of his mission, François felt like the first pawn advanced by a chess player at the beginning of a game. He might be sacrificed at any moment, or simply moved to deceive the opponent. Unlike a king, a knight, or a bishop, a pawn could not retreat.

"Will you supply us with the books we require? The Bishop of Paris is waiting for your answer."

Gamliel promised nothing. France's participation had not been part of the plan. It opened up a new front at a time when the campaign being waged with Florence and Milan had not yet extended to the rest of Italy, proceeding as it was in stages according to a rigorous plan. City by city, book by book. The rabbi nevertheless agreed to obtain an interview for them with his peers in Jerusalem. His letter of recommendation would get there in the morning by carrier pigeon.

Gamliel stood up. It was time for evening prayers. He was sorry he could not offer them hospitality but the rabbis of Safed were not accustomed to housing Catholic pilgrims. In order not to arouse the suspicions of the Mamluks, François and Colin would lodge on the edge of town with Moussa the blacksmith.

The secretary led the visitors back to their horses and indicated the way. Colin mounted, but François, his feet still on the ground, held his horse by the bridle. In the darkness, he made out Federico watching their departure from a small stone balcony.

13

F rançois and Colin reached the blacksmith's forge just as
night was falling. A broad-shouldered man was beating
the anvil with huge hammer blows. François hailed him
in Moorish, at least the little he remembered from the time
when he had shared his student garret with a man from Seville.
The blacksmith hastened to respond with a web of words
woven from the many customary courtesies, while eyeing the
two strangers suspiciously, especially the big one with the war-
like demeanor. Impassively, Colin sustained the Saracen's
searching gaze.

"Ask this damned boilermaker if he knows how to shoe
horses. Our animals' shoes have been scraped by the stones!"

Moussa retorted that he was the best blacksmith in the
Levant. The two travelers dismounted and entrusted their horses
to him.

"Aisha! Aisha!" Moussa yelled.

Amid the reflections projected by the fire of the forge on a
shack with whitewashed walls, they saw a low door. The thin
figure of a woman dressed in black came through it. She
advanced slowly, bent forward, avoiding looking at the visitors.
Without saying a word and with unexpected strength, she
seized the pouches and the goatskins, secured them on her
shoulders, forearms, and wrists, then motioned to the two men
to follow her inside. The main room was dimly lit by an oil
lamp. The tiny jingling of the small coins sewed on the fringe
of Aisha's veil was the only sound she made. Her bare feet

made no noise. She held out a surprisingly slender hand, indicating the guest room. François thanked her. She raised her head, and her eyes met his for a split second. In all that darkness, the pallor of her face, the delicacy of her features, and the piercing light of her pupils left the poet speechless. Aisha went out, closing the door behind her. Outside, Moussa was striking his anvil with such force that Colin regretted not agreeing on the cost of the shoeing in advance.

"Two oatcakes and a jug of water for our only sustenance!"

"I still have a few dry almonds left."

The almonds were the same oblong shape as Aisha's eyes. François placed them side by side on the surface of his bag. He stared at them for a long time, imagining the rest of the face, the pale cheeks surrounded by small coins.

Even though they were exhausted, Colin and François could not sleep. Colin kept going over the rabbi's words. He still didn't trust him. He was convinced that the Jew was up to something. His goodwill toward Christian men of letters was probably a cover. You didn't fight Rome with books as your only ammunition. All those printing works all over the place had to be arms caches and meeting points. As for Louis XI, he hadn't sent two cunning Coquillards such a long distance just so that they could bring him back a pile of old books. His library was overflowing with books. And besides, a few clever maxims certainly weren't going to add much to the glory of France!

François's ruminations were of quite another kind. The night smells filtering in through the small window mingled with the scent of Aisha. The line of the hills undulated in the moonlight like a hip draped in silk. The wind gently caressed the valleys in order not to wake the sleeping earth from its bed. The burning, feverish, fiercely desired earth. Often ravished, never conquered. For what lover was she still reserving herself? For which chosen one? Around Safed, the countryside fell silent, somnolent in the breeze. The whole night sighed sadly for the heart of a young woman of Palestine.

The oil had burned down in the clay lamp. The isolated howl of a jackal briefly covered the relentless chanting of the cicadas. In the room, the heat was suffocating. Colin and François both decided it might be cooler outside. Moussa was sitting beneath the arbor, dipping into a bowl of olives. The two men sat down next to him. He clapped his hands, and Aisha appeared immediately. He ordered her to bring dates, grapes, and a gourd. As she returned and put down the food and drink, the young woman felt François's gaze come to rest on her. She gave him a furtive, mischievous glance, and her fingers brushed his hand. Moussa observed this ploy with a stern air.

"A Berber slave," he said, "a little savage from Kabylia. Not for sale."

Colin struck up a Burgundian cantilena. His baritone voice made moles and field mice scurry away. François breathed in the night air, stroking the polished, rounded bark of the gourd with languorous gestures that exasperated Moussa.

14

T he day had barely risen. The room was still dark. François, who had finally fallen asleep just before dawn, woke abruptly. He saw Colin standing by the door, tense, his sword unsheathed. Shuffled footsteps and curses interspersed with entreaties and moans came from outside. Just as Colin was making a signal to keep quiet, the door burst open and two armed men confronted him. He was at least a head taller than them, and his bellicose air made them hesitate. One of them called in Egyptian for reinforcements. Swords were unsheathed.

"Caliph's police. You're under arrest!"

In the courtyard, other Mamluks were waiting. Moussa was on his knees in front of them, begging. Aisha had been chained to the big bellows in the forge. Her torn tunic revealed marks of burns and blows. A terrified grimace distorted her face, which had turned white, as if suddenly aged.

"Cowards, that's all you are!"

Colin's voice boomed like thunder. François tugged at his elbows to restrain him.

"Let's go quietly. It's the only way to save these people."

Colin threw down his weapon. Several men immediately rushed at him. François and Colin were tied together and forced to walk by those of the Mamluks already back in the saddle. Others loaded the prisoners' things on the horses, not without noticing that these were freshly shod.

"You're lucky. A good artisan deserves to live . . . "

Moussa was already muttering a thousand formulas of gratitude, but the soldier grabbed Aisha by the hair and winked roguishly at the blacksmith.

" . . . but not this bitch!"

He lifted Aisha and laid her, bent double like a puppet, across the back of his horse. Moussa waited until the riders had disappeared over the horizon before getting up. Brandishing a calloused fist at the sky, he groaned a bitter "May the plague take you!"

From the far end of the great courtroom, his stern voice echoing off the stone walls, the *qadi* of Nazareth read out the charges and the sentences. François found it hard to understand this foreign tongue uttered with such monotony, as if the legal document was unpunctuated. The *qadi* raised his eyes and looked at the prisoners for the first time. François thought he detected a thin smile beneath the gleaming mustache. As the guards were about to lead Colin and François to their cell, the *qadi* signaled to them to wait and addressed the two men directly, in Byzantine Latin.

"The provosts of Acre informed our agents of your arrival. One of them, a Frenchman, recognized your insignia."

The *qadi* pointed at the shell-shaped pendants around their necks.

"We have committed no crime, Your Excellency," François stammered in Moorish.

"Two days ago, an Italian merchant was robbed not far from Safed. The list of stolen items includes a detailed description of certain objects of value, including this one, which we found at the bottom of your bag!"

He brandished the book encrusted with a translucent butterfly given to François by Federico. Stunned, François tried to plead his case but the *qadi* ordered him to keep silent. Colin was shaking with rage. The *qadi* put the book down and then, as if forgetting all about the charges, adopted an almost friendly tone.

"I'm told you are skilful with your pen."

Taken aback, François nodded.

"The emir of Nazareth is a great lover of literature. Your rhymes may amuse him . . .As for your companion, he will provide us with quite another kind of spectacle. Take them away!"

The narrow cell was filled to overflowing. Some thirty prisoners were rotting there: Jews, Arabs, Persians, Turks. Colin and François had to find somewhere to put themselves. Nobody gave up his place to them, or even said a word. As Colin was asking François to translate the *qadi*'s sentence for him, two guards burst in, beating all those in their way. One of them brandished a whip with which he started hitting Colin at full force. The skin burst, revealing the naked flesh. Blood ran. The prisoners had no right to speak. That was what explained their silence. A filthy old man signaled to them to keep quiet by placing a thin finger on his dry lips. But Colin yelled, insulting his attacker and the caliph and the whole Mamluk Empire. François threw himself at the soldier's feet and received several blows in his turn. Weary of whipping these vermin, the guards went out again. François heard them laughing in the dark corridor. They did not return until that night, when they let a horde of starving rats out of an old crate. The beasts seemed as terrified as the men. A youth of barely fifteen grabbed hold of one of the bigger rats, twisted its neck, and planted his yellow teeth in the still warm flesh. François vomited. The old man let out a cracked laugh.

All night long, François made an effort to compose, in his head, an Eastern version of his most famous ballad, the *Ballad of the Hanged Men*. He was constantly distracted by the ghost of Federico, whose mocking laugh echoed off the walls of the cell. Colin covered his wounds with dry dust and spit, not flinching once.

Little by little, the rats withdrew from the cell in search of food, taking care to swerve to avoid the gluttonous youth. But he was already asleep, his fist clenched, the corners of his mouth stained with black blood. His pale complexion and dark hair made him look both innocent and wild, just like Aisha. Was she also asleep in another corner of the fortress? François preferred not to think about the fate the Mamluks had in store for her.

Nobody knew when morning came. There were no windows here. Only the length of François's nails indicated to him the relentless passing of the days. Three prisoners had been taken away, and two others had arrived. François was still trying hard to compose his poem. He dreamed of Aisha, of the ladies of days gone by, of the muses. He turned a crack in the wall into a ray of sunlight, the dark and damp wall into a starry sky, wisps of straw on the ground into meadows. The others also seemed to cling to life, even the shriveled old man. He would have loved to know their stories, to know where the youth came from. How long had they been there, these last vestiges of men?

Colin's wounds became hideously infected. François washed them in warm urine, which gave his companion the opportunity to deploy the complete range of his oaths and curses. The steaming, acid liquid seemed nevertheless to work. After a while, healing began. François scratched the circumference with a twig smoothed at length between his fingers to remove the dirt. Overcoming his own disgust, he squeezed the wounds in the middle to make the pus come out. Colin had stopped grumbling. He watched the gestures of his flea-ridden doctor with what might have been an air of gratitude. François, trying to keep up appearances, smiled nervously.

From time to time, a guard introduced a cooking pot and a jug into the cell. In spite of his condition, Colin always managed to be the first to run to it, followed by the youth, who was now imitating his ferocious attitude. The others had to be content with what was left, leaving the old man the privilege of licking the bottom of the pot.

At first the prisoner saw oceans, golden-haired women, giant flowers, snakes. And then, quickly, other images flowed past, one after the other: a piece of meat roasting on a spit, a huge piece of fruit overflowing with juice and sugar. The convolutions of the brain became a labyrinth of intestines, the whole body one big gut. It was then that it came, treacherous but liberating, the thought of dying. The prisoner pushed it away. Death still scared him. And then, one day, it spoke to him. It confided in him. He recoiled in terror, but it did not detain him. It waited . . . It waited for him to finish his poem. But he could no longer write, no longer recite. He stammered, bit his lip, gradually forgetting the words of his ballad. Death attempted a caress. It had the pale fingers of Aisha.

An affable, elegant man, surrounded by torches, entered the cell like a flaming star. He cautiously placed an inkpot, a quill, parchment, and candle wax at François's feet. The apparition was short-lived, but François recognized the *qadi*'s dark, finely-embroidered caftan.

Later, from out of the darkness, Colin's trembling voice whispered, "The ink is drying. You haven't written a line."

"I'm hungry."

"Then chew a little paper."

François hesitated. His stomach hurt. Gently, he put a sheet in his mouth and chewed. A kind of juice extracted from the wet paste added to his saliva. He handed a piece of paper to Colin, who thanked him with a courtly bow. The two friends feasted. A chorus of snores enlivened the meal. François took up his pen to pick his teeth.

Every day, two or three prisoners were dragged to the torture chambers. Their muffled groans echoed through the walls. They came back with bodies lacerated with gaping wounds that soon became infected and stank. François eventually lost all sense of time. For days on end he stared at the empty inkpot and the chewed quill, abandoned on the floor amid the sawdust and excrement. A brawl drew him abruptly from his lethargy. Colin was struggling with all his might and hurling abuse at the guards, who had grabbed him by the feet and were dragging him out into the corridor. An official stood impassively in the doorway of the cell, peering into the darkness as if looking for something, then addressed François.

"Where is your ode to the emir?" he said in surprise.

He made a sign with his finger, and François stood up and meekly followed him along the dark corridors. Ahead of them, Colin continued to stamp with rage and deliver a stream of curses at his jailers. The group walked down a long tunnel. At the end, servants armed with brushes and towels were waiting patiently. They all bowed when they saw the official.

"Get the dirt off these two!"

15

How could a man as fat as that have such slender fingers? François wondered. He looked at his own wrists, his verrucose palms, his unfiled nails, his skin scrubbed with soap and horsehair to make him presentable. From the low table around which tumblers and musicians crouched with him, François could only glimpse the emir, whose beringed fingers lay crossed over a huge belly. He did not yet know when exactly he would be called on to amuse that faceless mass of flesh sinking beneath brocades and insignia of rank. Glittering on the august belly, the precious stones of the rings were drowning in the heavy folds of a cheap silk robe that reminded François of Chartier's alb. The rolls of fat, whose presence you sensed, evoked casual authority, an indolent, cruel power. How to win over such a paunch?

François and his companions in misfortune hastened to devour the leftover food the slaves abandoned to them. They joyfully plunged their hands into the steaming entrails of a sheep and hulled chickpeas, almonds, and dates. François looked desperately for Aisha amid the throng of guests, but in vain. He could barely remember her face. Glimpsed in the space of one night, her white face was fleeting and hazy, like that of someone met once a long time ago. Only her dark eyes shone through the fog of forgetfulness. In the din of the banquet, the prison was also gradually moving away, toward the other end of another world. The old man, the youth, the guards were all ghosts now. Even death had withdrawn with dignity down the dark corridors, back to its lair. It was death, though, that was defied here, in the arrogance of the banquet, in this pathetic luxury. And to challenge it in this way, you had to stuff yourself like an emir. Or eat rat.

Women danced with snakes wound around their arms, dwarves rang little bells, brown fingers plucked at meager strings. The eye of a calf rolled to the ground. A guest picked it up and swallowed it.

The sound of the tambourines stopped abruptly. The only thing heard now was the solemn beating of a gong. From the far end of the hall, a huge warrior, his oiled body glistening in the torchlight, advanced to the percussive rhythm. He bowed briefly to the emir then turned. He was a Turkish slave, captured during a battle against the Ottoman sultan. His opponent followed, tall and thin, chin raised high, like a rooster. A cotton top covered his scars. He seemed less sturdy than the other man.

Most of the guests continued to scoff from the dishes. Performers and gladiators alike froze, tense, ill at ease. If the Christian won the day, the emir of Nazareth would not be pleased.

They nevertheless hoped secretly that the big Turk would bite the dust. As soon as he came within distance of his rival, Colin gave him a slap on the left ear followed by a poke in the groin. The Turk gripped Colin with force but the Coquillard, furious now, headbutted him. It was like a combat of stags, with its silent clash of heads, and it was only a matter of time before one of the two skulls burst. Just as the Turk seemed to be bearing up best under this unbridled hammering, Colin plunged his teeth into his opponent's nose and bit it off, much to the delight of the spectators. He spat out the piece of flesh, while the guests clapped and laughed. But the Turk held on, his big arms holding his rival tight, his fists crushing his back.

Suddenly, Colin flopped backwards like a puppet, his eyes empty, his arms dangling. François sat up on his stool, helpless to do anything. His friend had stopped moving. The Turk was pummeling him with punches. Colin, quite limp now, was about to fall to the floor. But in the middle of his fall, he suddenly leapt at the Turk's throat, again using his teeth, while his hands pulled the big man's ears, which seemed to amuse the emir. François clearly heard the Turk's throat crack under the pressure of his opponent's jaws. Lower down, Colin was hitting the Turk's belly with his knees, first the right then the left, as if he were running on the spot. It was nevertheless to his face that the Turk raised his arms. It was as if the pulling of his ears was the most intolerable thing for him, the most humiliating. The emir gave the signal, and guards separated the two fighters and took them promptly offstage. The music resumed.

Still openmouthed, François saw the *qadi* advance toward him.

"Your turn, poet!"

The instruments fell silent.

Even though they had dressed him in a long Egyptian robe and slippers, François had been determined to wear his tricorn. He made a questionable bow, immediately spoiled by his half smile. He remained prostrate for a little too long, and in too exaggerated and ambiguous a fashion, which made the audience feel ill at ease. The emir, too, was showing signs of irritation. Total silence fell. His tricorn sweeping the floor, François slowly raised his head to confront the tyrant's dark eyes. They shone with the same caustic gleam as those of Guillaume Chartier. François knew that expression well. Whether they wore helmets or skullcaps, whether they pouted condescendingly or turned up their noses, whether they had well-cut beards or hairless chins, prelates and knights, informers and tax collectors all seemed to come from the same mold, as if, beneath their various titles and appearances, there was only in fact one man. Yesterday, he had had the pale countenance of a bishop. Today, the pink complexion of a fat emir. But it was indeed him, always him, that François fought, under all of his masks, and whom he now decided to fight in his own way. The emir was no more fooled than François. He too had recognized, beneath the stranger's falsely affable face, that gleam in the eye, that hint of defiance at the corners of the lips. He had tamed more than one recalcitrant subject. This one was no different than the others.

The audience, which could feel the tension rising, was delighted. This skirmish promised to be as exciting as the bare-fisted fight earlier.

"It is in the French language that I wish to declaim the present ballad."

Brother men who live when we have gone
Against us do not let your hearts grow stern . . .

The emir took all this without flinching. Nobody present understood a damned word of French.

Chanting the lines of his *Ballad of the Hanged Men*, François let their rhythm sway him. The prosody, combined with the softness of the language, the secret spell of the intonations, and adorned with the Latinate gestures performed by the reciter's frail hands, seemed to cradle the audience, breaking with the vulgarity of the banquet and the violence of the fighting. The rhymes echoed from the walls, glided among the hangings, made their way between the tables, flowed along the candelabra. They were the melodious petition of a poor troubadour, but also the supreme act of arrogance of a condemned man, as if François were offering his neck to the hangman—an idea that was not disagreeable to the emir.

For if some pity on us poor souls you take,
The sooner then God's mercy you will earn . . .

François, having struck the fish, now reeled it in. He raised his voice, became more spirited, exaggerated his incisive urban accent. In an instant, he transported his audience to Paris, a Paris of the imagination, a Paris sure of its genius and its charms. The regular delivery of the lines evoked a trip on a river. The turns of phrase wound through the heart of the intrigued audience, just as the Seine plies its course across the valleys.

The wind changes, and we are blown
Hither and yon, at its behest without . . .

With the final verse, uttered in a grave, slow voice, the waters poured out into a wide estuary leading to an ocean of silence. François ended his melancholy recitation by addressing a broad smile to the ceiling, confident of the effect he was having. His lines had captivated many drunkards and prostitutes, innkeepers, gravediggers, carters, courtesans, and notaries, who knew no more about meter and prosody than did this emir and his henchmen. The force of a ballad did not lie in fine words or complicated rhymes, but in the voice that spoke, that sang, that caressed. It was the voice that brought men together, like a bridge. Or an outstretched hand.

The audience waited nervously. The emir was well aware how much everyone had appreciated the performance. Better to show mercy than to play the despot, which would cast a chill over a splendid evening. Torturing this prisoner would bring him no benefit. He applauded loudly, almost sincerely, which in turn provoked the audience to wild applause. Was he not a man of taste and discernment?

The Chinese acrobats came onstage. Escorted to the wings,

François got his breath back. He was always surprised by the effect his verse had on even the most mean-spirited souls. Simple words, a good-humored tone, a soft, barely accentuated melody, overwhelmed them much more than a tragedian's monologue or a tribune's passionate oration. His rondeaus had saved him from the gallows on more than one occasion—after attracting the wrath of the magistrates, admittedly. For they disturbed the officials far more than did the knife hanging from his belt. That was why he constantly refined them, just as if he were sharpening a blade. But were they sharp enough to sever the bonds that still tied him to Chartier? And to cut through the net of schemes and stratagems laid from Nazareth to Florence, behind which his true destiny was concealed?

As he left, François noticed a familiar figure among the guests. From a distance, he could not make out the features, but the elegance certainly stood out in this crowd uniformly dressed in Eastern tunics. All frills and brocades, and a broad hat with a plume—the attire of an Italian gentleman.

The next day, Colin and François appeared again before the court. A grim-faced Mamluk officer stood behind the *qadi*, a man with the hair and the arched back of a wild beast. His piercing eyes were separated by a pointed brass strip soldered to the rim of his helmet in such a way as to hide his nose. He looked the prisoners up and down, as if measuring them for coffins. Colin stared back at him defiantly. The Mamluk would happily have sunk his saber into Colin's belly. He put his hand to the pommel, threateningly. Delighted, Colin rose to his full height, ready for a fight. The officer, although also champing at the bit, restrained himself. But it was the other man's twisted grin that annoyed him the most. Beneath his ridiculous tricorn, he was looking at him with such an air of imbecility as to make him lose his temper. It was obvious that this good-for-nothing was used to both soldiers and judges. And it was equally obvious, by the way he was taunting one of the caliph's most feared representatives, that he wasn't afraid of them.

The *qadi*, on the other hand, seemed well-disposed. François remembered that nonchalant, almost amused, strangely benevolent pout. It was the condescending pout sometimes adopted by those who have the power of life and death over others. As during the first audience, the *qadi* neither raised his head nor spoke until he had given the documents spread in front of him a proper examination. He pointed out a paragraph to the officer, who nodded briefly in agreement.

"You fought well, infidel."

Ignoring Colin's hate-filled glare, the *qadi* continued to grin ambiguously. The officer stood to attention, devoid of expression. Both seemed determined to stick to the caricatures they embodied, as if, while assuming their roles, they were at the same time satirizing them.

"The reward offered by the provosts of Acre for your capture is paltry. It barely covers the expenses of procedure and detention that you have cost the caliphate. This big fellow would make a good galley slave. But you? Take them away."

Once the prisoners had gone, the *qadi* turned to the officer. "The ransom was paid this morning by Gamliel of Safed. Why would a rabbi untie his purse like that?"

"Jews, Christians, what does it matter? They're all unbelievers, venerable *qadi*. That's what unites them."

"I beg you, Suleyman, spare us that sanctimonious rot."

The officer rose to his full height, towering over the *qadi* with his warlike build, covering him with his threatening shadow. The *qadi*, still seated, remained imperturbable. The mutual disdain Egyptian officials and Mamluk soldiers had for each other was like a thread of hatred, one on which the whole of the caliphate balanced, a thread somehow firmer than one woven from feelings of warmth.

"These people share a certain affinity for books, Your Excellency."

"Nothing too reprehensible in that, as long as they don't undermine the teachings of the Holy Qu'ran."

The *qadi* stroked his beard pensively. Most of the carrier pigeons being intercepted in Jerusalem, Safed or Tiberias were carrying messages concerning the purchase and sale of books. These smuggling activities did not bother the police at all as long as they took their cut. The unexpected visit of the two Frenchmen, though, suggested that more vigilance was required. According to the provosts of Acre, they were notorious brigands. But during their incarceration, the two foreigners had not behaved like common criminals. They had appeared surprised, not to say shocked, at their arrest. No normal prisoner protested like that. That a rabbi from Safed should have stood bail for them so readily was equally troubling. In any case, the *qadi* of Nazareth was firmly convinced that this was much more than a simple case of receiving stolen goods. Rather than torture the two Frenchmen, he planned to let them go on their way to see where they led. So far, they had not taken the usual pilgrim routes. They had followed an itinerary that only someone who knew all the paths in the region could have supplied them with. Their journey through the Holy Land was clearly not innocuous. The *qadi* reflected for a moment then, without deigning to look up at Suleyman, ordered him to have the suspects followed.

16

François and Colin were led to the gates of the fortress and expelled without further ado. Gamliel's secretary was sitting in the shade of an olive tree close by the ramparts, waiting for them. He stood up to greet them, then pulled on a linen cloth to reveal a platter laden with food.

"*Shalom*, gentlemen."

While Colin and François threw themselves on the smoked poultry, oatcakes, and dried fruit, the Jew opened a bottle of wine with all the dexterity of a trained steward.

"My master has had excellent news from Jerusalem."

"Your master has brought us enough bad luck," Colin growled back.

As François undertook to explain the reason for so much anger, the rabbi's secretary listened to him with a distracted, almost amused expression, indifferent to the flush of rage on Colin's face. Federico's betrayal seemed not to surprise him at all.

"Your bravery is highly praiseworthy. You passed this test with a distinction that does you honor."

François and Colin were stunned. Such a denunciation overstepped the mark. It might have cost them their lives. What malicious pleasure did these people take in mortifying the king's emissaries in this way? François even wondered if the *qadi* of Nazareth, whose clemency he found hard to fathom, had not also been complicit in this charade.

"We had to make sure of your loyalty," the secretary continued in a neutral, disenchanted tone, as if bored by the thankless mission with which his master had entrusted him.

"While we have no guarantee of yours!"

The two Frenchmen were hardly in a position to demand anything. They could not return home empty-handed without risking the gallows and as long as they stayed here, lost and destitute, their fate depended on Gamliel's goodwill. The secretary did not therefore take the trouble to respond. He clapped his hands, and two Mongols appeared, supporting Aisha. Wild-eyed, she flashed a reproachful glare at François and Colin. Her body bore the marks of the abuse she had endured.

"The poor thing has been harshly treated. It's best if she doesn't go back to Safed. She won't be well received there. Whether or not she was raped by the guards, she'll be seen as defiled."

François clutched his crumpled hat in his clumsy hands. He leaned toward Aisha and kissed her fingers. She leapt back in terror. François turned to Gamliel's secretary. Defiled or not, he refused to abandon her to her fate. Colin threw François a disapproving glance. A woman was bound to bring trouble down on their heads. Unconcerned by what would befall this slave, the secretary decided he would hear no more. He was hoping to expedite his task as quickly as possible.

"Take off those rags. Two Mongols will wear your prison grab in order to create a diversion. They'll leave for Safed this evening. Here are fresh clothes and shoes."

"I'm sick and tired of all your precautions!" roared Colin.

The secretary remained calm. "We have to be careful. Not because of the Mamluks. The Vatican has agents in Nazareth. They must have had wind of your arrival in the Holy Land."

"Have you forgotten that I have the support of the Bishop of Paris?"

"But what rabbi would trust the Bishop of Paris?"

François grabbed hold of Colin's arm before he could knock the wretched fellow out. Taking several steps back, the secretary pointed at a tall thin man leaning against a tree, wearing torn and frayed pirate breeches and with a red scarf tightly knotted around his skull. Two big toes, the nails black, poked out of the ends of worn boots that looked as if they had seen better days—and a better owner. He was kneading a piece of straw between two rows of carious teeth.

"Djanoush will be your guide. On the roads, a nomad attracts less attention. His mission is to take you to the Holy Sepulcher. From there, we'll take over."

At a signal from the secretary, Djanoush approached, two donkeys tied to his horse. Colin refused the bridle the gypsy held out to him. Djanoush insisted. Colin cursed. Djanoush lost his temper. All this lasted a while.

"Let's just gratefully accept," François said.

"I'm not going to ride through Galilee on a donkey!"

"Our Lord did."

"This one's all lopsided, I'll take the other one."

The secretary watched helplessly as the scene unfolded. These two foreigners were constantly squabbling over trifles. They never talked about anything serious, not even their mission. And they drank too much wine. The King of France must be a poor monarch indeed. You just had to look at his emissaries. And yet Rabbi Gamliel gave them a good deal of respect. He even claimed that they had been sent by Providence. It was to make sure of this that he had put them to such a hard test. He saw their coming here to Judea as a sign from God. As for Master Federico, he had been certain they would pull through.

"My master has obtained permission for the gate of the Holy City to be opened to you."

"Any camel driver can go through those gates any day of the week!"

"Not this gate."

"Which gate is that, then?"

The Jew looked Colin and François up and down one last time, increasingly irritated by their insolence. "The gate to the secret Jerusalem."

17

Colin almost fell backwards as he mounted his donkey. His legs were so long, they touched the ground on either side of the poor animal. Refusing François's help, Aisha nimbly mounted behind Djanoush. Guided by the gypsy, the survivors at last said goodbye to the dungeons of Nazareth and reached the shelter of the first orchards. Colin held himself tensely on his donkey, grimacing whenever one of his bruises played up. François trotted cheerfully along, breathing in the air with its scents of prickly pear and wild lemon.

It was the hottest part of the day, and there was not a soul in sight. In the fields, the flocks seemed abandoned while shepherds and dogs slumbered in the shade of the olive trees. When the sun began to sink, granting a last caress of light to the surrounding hills, it was not replaced by any beneficial coolness.

For a while, Djanoush led them along the ridge road, then started down the steep slope that led to Lake Tiberias. Making his way through the undergrowth, a young shepherd was following the riders. He suddenly crouched behind a bush. Then, once he was sure that the gypsy had turned due south, he leapt to his feet and ran off like a hare to go and inform Suleyman.

Slowly advancing across the still burning scrubland, through ravines over which darkness was spreading, Djanoush at last reached a promontory from which the outline of the lake could be seen in the distance. His traveling companions gazed down at the fabled landscape in silence. A sparrow hawk hovered, describing broad circles, weaving his flight in the invisible weft of the sky, patrolling the sheet of water in search of prey. The Sea of Kinnereth, as the Hebrews called it, stretched as far as the horizon, lined with wild rushes and willows. The white domes of Tiberias glittered on the western shore. To the east, the grim mass of the Golan rose into the clouds, covering the tranquil waters with its threatening shadow. Opposite, in the distance, where the haze of the lake gave way to a sand-filled mist, Judea began.

When night had fallen, the men rested by a fire, sitting cross-legged. Weak and shivering, Aisha kept her distance. François gave her the piece of wool that protected his donkey's back from the rough leather of the saddle. Djanoush, taking care not to scare her away, placed a goatskin canteen on the ground.

François poked the fire with part of a branch. The blaze of the burning leaves reminded him of Master Federico's gaudy attire. The Florentine's devilish laughter taunted him in the crackling of the dead wood. He kept trying to understand the reason for that denunciation, in which Gamliel had evidently been complicit. The clear purpose of their stay in the Mamluk jail had been to put Colin and François at the rabbi's mercy. It was an outrageous insult to Louis XI. All the same, it seemed that the negotiations would continue as planned. That was why François suspected Gamliel of having had some other purpose than merely to intimidate him. He thought about his journey, from Rue Saint-Jacques to Genoa, from Acre to the monastery in Galilee and to Safed, and above all about this ride that was now taking him across the Holy Land, toward Jerusalem. This long route had not been drawn up at random. François even wondered if Aisha's sudden appearance on his path was as fortuitous as it seemed.

From the market stalls of Tiberias to the farms of the Jordan valley, Djanoush and Colin left a trail of petty thefts in their wake. They stole hens, eggs, cloves of garlic, peppers hanging in the doorways of barns, and, for Aisha, fresh linen drying in the sun. François was surprised that, in spite of their misdeeds and their shabby appearance, none of the patrols had seen fit to stop them. They were known to rob pilgrims and wandering peddlers at every opportunity. He told himself there was probably nothing to fear from the Mamluks as long as they had no idea why he was here. Unless Djanoush was in league with them. As recently as the day before yesterday, Colin had surprised the gypsy in conversation with two soldiers who had quickly disappeared at his approach. The incident had left him puzzled, but little by little the road wiped out any lingering resentment.

François had no idea by what marvels of gesture, raucous laughter, and pokes of the elbow Djanoush and Colin managed to make themselves understood to each other. They spoke about knife blades and the training of horses, boot leather and bare-knuckle fighting. They compared scars and gashes like connoisseurs, feeling each other's biceps with mutual appreciation. To fill the silence of gestures and grimaces, they laughed, clicked their tongues, let out cries, constantly hailed each other: Hey, Januch! Hey, Colino!

Whenever the animals grew tired, Djanoush and Colin walked nimbly in front. François and Aisha trailed behind, avoiding each other and yet coming closer according to the rules of a secret game. A wink forced the adversary to look down, a timid touch provoked a quiver, a flower gently picked was accepted without a smile. Having previously been courted by the awkward young peasants of Safed, Aisha now discovered the ardor of a gallant's attentions, at once gentler and more masculine. Her mountain girl vanity, her sometimes melancholy eyes, her delicate gestures, which the rigors of slavery had not withered, all disarmed François, veteran of the boudoirs and seducer of consenting prey that he was. The game was an unequal one. François doubted, hesitated, sighed. He took care not to commit any blunder, whereas Aisha, innocent and wild, had never been so sure that she was liked. She trod the hot earth, feeling, for the first time, mistress of her own fate.

On the third day, the little group reached Beit She'an. Reluctant to enter the town, access to which was guarded by sentries of the watch, Djanoush led his companions to a caravan that was just then bypassing the ramparts. The line of camels and beasts of burden stretched to the horizon, raising a huge cloud of dust. The cries of the people, the lowing of the animals, the hammering of hundreds of hooves, the jingling of the harnesses made an almighty din. Nobody even noticed the four newcomers joining the procession.

The camel drivers had the slanting eyes and weather-beaten skin of men from Asia, while their slaves, tied together by ropes, seemed to come from the four corners of the earth. François looked in amazement at the spices and silks, the studded chests stowed on the embroidered saddles of the dromedaries, the sumptuous cloaks of the merchants as they swayed from side to side on mules adorned with charms and multicolored tufts.

From a promontory, a Mamluk detachment watched the column. François thought he saw an officer point at Aisha and snigger. Turning red, the girl lowered her head and stared obstinately at the ground.

François looked intently at the landscapes he passed through, wishing he could shatter the silence of this country. He heard it sometimes whispering in the rustle of the foliage, calling to him with a beating of wings, urging him on with a gust of hot wind. But he did not understand what it was telling him. He listened to the travelers talking, praying, yelling around him, in Syriac or Hindi or Phoenician. Did one of them speak the mysterious language that was still unknown to him?

Aisha rode close by. She moved with ease, her indolent figure swaying as the road twisted, her black hair floating in the heat haze, as if she were letting herself be cradled by a music that she alone could hear. Her eyes peered into the scrub, lingering sometimes on a heap of stones, coming to rest on the tracks of an animal, rising suddenly to look at the branch of an almond tree. She seemed to see many things that escaped François, as if the language of the brambles and the sand were familiar to her.

François gazed at the orchards stretching at the foot of the hills, the slopes' streaked vines and, higher up, the brown rock of a cliff, trying as of now to see this land through other eyes. Those of Aisha.

At dawn on the fifth day, Djanoush broke away from the caravan, which continued on its way to the port of Jaffa. He turned left, into a ravine that wound in all directions through the arid rock. It was the dry bed of a *wadi*. With each bend, its walls grew increasingly bare, until all vegetation faded away in discouragement, as if the thorny bushes had at last realized that this bottleneck led nowhere. But Djanoush followed its twists and turns with confidence. He only emerged after several hours, forcing the horses to climb a steep slope covered with fallen rocks, which rolled down beneath the animals' hooves. At the top, the gypsy, half asleep on his exhausted horse, pointed to a plateau in the distance, ablaze with blinding light. On it, a line of fortifications could be made out through the haze. Hoarse with fatigue, Djanoush almost whispered, "Yerusalem . . . "

18

T he narrow alleys twisted in front of them. Furtive figures scurried along the walls. The few children to be
seen outside were lame or scrawny with rickets. They
played in the dirt, yelling in Arabic, in Hebrew, in Armenian,
in Greek. The older ones insulted a pompous-looking passing
soldier, then ran off through the courtyards, yelling. The
younger ones stood huddled in a doorway, busy torturing a
skinny cat. Odors and noxious air whirled through the dark,
stifling alleys. The stone of the houses was crumbling, the
slates on the roofs were cracked, the few windows were like
gaping holes. The sky, glimpsed stubbornly between two gutters, was higher here than elsewhere. At the corner of a covered street, a peasant woman in a plaited hat was kneeling in
front of a heap of peppers covered with flies. Disheartened, the
visitors followed Djanoush through this gray maze of poverty
and neglect.

Bells began ringing out. The gypsy moved faster now,
guided by the pealing of the bells, and came out onto a small
esplanade where hens frolicked. He tied the animals to a stone
boundary. A monk descended from a ladder, a bundle of straw
over his shoulder. As soon as he saw the strangers, he threw the
bundle to the ground, quickly dusted his habit, rubbed his
hands, and, assuming a dignified air, muttered a few words of
welcome in bad Latin.

"Come, this is the tomb of Christ."

The travelers obeyed meekly, going in through a rusty gate,

stumbling in the gloom, making their way amid the dark
recesses of the chapels, the lecterns and pews, past walls laden
with blunt-edged stelae, candlesticks without rings, silver
censers, frescoes filled with angels and ghosts. François and
Colin kept crossing themselves devoutly. Something undefined
had entered their bodies. Their eyes peered greedily into the
dark nave. He was here, somewhere, in the middle of the spi-
ders' webs and the spent candles: the son of God. They looked
for Him in a ray of light falling through a stained-glass window,
in the gleam on the gilded frame of a triptych, in the curve of
the arches. He must be here. They called to Him from the
depths of their souls, hungry for His love. The monk had
already reached the sepulcher and was muttering hymns. Colin
held himself as stiffly and numbly as if he had just been
knighted. François knelt, hands joined, and gathered his
thoughts, but found himself unable to pray. He thought about
Aisha, whom he was trying in vain to pursue, and about Jesus,
whom he was trying in vain to hold on to.

Until he came to this sepulcher, François had not thought
he was pursuing a specific aim. He did not care about
Chartier's schemes, Gamliel's stratagems, or the interests of the
kingdom. He had seen his mission merely as an excuse to roam
far and wide. But now he saw the hand of fate in it. And perhaps an end to his wandering. The Holy Land had been awaiting him forever. Its strange landscapes were slowly enclosing
him in their folds just like the enchanted letters embracing the
Medici coat of arms. François was sure he had come all this
way to fulfill a sacred duty. As he bent to meditate, he saw his
own face reflected in the silver border around the tomb. An icy
breath touched his cheek, like a whisper. He pressed his ear to
the tombstone as if the Savior were going to whisper to him the
answer he had come looking for. But just as he managed at last
to imbue himself with the holiness of the place, the strange,
almost complicit intimacy that suddenly linked his fate as a

rebel, a man condemned to death, with that of Jesus, two men, their faces hidden beneath large hoods, entered the basilica and signaled to him and Colin to follow them.

The two guides strode ahead, leaving no choice other than to scamper hurriedly after them. They went along winding passages, cut through backyards, and crossed vegetable gardens to throw off any possible pursuer. The greyness of the houses, the black holes of the doorways and windows, the sullen air of the sky took on an ever more sinister appearance as they entered the entrails of the city.

At a crossroads, one of the strangers turned right, ordering Djanoush and Aisha to follow him. François intervened. Not knowing in which language he would be understood, he grimaced and gesticulated, holding Aisha back by the sleeve. Colin came to the rescue, fists at the ready. Djanoush brought up the rear, brandishing his knife. The first man threw back his hood, revealing a Mongol's shaved head. He held himself in a strange position, his knees slightly bent, his arms raised to his chest, his open hands quite vertical, fingers together, as slender as blades. He twisted suddenly on one foot and struck Djanoush on the wrist with the other. The gypsy let out a roar of pain, and his knife went flying. The Mongol immediately resumed his former position, ready to leap at Colin, but his associate intervened and now also uncovered his head.

"Be reasonable, Master Villon, I beg you."

François froze, astounded to see Brother Paul's courteous smile. He held Aisha close to him. "This woman has suffered enough!"

"And you intend to protect her, do you?"

It was Colin who replied to the prior's sarcasm. "What do you fear from this slave girl? That she might turn his head? In that case, you're too late!"

The monk looked closely at Aisha, then at François. The

Frenchman's openly stubborn air bore witness to a resolve that the prior found not unpleasing. If they ran into any trouble, the presence of a woman might prove useful, whether she served as a decoy, as bait, or quite simply as a bargaining counter. Above all, the girl provided an excellent way of putting pressure on François.

"She can wait outside, she'll be well guarded."

Brother Paul dismissed Djanoush, slipping a few crowns into his hand. The gypsy took his leave with a brief nod of the head. The Mongol gave him back his knife, pushed him forward, and showed him the way. The prior took the opposite direction.

François followed, Aisha clinging to his arm. With a shrug, Colin brought up the rear.

A young man was sitting on a rock, in the middle of a small square with granite flagstones. Two olive trees shaded him with their majestic branches. Brown roots and wild ivy wrapped around their giant trunks. This esplanade was at the same height as the ramparts, located on one of the terraced roofs that overlooked the lower town. It was interspersed with barred windows that snatched the light and dispensed its rays to a subterranean world of shopkeepers and artisans, huddled in the booths of a covered market, their backs stooped over stalls and workbenches, forever angry with heaven.

François preferred to forget the galleries of the cursed city into which men and gods, priests and slaves, mangy dogs and prophets were crammed willy-nilly. Instead, he drank in the soft, limpid air of the little square, where swallows fluttered just above the still burning ground. The young man was enjoying himself, throwing them pieces of oatcake. Behind, in the distance, the bright colors of the gardens of Gethsemane danced in the setting sun. Lower down, sickly scrub descended the sunny slope, rolling with the stones as far as the dark recesses of the valley of the Kidron. In the gathering dusk, a salt-laden breeze blew in from the Dead Sea. It was here that an apostle might at last appear, leaning on his stick, take you gently by the hand, and lead you toward the stars.

François could almost feel it, this invisible hand drawing him on, leading him into the heart of Judea. He was certain he was here for something other than to traffic in books. When it came to contraband, Colin could handle things perfectly well by himself. Brother Paul grabbed hold of François, drawing him out of his daydream. Come on, let's go! François let himself be pulled by the sleeve, all the while peering up at the sky in search of a clue.

As soon as he saw the little group, the young man jumped down from his rock, handed Brother Paul a key, then, without saying a word, returned to his post. The monk took some pieces of material from his pocket and blindfolded the three visitors. Holding each other by the hand like children, they let themselves be led through an invisible labyrinth. Colin had the distinct impression that the monk was taking them around in circles. The chirping of the swallows faded and returned on several occasions. The last rays of the sun warmed his right cheek and left cheek alternately. Beneath his feet, he could still feel still the hard, flat granite of the flagstones.

A door creaked. The heat from outside gave way to a pleasant coolness. After a few paces, Brother Paul lifted the blindfolds then continued advancing. A narrow corridor led to a spacious room where oil lamps hung from the ceiling on brass chains and a multitude of strange objects jostled for attention on shelves inlaid with gold and mother-of-pearl. Indian papier-mâché puppets, ivory abacuses, Venetian masks, Ethiopian javelins, Etruscan vases, fibulas, perfume burners, and jade statuettes basked amid silks from Damascus, carpets from Samarkand, and lace tablecloths from Flanders. Behind a

counter carved with imps and unicorns, a white-bearded patriarch was cleaning a binding with wax and a cloth. In between
blowing on the precious volume, his lips moved quickly, muttering psalms. Opaque eyes, whitened by cataracts, rolled
beneath his lids like two marbles.

"Good evening, Brother Paul. I'm just getting Master
Federico's order ready."

Colin jumped at the mention of the Florentine. François
addressed an inquisitive look at Brother Paul, who raised a finger to his lips to indicate that now was not the time.

The old man stroked the covers and breathed in the odor of
the leather then, opening the book, sniffed the ink and rubbed
his nose on the parchment, his nostrils quivering above the
illuminations. He moistened his thumb, passed it over the
crimson surface of a miniature, and licked the rubbed-off
gouache with delight.

"A fine Byzantine edition, in faith. Somewhat faded in style . . .
I doubt these dull, diluted colors would tempt the Italian.
They would be better suited to more austere tastes, those of a
prelate in Cologne perhaps or a burgher in Ghent. But they are
done with a sure hand, trust a blind man's touch."

Impatiently, Brother Paul entrusted Aisha to the old man,
assuring François she would be well treated. The woman
would not let go, squeezing François's hand hard, while he
furtively kissed hers. Brother Paul went behind the counter
and approached a tapestry depicting a Persian banquet in a
park with fountains. Barely touching the thick fabric of the
tapestry, he inserted his key in the mouth of a lion that was
spitting out a jet of water. The wall revolved. Brother Paul
immediately reached in through the door and took hold of a
torch, thus illuminating the steps of a broad stone staircase.

Outside, on the square, the young man finished nibbling his
oatcake. The swallows had gone. A low moon had come to rest

on the tops of the olive trees. A cat scurried away, frightened by a slender shadow gliding nimbly along the walls, head covered in a kind of helmet.

19

The staircase kept endlessly descending. The walls were smooth and polished, bearing no trace of the ax. At regular intervals, chinks held sticks of incense, the fumes from which chased away the smell of resin given off by the torches. Tunnels led off from each landing, but access to these was barred by guards. They all had dark skin, black curly hair, and long, thick, square-cut beards. In spite of their war-like demeanor, they bore no arms or insignia.

Brother Paul hurtled down the steps, head bowed, until the rock in which the staircase had been bored suddenly widened out into a vast platform. Dozens of young people—boys and girls—were bustling in all directions. Some were drawing water from a large well, others were leading goats and sheep to a manger. In the middle of a ring of fine sand, a small group was training in unarmed combat. Behind them, two women were throwing knives at a target made of braided reeds. Small huts carved in the sides of this cave marked the perimeter of the space, the ground of which was covered in carefully raked gravel.

This place, which came as such a surprise to François and Colin, was less unusual than they thought. The bowels of the Holy Land were riddled with these subterranean networks. Latin historians and Jewish chroniclers, including Flavius Josephus, numbered them in the hundreds. Beneath the soil of Judea, wells and water tanks from the days of King David,

Roman pipes and sewers, dungeons and thieves' dens, cata-
combs and crypts, met and crisscrossed in an impenetrable
labyrinth. This one, dating from the time of Vespasian, had
been dug by Jewish rebels who had lived there for months,
harrying the emperor's legions until his son Titus crushed
them. Soon after this defeat, others came, also to flee Roman
oppression. The first disciples of Christ, like their predeces-
sors, set up oil presses, bread ovens, dovecotes, and schools.
Then came the turn of the brotherhood of which Gamliel was
a member. It had its headquarters here, where it had been
training an invisible army for almost twelve hundred years.
This clandestine command post was neither a government in
exile nor a den of rebels. It ran the many networks that
ensured the cohesion of a dispersed people, providing supplies
to communities in distress, keeping an eye on hostile govern-
ments, trying to ward off the perils constantly threatening the
Jews. The existence of this secret organization was mentioned
many times, surreptitiously, in the annals of various periods, in
travelers' tales, in pious manuals. This was the "invisible
Jerusalem" of which Talmudists and commentators spoke—
taking care never to describe it, nor to say exactly where it was
located.

Two sentries saluted Brother Paul. One of them escorted
the visitors along a series of corridors until they came to a long,
rectangular hall with a low vaulted ceiling. The walls were
lined with maps. Bathed in the diffuse light of the oil lamps,
some twenty figures, their faces barely distinguishable, sat
around a massive table. François made out rabbis' skullcaps,
Bedouin keffiyehs, and the sturdy heads of warriors among this
heterogeneous audience, the composition of which he found
hard to fathom. There seemed to be nobody presiding over the
session. One chair higher than the others, at the end of the
table, remained respectfully unoccupied. Even though vacant,

this chair imbued the place with the manifest authority of whoever had the right to take his seat there. Its back was carved
with a Hebrew motto, the same one that surrounded the
Medici coat of arms on the bindings that François had seen in
Paris and in Galilee.

François regretted the fact that the head of this Brotherhood had not seen fit to be present at the meeting. Colin found
his absence frankly offensive. The opportunity to negotiate
with the representatives of a monarch surely deserved more
consideration. He wondered if he should tolerate such an
insult, cause a scene, or ignore it. Emerging from the gloom,
Rabbi Gamliel warmly held out his hand.

"Welcome to Jerusalem, Master Villon."

In spite of the rabbi's friendly demeanor, the two men felt
ill at ease, chilled by the impassive faces scrutinizing them.
Accustomed to the obsequious bowing, furtive glances, and
nervous smiles of the Jews of Bordeaux or Orléans, François
and Colin suddenly felt the unease they themselves had so
often inflicted on the stranger, the pariah. Even alone and on
foot, a true-born Christian could walk the alleyways of a Jewish
quarter with confidence, knowing he was the uncontested master of all he surveyed. Not here. For if there was no doubt of
the supremacy of the French over Paris, or that of the
Germans over Frankfurt, whose fiefdom was Jerusalem truly?
Unlike with Frankfurt or Paris, this question preoccupied even
those who had never seen the Holy City nor would ever tread
its soil.

Disconcerted, the two Coquillards raised their eyes to the
assembly. Its members had the confident demeanor, the
haughty, almost arrogant look of lords and people of class.
Actually, their lineage went back to Alexander the Great and
Ptolemy, who had recruited their ancestors to fill the shelves of
the imperial library. Mastering languages as diverse as Greek,
Persian, Syriac and Aramaic, trained to study texts, the Jews

were excellent at tracking down knowledge. After the fire that
ravaged Alexandria, the Brotherhood of Book Hunters went
and sold its services elsewhere, to all the tyrants and high
priests hungry for knowledge and power. Its agents crossed
continents and oceans to unearth the rare or valuable writings
sought by their paymasters. But they also found a source of
income quite other than keeping temples and palaces well-
stocked. Heretics, alchemists, and bold scholars employed
them to save their writings from the flames. But to keep any
work safe from the hands of barbarians, it was not enough to
put it in a cave. Its meaning and significance had to be understood, which obliged the book hunters to keep a kind of com-
prehensive catalogue of human thought. And so it was that,
from generation to generation, these mercenaries became, of
necessity and without having ever wanted it, the guardians of
wisdom.

The cellars of the *Archivum Secretum Vaticanum*, access to
which was so jealously guarded by the Papacy, contained documents gathered since the establishment of the Holy See. The
collections of the Brotherhood in Jerusalem, though, dated
from before Rome itself. They covered three thousand years of
history. The Brotherhood held decrees by the Pharaohs,
Cretan and Assyrian edicts, Chinese, Ethiopian and Mongolian
annals, travel diaries and logbooks, manuals on war, treatises
on medicine and astronomy, philosophical works from the four
corners of the earth—and even the final statement of Jesus, as
transcribed by the high priest Annas just before he handed the
Savior over to Pontius Pilate. This document was the true testament of Christ.

François could not remain indifferent to this last detail. Of
all the works mentioned, it was the only one he wanted to read,
or even just touch. The only one, probably, for which he had
come. He remembered the caress of the air in the Holy
Sepulcher, friendly and inviting. Like a call that only he could

hear. Had he not himself composed his own poetic testament? He peered into the gloom. Where were all these books hidden? And how on earth to get his hands on the one containing the last words of Jesus? All the same, François couldn't help wondering if Gamliel wasn't perhaps exaggerating.

"So the last wishes of Our Lord have passed into your hands?"

The rabbi assured that such was indeed the case. The Brotherhood carefully checked the authenticity of each document. This was the daily task of the monks directed by Brother Médard, the pious students of Safed and, in Florence, the scholars of the Platonic Academy founded by the Medicis. The book hunters owed it to themselves to scrupulously corroborate every piece of information, because the volumes housed in this "invisible Jerusalem" were not merely trophies for collectors. They were a war arsenal.

Gamliel gave François and Colin what he hoped was a reassuring a smile. But his benevolent expression did little to calm them. Colin, who had never seen so many Jews in his life, wondered how Chartier would take it. Somehow he couldn't see the bishop congratulating him on associating the diocese of Paris with the machinations of some kind of Judean secret society. As for François, he had been expecting to enter a temple with porphyry columns and converse with elderly scribes, white-bearded sages, philosophers—even talk with them about poetry. This place was hardly appropriate for that. It was more like a den of brigands. Worse, it was a nest of spies. And they were keeping Christ's word hostage.

A few feet away, the visible Jerusalem was dozing peacefully. The little square with its granite flagstones was deserted. The young man guarding it had just left his post in pursuit of the furtive figure he thought he had glimpsed a few moments earlier. Choosing to take the alley from which Brother Paul had emerged that afternoon, he moved forward cautiously, sniffing the warm air, hugging the house fronts, listening for the slightest sound. He could hear nothing, not even the meowing of a cat, not even the scamper of the rats that stole in packs along the walls at night. It was as if the alley had been gagged. The silence that usually reigned in it was completely different from this total absence of noise. Fleeing an invisible threat, the young man began walking more quickly. He stumbled over a stone boundary marking the entrance to a large building. As he tried to get shakily to his feet, he felt a sharp burning sensation in his insides. In his fall, he caught a brief glimpse of his attacker's cruel face then, behind the helmet glinting in the moonlight, the starry firmament falling silent. Other soldiers emerged from the doorway and carried off the body. Suleyman and his men crept into position around the little square. A Saracen scout softly approached the houses lining the esplanade, listening at the doors or standing on tiptoe and peering through the cracks in the shutters to try to see inside.

Lying flat on his stomach on a roof, a Mongol sentry watched the scene, holding his breath. When the moment was right, he let out a languorous meow, like an old cat. He waited and listened. Almost immediately, another meow responded to his, shorter and sharper, like that of a young she-cat. The alarm had been raised.

20

Two young girls brought tea, almond biscuits, and dried fruit. The collation was an opportunity for François and Colin to converse with their table companions, who, surprisingly, seemed quite alarmed by Louis XI's recent setbacks in his struggle with the provincial barons and dukes. They seemed well informed of the threats from Charles the Bold, Jean of Clèves, and Pierre of Amboise looming over the crown, and even stated that, in their opinion, the king should beware of his own brother, the Duke of Berry. It struck François that these comments were probably a way of demanding guarantees. What would be the point of signing an agreement with Paris if the city was besieged? He leapt indignantly to his feet. He'd had enough of insinuations, mysteries, bargaining. Colin and he were the envoys of a monarch who was still in place, a legitimate monarch who—they did not doubt for a moment—could put down this rebellion of scheming country squires. They hadn't come all this way to be told how to manage the affairs of the kingdom—and certainly not by mercenaries who lived in hiding in the sewers of their own city, survivors of a people who had let themselves be enslaved and mistreated for centuries without offering the slightest resistance. Excellent counselors, indeed!

Colin stiffened, ready for a fight. But the gathering remained silent, listening to François with rapt attention. Gamliel even seemed delighted. François continued to hold forth.

"King Louis already has all the ministers and armorers he

needs. We haven't come here for halberds or cannons. Or for vain talk!"

But books, François said to himself, surprised by the strangeness of such a request. Only books? François was hardly one to deny the power of the written word. In Fust's printing works, he had seen the heavy presses beating ceaselessly, inking page after page, making the boldest texts suddenly appear on hitherto blank paper. But he had also seen Chartier there. It was the bishop's well-known scheming nature that made François doubt the legitimacy of his mission. What was the point of flooding the place with treatises on science and philosophy, with odes and fables, if it was to be the clerics and rulers who decided what everyone should read— and think? François knew that better than anyone. His own verses were either applauded or outlawed by lords and burghers alike, depending on whether they found their rebellious overtones annoying or amusing.

And now, in this military headquarters, his angry speech also seemed to please rather than shock. He had the impression that he was stupidly allowing himself to be a spectacle once again, just as he had done in the drawing rooms of courtly ladies titillated by his satires and delighted with his insidious tone. Gamliel would no doubt have been disappointed not to see François fight back. He had clearly been counting on that rebellious streak of his. And on Colin's aggressiveness. Weren't the two Frenchmen the perfect partners for these book hunters? Dissidents and outlaws like them.

François regretted having said out loud what had been on his mind. He vowed to be more perceptive in the future. He still lacked too many elements to pull off the kind of trick of which he alone had the secret. He sat down again, looking suddenly calmer. Colin seemed to have understood, and also became less hostile.

Considering that the storm had passed, one of those present asked permission to speak. He bowed to the empty chair of the commander of the Brotherhood as if expecting his consent. But it was Gamliel who signaled to him to begin. The man was quite young and full of spirit. He spoke quickly, raising his voice as if the august older members of the gathering were hard of hearing. He might not have been wrong. Slumped on his bench, Brother Paul was dozing peacefully, arms folded over his belly, a blissful smile on his lips. This confirmed François in his opinion: the prior was as indifferent to this masquerade as he was. He was here for another reason, although what that might be, François had no idea. What did the monk know that he himself didn't yet know?

The young man continued, giving a broad outline of the operation for the guidance of François and Colin. He described the campaign phase by phase, citing the principal works chosen by Cosimo and Gamliel, the names of the printers and peddlers who supported the cause, the cities to be targeted as a matter of priority. This was an all-out offensive. Colin feared its extent.

"It isn't only the Pope you're attacking by inflaming minds in this way, but the whole of Christendom!"

"Do you fear for your faith? Isn't it strong enough? I bless every opportunity to put mine to the test."

The acerbic tone in which the young man had retorted sent a chill through François. It would be much harder to escape the clutches of these people, he thought, than those of Chartier or Louis XI.

To win them over, Gamliel reminded them that the Medicis, who were fervent Catholics, had unreservedly subscribed to the Brotherhood's plans. In any case, it was not up to Colin to debate the strategy, merely the methods, should Paris decide to join Florence and Jerusalem in this adventure.

François grasped the opportunity to inquire about the conditions the book hunters were laying down. He was convinced that they were expecting a repeal of the decrees banishing the Jews from France. In Tuscany, the Brotherhood had obtained a reduction in the taxes imposed on the Jewish community as well as greater freedom of movement for peddlers and traders. In exchange, prominent Jews had committed themselves to financing the purchase of presses, hiring binders and copyists, providing accommodation for agents who had come from the Holy Land to prepare the operation. But Gamliel was not demanding anything like that from the French. He did not even require an exemption from the wearing of the *rouelle*, a piece of yellow material that the few Jews in the kingdom had to sew on the front and back of their clothes. This surprised François, given the risks they were incurring.

"If the secret is discovered, your brothers will be the first to suffer the wrath of Rome."

François was taken aback by the rabbi's brief reply, the sudden curtness of his voice, mixed with a certain arrogance, which echoed the insolence of the young man who had responded to Colin.

"The gates of Zion have always been open to them."

In fact, Gamliel had only one request: the king of France had to guarantee that, during his reign, no new crusade would be undertaken. François found it hard to hold back a sardonic smile. Louis XI's promises were worthless. But Gamliel kept going, boldly asserting that noncompliance with this clause would result in serious consequences.

François and Colin could hardly believe their ears. They exchanged amused winks. To curtail their sarcasm, Gamliel told them of the advantage the Brotherhood had gained from the conquest of Byzantium, just ten or so years ago. It was its soldiers, hired as sailors and mapmakers, who had sabotaged the Venetian ships that had moored off Constantinople to challenge the Turkish fleet. In return, the sultan was now granting his protection to those Jews who, fleeing persecution, were trying to get to the Holy Land. The situation of some Jewish communities was in fact becoming increasingly worrisome, especially in England and Spain. Foreseeing the possibility of a massive exodus to the East, Jerusalem had promised to help the Turkish ruler chase the Mamluks out of Palestine.

Of course, François told himself, there was a good deal of bravado in the rabbi's words. The stratagems Gamliel had just mentioned did not surprise him. Spies and informers always behaved in the same way. Even though Louis XI's secret police were well known for their efficiency, François had frequently eluded the traps they had set for him. So these sycophants couldn't teach him anything. In fact, he was planning to teach them a lesson they wouldn't forget in a hurry.

One aspect of what Gamliel said, however, did surprise François: not so much the scale of the mission as its significance. It was a fateful turning point, which had nothing to do with military conquest or even political maneuvering. The book hunters had been waiting a long time for the right moment, for a sign, to go into action. The fall of Byzantium had been that unmistakable sign. It had marked the end of a dark and terrible era. All they had to do now was give that era the final deathblow.

In the shop, Aisha was busy looking through the closet the old antiques dealer had opened to distract her, stroking the satin gowns, plunging her hands into chests filled with trinkets, sniffing the perfume bottles one by one. From time to time, she would pin a brooch to her chest or put on an embroidered shawl, then go and look at herself in a large Venetian mirror, putting on the airs of a princess, giggling with surprise. She strutted and sang to herself as the old man watched indulgently. She turned and whirled amid the gleam of the crystal vases, the glitter of the amulets, the sheen of copper. Her partner in this imaginary dance had a face without eyes or nose, merely a strange half smile. She was surprised by her own choice, still refusing to admit it. She kept asking other partners to dance with her—tall, brown-skinned young men, nimble athletes whose muscles glistened with sweat, sweet, tender-eyed Adonises—but somehow he always stepped in ahead of them, with his crumpled tricorn on his head, and took her hand.

21

Brother Paul, who had dozed off, now woke with a start, almost falling off his chair. A huge fellow, his face cross-hatched with gashes, his left eye covered with a leather patch, had just burst into the room. He walked around the table, went up to a thin, patrician-looking old man in a beige tunic with blue stripes, and whispered something in his ear. Although this austere figure listened attentively, there was no reaction to betray what he was feeling. He responded briefly, inaudibly, but it was clear that he was giving orders. The man with the gashes responded with a military salute and went out as abruptly as he had come in. The patrician-looking individual at last deigned to inform the gathering as to the reason for this interruption. Gamliel translated immediately.

"The Mamluks have surrounded the esplanade."

"The gypsy betrayed us!" cried Colin.

Brother Paul seemed surprised. How could Djanoush have eluded the vigilance of the Mongol who had been escorting him out of the city? The prior threw a reproachful look at Gamliel. The rabbi had assured him of the gypsy's loyalty. His tribe had been living in Safed for decades and hated the Mamluks, who constantly mistreated them. The news saddened François and Colin, who had grown fond of Djanoush.

The blind old man gave a start and pricked up his ears. Furtive, hurried steps could be made out scampering over the flagstones of the little square. Standing right up against the shutters, he heard a voice whisper, "Aisha. Aisha?"

The girl froze. She looked at the antiques dealer out of the corner of her eye. The old man quietly opened his desk drawer and took out a dagger. Terrified, Aisha rushed to the door, sprang the latch, and rushed outside, hurling herself straight into the arms of the soldier who had just whispered her name. Startled, the man did not know what to say. Emerging from the semidarkness, Suleyman planted himself between the soldier and the young slave.

"It's here, it's here!" said Aisha weeping.

Suleyman immediately entered the shop with his men. They spread out, swords in their hands, smashing the vases, overturning the furniture, stooping to avoid volleys of arrows and knife thrusts. They fought duels with the dancing shadows of the Greek statues, the porcelain dragons, and even a Gascon suit of armor. Several threw themselves to the floor. When they looked up, they saw nothing but their own reflections in a mirror from India or Turin. Just as one halberdier was about to assail the belly of a stuffed crocodile, a barked order from Suleyman put an end to the attack. Behind him, crouching in a corner, Aisha heaved a sigh of relief. There was not a soul in sight. The old man had disappeared.

The attackers searched the shop from top to bottom. No partition sounded hollow, no chink revealed a trapdoor, no lever gave access to a secret passage. In his rage, Suleyman slapped Aisha, but could get nothing from her. She raved, talking of witchcraft, pointing to a thick wall covered with a Persian tapestry, swearing she had seen Brother Paul and his protégés walk right through it like ghosts. The soldiers tore down the tapestry. Their hatchets rained down on the wall, but barely scratched the rock. Suleyman ordered them to stop. He struck Aisha even harder. How could this wall lead to a corridor or a tunnel? It opened onto emptiness. It was the back of the cliff that rose sheer above the Kidron.

The soldiers hurriedly collected jewels and items of silverware, throwing everything willy-nilly into a large canvas sack, then set fire to the hangings. Suleyman was the first to leave, holding Aisha firmly by the arm. He looked around the esplanade, ill at ease, sensing an invisible presence.

The flames rose quickly. Dolls and papier-mâché masks twisted and shriveled. A wax figurine melted to a brown teardrop that ran slowly over its little wooden plinth. The pages of a psalter rose like imploring arms, bubbles of boiling ink forming on the parchment and sliding over it before exploding into tiny crackles. A bronze Pegasus galloped one last time through the smoke, its varnish trickling in gray-green beads of sweat over its taut back, its muscles rippling in the vapors of the fire, freed at last from their metal yoke, its throat contracted in a mute whinny. At last it vanished in a whirlwind of soot.

Exasperated, Suleyman screamed the order to retreat. Much to the annoyance of his sergeant, he left Aisha behind. She was of no more use to him. She had been forced to obey in order to spare Moussa, whom Suleyman threatened to have impaled at her first slip. The small pieces of material she had hung on the branches or stuck between the bricks of the houses had led here, confirming the *qadi*'s suspicions beyond the shadow of a doubt. He had only left her alive to disconcert the adversary, especially Villon.

The Mamluks plunged into the alleys that lined the square. There, they recovered their horses and set off eastward at a gallop, in the direction of the valley of Kidron, the only other possible escape route.

The esplanade was now deserted. Aisha approached the ruins of the shop. She bent over the embers, her eyes wandering amid the still burning rubble. A hand took hers, gently, so gently it was as if she had felt nothing. But she let herself be led. After a few steps, the other hand let go. Hesitantly, Aisha straightened up. It was dark. The Mongol lit a candle, then passed in front of her to show her the way.

22

At dawn, Suleyman and his men crisscrossed the valley of the Kidron, slashing through the bushes with pickaxes and striking the rock with the pommels of their swords, while the Bedouins looked on in terror. Shepherds drove their flocks toward the sun-drenched slopes, women vegetable sellers emerged from their shacks to go to market, and ragged children ran after the riders, yelling at the tops of their voices, delighted with this spectacle so early in the morning.

The horses kicked and snorted, sensing the nervousness of their riders, who were whipping them mercilessly. As it galloped, the detachment almost knocked down a beggar who happened to be in their way. Suleyman's stallion reared, and its hoof sent the poor fellow sprawling. Suleyman followed this up by landing the man an angry lash of the whip. Startled, the beggar stared for a moment as the officer spurred his mount and charged straight ahead. The rest of the patrol followed, bypassing the unfortunate man, not without spitting to their right to protect themselves from the evil eye. As soon as the Mamluks had vanished in a cloud of dust, the beggar laboriously picked himself up. He whistled in the direction of the undergrowth. Three ragged figures appeared and came to meet him. Just like him, they wore filthy headbands rolled around and around like *cheches*. Even Aisha.

Confident that Brother Paul would make sure the two Frenchmen arrived safe and sound, Rabbi Gamliel decided to leave Jerusalem as soon as possible. The ship on which Federico planned to leave would set sail in a few days, with the precious texts that would make Rome yield. Gamliel would have liked François and Colin to join the expedition. The Brotherhood having decided to meet Guillaume Chartier's demands, there was nothing more for Louis XI's two emissaries to do here.

The rabbi walked in the shadow of the gibbets that lined the ramparts of the holy city near the Damascus gate. He walked faster, trying not to look up at the hanged men rotting in the sun. He held his nose. A swarm of flies buzzed around a blackened corpse. Further on, at the foot of a gallows, a widow was waving a straw broom to chase away the crows, which flew off then immediately returned to the attack. Gamliel approached and murmured the prayer for the dead. The woman held out her hand. He favored her with an offering. She was young. Her beloved's dislocated body swayed at the end of the rope, muscles tense as if he were still struggling. A bright red patch in sharp contrast to the greyness of the walls attracted the rabbi's attention. The morning light forced him to squint. He found it hard to make out the dead man's features. Only the red cloth could be distinguished clearly. Gamliel let out a groan of distress when he recognized the gypsy's scarf.

23

A slight breeze caressed the courtyard. Leaning on the coping of the well, Federico supervised the loading of the wagons. Brother Médard hopped up and down and stamped his feet, pulling on the string around the packages and yelling at the muleteers, reprimanding these limbs of Satan for having tied them so badly. Federico dabbed at his cheeks with a handkerchief soaked in water, then continued reading the inventory. The manuscripts would only be wrapped at the last moment. They were sleeping in the cellar of the chapel. It was quite another arsenal that Brother Médard was currently busy putting in crates. Molds of fake patents, lead seals imitating those of the censors, fonts of characters with slight defects that would make it impossible to identify printers like Fust whose fonts were known to the inquisitors, acids to age the ink, tanks and sieves perforated with signs of the dolphin or the lyre with which the sheets would be watermarked in order to cover their tracks. All the crates in this consignment bore the Medici coat of arms surrounded by kabbalistic signs. The arms testified to the support of powerful protectors while the lettering in Hebrew would distract the attention of customs guards and men-at-arms, launching them on a trail that led a long way from Italy or France, beyond the seas, to the Holy Land, where they had no authority or power.

Federico was impatient to leave, but, as well as the supplying of Florence, it was now necessary to plan a second consignment intended for Fust and the booksellers on Rue Saint-Jacques. He smiled as he thought about the two Frenchmen. Against all expectation, they seemed to have made a good impression. Who would have thought that these vulgar fellows from a barbaric land, sent by an unremarkable young monarch, would become the valiant allies of the Medicis? And, through them, of Jerusalem? Master Colin was hardly a man of wit. As for Master Villon, he played the simpleton too well to actually be one. Was he wearing a mask, just like Federico? The mask of those who, being ahead of their time, chose to play the fool rather than be taken for prophets?

As Federico looked at these wagons overflowing with equipment, he felt a sense of discontent. He was aware that it was neither from Gamliel nor from the Medicis that the upheaval they planned to bring into the world could be expected to come. Basically, in the long run, the burghers would take the place of the lords. And whether Plato replaced Aristotle or not, the printers would make just as many spelling mistakes as the copyists, but in thousands of copies. It was not they who would change the situation. Injustice would continue to flourish beneath the layer of civility with which all these enlightened people claimed to smother it. No, in order to advance, much more than that was needed. Or much less. Oh, yes, much less! Hadn't Federico seen with his own eyes how Villon, after having humbly swept the ground with his tricorn, chanted his French ballad at the most formidable governor in the caliphate? Oh, yes! Federico could have slapped himself.

24

L ounging on a divan, the emir scratched his armpits. These mosquito bites were unbearable! To his right, Monsignor Francesco, the Archdeacon of Nazareth, was nervously waving a black lace fan. To his left, the *qadi* was filing his nails with a shell-bladed stylet. Sitting cross-legged at the foot of the dais, counselors and marabouts were making an effort to assume a solemn and reflective air beneath their tangled turbans.

The steward ushered the slaves out as soon as Suleyman's messenger appeared, out of breath after his long ride. The young soldier, eager to please the distinguished gathering, launched into a hurried account of what had happened. An interpreter whispered in the ear of the archdeacon, who immediately put down his fan. Without deigning to look up or interrupt the cleaning of his nails, the *qadi* hissed at the messenger to come to the point. The reprimanded soldier's cheeks turned red, making him look like a male whore, an effect the emir found not unpleasing.

It was clear that the anxieties expressed by the *qadi* had been confirmed. The skilful way the two Frenchmen had been spirited away, in the very heart of Jerusalem, under the noses of the Mamluk guards, proved once again that Colin and François were not mere receivers of stolen goods.

That Suleyman had failed to discover the entrance to the Brotherhood's mysterious headquarters did not greatly upset the emir, who thought it preferable not to intervene too early in this business. The more incriminating evidence they gathered, the easier it would be to confound Gamliel and his accomplices. Because what they still lacked was a charge that would stick.

"If, as you say, these conspirators meet in secret merely to discuss science and philosophy, I'll invite them here to the palace to discuss these things with our scholars."

The caliphate tolerated Gamliel's activities for the simple reason that they were only aimed at the foreign censors, thus manifesting a praiseworthy hostility toward the common enemy. To stop them would be ridiculous. That would be tantamount to disciplining the Jews of Palestine on behalf of Western Catholics. This time, though, the book hunters seemed to be declaring a more general, more universal rejection of all established authority, and therefore also of Islam.

The archdeacon smiled to himself. He did not share this opinion. Jerusalem could not threaten any religion. It had already manufactured at least three all by itself. But what he dreaded was the participation of an unexpected rival, dangerous in quite a different way from the Jewish rebel: an adversary from within the ranks of Christendom itself, a pariah. Villon was an inveterate rebel. Nothing good could come of his encounter with the Holy Land. This passionate, pugnacious country was too well suited to his bad character for some terrible misdeed not to be the result. Sooner or later, the desert would get his blood up. Liberated from both scholarly austerity and courtly frivolity, his eloquence might play more than one trick here. If necessary, the emir would have the cursed poet impaled, and the incident would be closed. But this rhymester was merely the spokesman for a malign wind that corrupted men's souls, a malaise eating away at their faith from the inside and already spreading over much of Italy. It was only a growing impulse, still immature, and therefore easy to guide on its first steps. From this very place, for example. The emir and the *qadi* were far from seeing how well-founded their suspicions were. And the archdeacon was certainly not going to tell them. Monsignor Francesco was sorry. His hands were tied. All he could do was inform Rome and try to convince the Papacy of the danger threatening it.

The *qadi* put away his file and dismissed the assembly. A slight smile lit up his arrogant face. Villon's repeated insults to the guard of the caliphate were not without flavor. They amused him rather than worried him, especially when he thought of how Suleyman must be feeling at this moment. The emir seemed equally untroubled by this affair. He crushed a mosquito with a quick blow of his hand and brandished the crushed corpse of the insect with a triumphant air. As for the archdeacon, he was already trotting along the galleries of the palace, the heels of his shoes nervously striking the marble flagstones and echoing down the colonnades. He was on his way to write his letter to the Pope.

25

The hostelry was filled with pilgrims. Some twenty Spaniards sat around the table singing a lament, their voices rising to a painful howl whenever the chorus came around. Four windows looked out on a large courtyard where a few donkeys were resting. The drafts that ran between them, instead of chasing away the smells of sweat and food and fermented wine, brought the odors of the farmyard inside, the stench of manure, the aroma of burning hay. They also however let in a little of the coolness provided by the enchanting shade of Mount Tabor. Christian visitors came here in large numbers to climb the steep calvary, cut in the rock face, in memory of Christ's Transfiguration.

Situated on the Via Maris, at the junction of the caravan routes that crossed the Jezreel Valley, this way station over-flowed with activity day and night. Brother Paul had thought it more prudent to melt into the crowd of pilgrims from all over than to try to make his way through the scrubland and undergrowth.

François was swallowing mouthfuls of bitter cider, one after the other, and they were starting to go to his head. The din of conversation and laughter broke in waves over his temples. The shadows of the guests swayed in the candlelight, dancing a macabre farandole on the cracked walls. François saw his own shadow twisting among the others like a lost soul in Dante's Hell. Separate from the rest, another shadow approached and moved feverishly against his on the reddening wall.

Who exactly was this Aisha? A Bathsheba, a Magdalen? Wasn't she rather the face he had been trying in vain to give this land since he had first set foot in it? The Holy Land was silent through her. She had made herself its mysterious accomplice. Like a sister. She had the gentleness of its contours, the brightness of its skin, the fascinating beauty of its gaze. And the same placidity. Unlike the faithful praying fervently for it, the soldiers mounting guard over it, the conquerors, the empire builders, Aisha did not behave as if she owned the place. She was just here, sitting beneath an olive tree, crouching by a *wadi*. Without saying anything, without making proclamations. She came from a far distant world, that of the Atlas Mountains, where men were tough and stubborn and took immense pride in their mere presence. Not claiming a single patch of land for themselves, they went back and forth across the expanses of stone and sand, circumscribing an invisible territory in which their tracks were immediately erased by the wind.

Sated, Brother Paul took it upon himself to thank the Lord. He began bawling a liturgical chant with exaggerated pomp and in a doomsday voice that exhorted the assembly to join him. Everyone turned respectfully toward this fat bard and recited the thanksgiving with him, profuse with blessings and litanies. In all this pious din, none of the pilgrims noticed that, beneath the table, two of the travelers were gently holding hands.

26

Rabbi Gamliel left the synagogue at nightfall, waving farewell to the faithful wrapped in their prayer shawls, distributing alms to the beggars that haunted the streets of Safed, blessing the little children, bowing whenever he passed an old man. The softness of the air made him feel carefree, even though the Law ordered him to rush home to study and not let himself be distracted by the witching charms of twilight. Not that the young rabbi had never violated the Law, may God forgive him. At the age of thirty, he was still a bachelor. The daughter of the *gaon* of Yavne was betrothed to him in marriage, and she was already twelve. But he had not waited to taste the pleasures of the flesh. Copulation with a prostitute was tolerated by the Torah. And monogamy had only recently been established by the elders. Many Jews were not yet practicing it.

His conduct often puzzled his flock. More than once, in the dead of night, he had been heard singing and dancing alone around his desk, talking to his books, screaming psalms at the stars. He sometimes disappeared without warning, merely leaving a few instructions to his secretary. He would suddenly reappear a few days later, enter the *yeshiva* of which he was the master, and resume his classes where he had broken them off, congratulating his studious pupils, reprimanding the idlers who had taken advantage of his absence to daydream, although nobody knew how he could so infallibly tell one group from the other.

What his disciples did not know was that he had read the Gospels in the company of Brother Paul. He also knew by heart the last words of Christ, which the Brotherhood held secretly in its cellars. He had studied them with great care, seeing nothing to disagree with. Nothing that contradicted his own faith. Except for that annoying Trinity . . . If it had not been for that, the Brotherhood would have made public this final message, this overwhelming testament dictated by Jesus to the high priest Annas just before his arrest. The Church had been looking for the document for centuries. In vain. And yet Gamliel had received orders to reveal its existence to two brigands from Paris. There wasn't much to fear from Colin. But God alone knew what Villon planned to do with such information. He might sabotage the whole operation, if only to take revenge for the imprisonment that had been inflicted on him as a test.

But it was precisely on Villon's cunning that the commander of the Brotherhood was banking. He knew perfectly well the poet would not submit blindly to the orders of Guillaume Chartier, let alone those of Jerusalem, and he was counting on that. Not that the unseen head of the book hunters had deigned to reveal his plan to Gamliel, but the rabbi guessed that Villon was one of its chief components.

Gamliel walked up and down the sleeping streets, for the first time doubting the legitimacy of his mission. When he reached the doorway of his house, he stopped for a moment or two at the foot of the steps and murmured a prayer. A thick cloud passed over Safed, covering the moon, plunging the town into darkness.

27

From the top of the bell tower, shielding his eyes with his hands, a Mongol sentry looked down at the valley. Four travelers had just appeared on the horizon. The first held the tails of his alb lifted so that his huge calves could pass unencumbered. He was trotting quickly, crushing the scrub, tracing a furrow as wide as that of an oxcart. Having recognized the prior's inimitable gait, the sentry left his post to go and inform Médard.

It was not until late afternoon that Brother Paul's glistening cranium emerged from the brambles that lined the edge of the cliff. Having arrived in the courtyard of the cloister, the visitors, out of breath from their journey, pulled down their hoods, much to the dismay of the monks, who suddenly discovered the gentle face and glossy hair of a beautiful young girl dressed in the habit of their order.

Paul hugged Médard, crushing him in his arms. The dwarf wriggled, two feet from the ground, trying to break free and regain terra firma. Federico was standing slightly to one side. He held out his hand to Colin, who immediately lifted his own high, ready to strike. Federico only just dodged the blow. He stepped back and plunged his arm into his tunic. Colin took up position, ready to parry a knife thrust, but Federico turned nonchalantly to François and held out the book with the butterfly wings, for the "theft" of which he and Colin had been imprisoned. François did not move. Even though he was bowing obsequiously to give him back the volume, the Italian had the same crafty smile as the first time, as if he were setting a new trap. François aimed a nimble kick in the direction of his bladder, which Federico parried with the book. Under the impact, the translucent butterfly came free of its binding and hovered for a moment in the breeze as if it were really flying, its wings ablaze in the reddening glow of the sunset. It stayed up a little longer, turning hither and thither, before gently coming to rest on a heap of straw. Federico and François both stopped to pick it up and their heads crashed into each other. Neither man moved for a moment, stubbornly remaining in the same position, forehead to forehead. It was Federico who bent first and recovered the butterfly. He tried to put it back into its leather chrysalis, but without success, and gave an almost embarrassed smile.

"Never mind. I still owe you reparation."

In the gathering darkness, François's narrow grin widened just slightly. Was he forgiving him, or rejoicing at the nasty trick he was preparing? With that enigma, the two men separated. Colin was sorry no blood had flowed. As for Aisha, she was disturbed to discover the brutal strength smoldering beneath François's amiable features. Given that she was under his protection, such strength should have reassured her, but she couldn't help dreading his obstinate ferocity, which would not easily be tamed. What would she do if François was too stubborn to follow her where she wanted to take him, the place where she could finally show him the way he had so long been seeking?

Médard waved his bronze key, like a baby shaking a little bell, already scampering toward the chapel, pulling the prior by the sleeve. Brother Paul let the dwarf scold him. He just had time to instruct the others to follow him. A wicked smile lit up his round face. He too had missed nothing of the spectacle. That joust had not been fortuitous, he was sure of it. The Italian had been counting on it. It was as if he had wanted to make sure of something.

Reaching the far end of the nave, Médard nimbly opened the door that led to the cellars. At the foot of the steps, he lit the torches in the wall one by one. A gentle odor of sawdust and camphor came in through a window. The air was surprisingly dry here, the temperature pleasant. At the entrance to the main room, a slight breeze caressed the visitors' cheeks. This slight coolness, combined with the smiling white of the walls, made them feel strangely at ease. The place was neither solemn nor austere. A kind of gaiety emanated from the brightly-colored bindings that stood close together on the shelves. On the floor, tall thin vases, containing scrolls of papyrus, rubbed shoulders with heavy nailed chests. There were no benches, no tables. This was the kingdom of books. Mingled thus in a kind of mute, meaningless dance, they did not seem like the works of man, or even for man, but endowed with their own life, freed from the very texts they contained.

François spotted a splendid binding stamped with animal motifs. Monsters and wild beasts frolicked on it, oblivious of their leather yoke. Aisha followed the direction of François's gaze. There was something physical, sensual even, in the way he eyed the book and caressed its cover. She noticed the same gleam of greed in Federico's eyes as, with a quick glance, he established a rapid inventory. There was so much here, it was worth a fortune.

Colin stopped in front of a clay statuette painted in several colors, with black lines that outlined the parts of the human body. The skull was covered with numbers drawn in ink. Beside it, a baboon's fetus was swimming in a jar filled with a foul-looking yellowish liquid. Further on, Colin stumbled over an assembly of iron hoops intertwined around an axis. Each of the hoops bore a brass ball. Colin tapped one of the balls with his finger, and to his surprise set the thing in motion. The hoops started turning slowly around each other, Roman numerals paraded to the rhythm of this meticulous ballet of arcs and balls, while, on a blue dial dotted with stars, a mother-of-pearl half-moon pursued a little brass sun, without ever catching it.

Brother Paul smiled with more than a hint of pride at his guests' dazzled reactions. But Médard was still in a foul mood. Upset at having introduced these intruders into his domain, he indicated the copies chosen for the mission with a casual gesture of the arm. They were marked with little crosses hastily drawn in chalk.

François wondered about the motives that led these monks to lend their hand to Jews from "the invisible Jerusalem." The book hunters were clearly trying to help a wind of apostasy blow through the Christian world. And yet there was no doubting the religious fervor of the Medicis, the Sforzas, Médard, or even Guillaume Chartier.

Noticing François's confusion, Brother Paul disappeared for a moment, then came back with a bundle of manuscript sheets. The parchment was blackened with serried lines, filled with crossings out, encumbered with feverish penciled notes that gave the whole a tormented appearance. A feeling of panic emanated from it, as if the author had feared he might not be able to finish his task in time. The jerky strokes and absence of punctuation revealed either a deranged soul or the anxiety of a visionary afraid of seeing some vision escape him before he had been able to describe it. François recognized the heavy characters of the Gothic, even though he was unable to decipher them. He looked up at the prior, who simply declared that a Christian was not obliged to speak to God in Latin.

In England, in Germany and in the lands of the North, the faithful found it hard to be inspired by a language whose sounds, so pleasant to the ears of a Spaniard or a Frenchman, were in no way melodious to Teutons and Saxons. These barbarian converts in the Rhineland or Scotland felt no affinity with Rome. After all, it wasn't the Italians or the Castilians whom the Lord had chosen to ensure the coming of His kingdom. And it was not in the language of the sacristy that Jesus and his apostles had spread the good word. From there to questioning the precepts of papal dogma, there was only one step.

Having always lived in the Holy Land, Paul and Médard also felt less and less need for Papal intercession with the Savior. They rubbed shoulders with Him every day in this very place, on the roads of Galilee, amid the dry ravines of Judea, in the fields of Samaria. Not that they fully grasped the significance of the text that François held in his hands. The heads of the Brotherhood, though, being better informed, had seen in it a mystic ardor capable of fanning a raging fire, even a war of religion. Written by an obscure priest in the Black Forest, it was merely a first, faltering step. It proclaimed a new kind of Christianity that repudiated Catholic doctrine. By chance, it was precisely the cities on the banks of the Rhine that counted the most printers and booksellers indispensable to its distribution.

Colin was the only one present to scent the danger. Those heavy Germanic letters, almost chiseled into the skin of the parchment, made him ill at ease. He was no great reader but he was familiar with the handwriting of his good friend François, so light, so playful, laying down the stokes so nimbly, gliding over the paper. The sturdy characters of this German script hardly lent themselves to the madrigal and the rondeau. On the other hand, they perfectly suited the heated exhortations of a preacher. Repelled by the impetuousness of the upstrokes, the brutality of the downstrokes, the stiffness of the lines, Colin instinctively perceived their intransigent fanaticism.

Driven by more down-to-earth considerations, Federico was wondering if he had allowed for enough cases. He judged that he would have room in the false bottoms of the wagons, the inner pockets of the provision sacks, the cavities hollowed in the lids of the barrels, to hide the most compromising works. Not to mention his own rich wardrobe. The astronomical maps could be sewed between the flaps of his winter cape, the marine charts of the Aegeans in the sleeves of his hunting doublet, the pamphlets of Aesop in the rim of his hat. Cotton balls, sawdust, and several dozen cheap books would absorb the damp in the hold of the ship. Camphor, acids, and traps would protect against rats.

Federico went to a package tied with red ribbon for which he had not yet chosen a place within his cargo. Brother Médard tried to hold him back but the Italian, holding the package firmly, made an abrupt about-face and walked up to François. He set aside the crumpled paper, revealing the contents with theatrical slowness.

It was Colin who gave a start first, immediately recognizing the familiar handwriting he had just been thinking about. Speechless, François looked at the first page without daring to touch it. The last time he had seen that sheet, the constabulary had just burst into his garret and grabbed him by the elbows, ready to haul him off to prison. Although they had searched his lodgings from top to bottom, they had not found the knife that Master Ferrebouc, a respectable notary, had accused François of using on him during a nocturnal brawl with the Coquillards. Having been unable to identify his assailants in the darkness, the accursed notary had quite simply denounced the most famous member of the band. Counting on the clemency of his protectors, Louis XI, Charles of Orléans and Marie of Clèves, François had offered little resistance. Risking nevertheless the death penalty, he had thrown a last desperate glance at the scattered and trampled sheets of paper, resigned to the idea that they were his only testament. And now here were his last rhymes in the hands of the Brotherhood, just like the last words of Jesus as recorded by Annas. Were they also hidden here, in this very cellar?

François gently passed his hand over the pages he had composed, remembering every line, every crossed-out word. Colin demanded an explanation, and Federico obliged him. Whenever they learned of the arrest of a tendentious author, a renowned scholar, or a humanist, the book hunters hastened to intervene, hoping to get their hands on the manuscripts hidden by the suspects. Most left them with a person they trusted, and it was sufficient to track that person down. In Villon's case, the task had been much easier. Since he was being pursued for a common crime rather than for his writings, the men-at-arms had come to his dwelling, not to seize his ballads, but to search for a weapon. The pages had simply had to be collected and taken away.

François handled his work with tender care. Suddenly, he noticed that his fingers were white with chalk powder, and he tuned red with anger. His manuscript had also been marked with a cross! It, too, was to be shipped off!

Médard was visibly embarrassed, Federico frankly amused. Brother Paul hastened to specify that it was up to Gamliel to explain to François the reasons for this choice. François was outraged. The prior painted in glowing colors the possibility of a successful edition printed by Fust, with the royal seal of approval. All to no avail. François demanded that his property be restored to him immediately. Deeply offended, he grunted and gesticulated. He was puzzled, too. This reunion with his own poetry, after all this time, and so far from Paris, could not decently be put down to chance. His manuscript had preceded him here to the Holy Land. It had even arrived well before him, since the action brought by Ferrebouc dated from that damned Christmas of 1462, more than a year ago. These pages had therefore been in the hands of the book hunters before Chartier had visited him in prison. Had Gamliel read them? Whether he had or not, he had certainly known who François Villon was before he set foot in Safed.

Federico smiled. "My late master Cosimo was delighted to read your rhymes."

François's whole body stiffened. Yes, his poems had not only preceded him to the Holy Land, they had passed through Florence first, even before Fust had opened his shop on Rue Saint-Jacques or Chartier, knowing nothing of the existence of a clandestine Jerusalem, had condescended to send two obscure Coquillards to Palestine. François had to face the truth. Nothing had been negotiated here that could not have been concluded without his intervention, and in the highest circles too. He had never been the official emissary of the kingdom. All these arrangements with Fust and Schoeffer, and with the Bishop of Paris, had come later, after the arrival of his ballads in the Holy Land! And after his arrest! That time in Paris, it had not been his own cunning that had helped him to avoid the gallows, nor Colin's intercession. It had been the book hunters.

From the start, it was him they had wanted, François de Montcorbier, known as Villon. François tried to regain his composure and think. Dozens of questions were going through his head. Why had the Brotherhood hidden the presence of his manuscript from him for so long? Why was Federico showing it to him now? What did Jerusalem want of him?

With an authoritative clap of his hands, Paul announced that it was time for vespers. Federico offered his arm to Aisha. Colin, starving after that afternoon's long walk, nimbly got in ahead of them. François resigned himself to following behind them. There was one question that kept going around and around in his head, tormenting him more than any other. What was the king's role in all this?

Alone now, Médard extinguished the torches one by one, plunging the cellar into darkness. He hopped up the steps that led to the nave. Out of breath, he turned one last time, like a lord inspecting his fiefdom, then closed the door behind him, returning the books to their deep slumber.

L arge brass chandeliers hung from the ceiling, but it was dark. Two big oak logs blazed in the central hearth, but it was cold. Seen from the entrance, the huge hall seemed almost deserted. At the other end, though, several rows of officers and dignitaries pressed in front of the throne. Their words were lost in the din of the rain hammering the stained-glass window. The king listened, stroking his dogs with a distracted hand. He was dressed simply, in a brown tunic. His rough hair bore a small crenellated crown of matte gold, without stones or engravings. A long knife hung from his belt, clearly visible.

A lackey pointed to a bench against the side wall, and Fust took his seat, taking care not to make the slightest noise. He looked around at the damp walls, devoid of ornament, the rough flagstones, scrubbed with water, the dust-covered beams. He remembered the polished marble of the palaces of Mayence, the tapestries evoking the luxuries of the court and the pleasures of the heart, the glittering draperies, the walls laden with trophies: the shields of vanquished enemies, the heads of bears and stags and boars, stuffed falcons on silver perches. But Fust did not regret his choice. Paris glowed with quite another fire than did the cities of Germany or Italy, which were devoted to glory and beauty in too flagrant a manner. A concern for good taste reigned on the banks of the Seine just as it did elsewhere, but with a natural, somewhat nonchalant elegance, which, instead of always bowing down before genius, was also able to let itself be won over by subtler, more mischievous talents.

In his opinion, the book trade would blossom much more here than in Madrid, Turin or Frankfurt. So far, Louis XI had been more astute in his choices than the Italian princes or patrons from the German aristocracy. Cosimo de' Medici had appointed a philosopher, Marsilio Ficino, director of the Platonic Academy. He had not hesitated to open its doors to the Talmudists, to encourage the researches of Phoenician astronomers and Arab mathematicians, to finance the work of doctors and alchemists. In Mayence, Gutenberg only survived by publishing grandiose bibles and tedious commentaries. But the King of France, against all expectation, had developed friendly feelings for a maker of rhymes whose escapades he had pardoned more than once. And Fust thought he knew why. Villon helped Louis XI in his plans as no brilliant theoretician or faculty heavyweight could have done. In speaking of his life, of women, of his sorrows, of Paris, he invited the subjects of the kingdom to all share the same destiny. His song united the French, be they from Poitou or Picardy, in a single anthem, a single language, which transcended dialects and coteries. Unlike the Medicis, Louis XI was not steeped in Greek and Latin but in the language of his country, as handled so well by Master François. The king was not a great lover of poetry. He quite simply saw Villon as the bard of a nation in the process of being born.

Nevertheless, Fust was plagued by doubt. The subject he had come to discuss today was of little interest to a monarch who was under attack on all sides. The rebellion of the nobles was taking on an unexpected scale. Charles the Bold, Count of Charolais, now at the head of an impressive coalition of dukes and barons, had just openly declared war on the crown. Bretons, Burgundians, and other provincials jealous of their prerogatives, hoped to dismiss their ambitious monarch and remedy the problems of government by placing on the throne an eighteen-year-old boy, the Duke of Berry, who was none other than the king's brother. To put down this rebellion, Louis XI had called on his surest allies, the Italians. With the Sforzas and the Medicis entering the battle, Fust found it hard to see how the book hunters' operation could be properly launched. If Louis XI was ousted, the Brotherhood's secret agreement with France would be rendered null and void. The defeat of Paris would be much more serious than a simple political reversal. It would give the dark forces that had governed Christendom for centuries a highly regrettable reprieve, pushing back the deadline once and for all. A fatal blow must absolutely be dealt to the demons of this abject past that would not resign itself to die. The young king's possible victory against the lords would not be complete if it did not also ring the funeral bell for the age of chivalry. A military victory was not enough. If the rebellious knights and paladins perished only by the sword, their deaths would be glorious, their bravery legendary. Unless a soldier from quite another legion denied them this final honor. While composing their elegy, he would dig their grave. He would bury them once and for all with a melancholy stroke of his pen. And it was on Villon that Louis XI was counting to deal this fatal blow.

Waiting to be called, Fust did not move from his bench. The king had not made any announcements on the measures to be taken. He had given no orders, being content to amiably thank the speakers and now and then whisper a few mysterious instructions to his aide-de-camp. The dignitaries and the captains gradually withdrew. It was getting colder and colder, darker and darker, in the great council chamber. Only the Bishop of Paris remained in his place. Once everyone had gone, Guillaume Chartier began an inaudible dialogue with his monarch. His Majesty, who until then had appeared impassive, bent forward to hear better, interrupted the bishop on several occasions, and even smiled with a crafty grin that reminded Fust somewhat of François.

At last summoned to join in the discussion, the bookseller rose laboriously and approached, leaning on his cane. He prostrated himself awkwardly in what he hoped was a bow, then conveyed greetings to the king from Jerusalem. This tribute did not fail to disconcert Louis XI, who remembered suddenly, with a certain embarrassment, that he was negotiating with Jews. Should he consider this mark of their deference as a courtesy of protocol or be offended by such arrogance? Since when had these godless people without a land of their own had ambassadors? True, he did not trust his own courtiers, nor indeed his own brother. But the Jews? After helping him to undermine the power of the Pope, they would no doubt try to erode his own. Even though they had been recommended by the Medicis, Louis XI suspected Fust's patrons of having aims that were quite different than those of Florence or Paris. He thought of the only Jews he knew: moneylenders richer than Croesus, a doctor from Toledo who had cured his dislocated shoulder, and a few unfortunates burned in the public square.

Fust tried to present the Brotherhood's plan as best he could. After the imposing parade of soldiers and diplomats that had just taken place, it was not easy to come here and boast of the merits of an offensive involving books. To weaken the papacy without setting off an actual conflict, the Brotherhood had carefully chosen the texts to be disseminated. But it was first of all the books themselves that the operation aspired to change, their form, their weight, their appearance. It would liberate them from the yoke of the cloisters and the colleges. Printers, engravers, binders, and peddlers would make them easier to handle, lighter, less expensive. And much less serious. Instead of attacking scholasticism head-on, they would drown it in a stream of works of all kinds, flooding the marketplace with accounts of journeys, treatises on physics, tragedies and farces, manuals on algebra or boilermaking, historical chronicles, tales and legends. And above all, the booksellers would encourage the use of French, Italian, and German. Latin would no longer be a sacred idiom but simply the language of Livy and Virgil.

Guillaume Chartier seemed to approve. By diminishing the influence of Rome, the clergy of France would strengthen its position within the kingdom. The goods of the Church would at last be in its full possession rather than filling the pockets of the Pope. The expenses incurred in fighting the rebellion of the barons would rapidly place the royal coffers at the mercy of the ecclesiastical finances. And so the Bishop of Paris would become at once spiritual head of the country and principal treasurer to the court.

The king, who had begun stroking his dogs again, did not deign to express his opinion on the proposed strategy and dismissed Fust. His indifference, whether feigned or not, made the printer ill at ease. The light was gradually going out in the melted wax of the candelabra, plunging the chamber into darkness. As a majordomo escorted Fust to the exit, Louis XI suddenly spoke up. The German turned, tense, all ears.

"Tell Jerusalem to take good care of Master François."

29

A isha sat down on the coping of the well, hoping it would provide a little coolness. François remained standing, facing her. As soon as she took his hand, an animal heat, both burning and delicious, spread through the hollow of his palm.

"Are you as good a poet as they say?"

Aisha's innocent question made François smile. He would have liked to lay the girl on the ground and take her right here. He raised his head and examined her for a long time.

He could not help thinking that the presence of this nomad by his side was far from being fortuitous. Every time he wanted to detain her, the rejection he met with was merely formal—or feigned. She was more than just bait, he knew that. She was his guide through the paths and *wadis*. Or else an enchantress in the pay of Gamliel.

A stroke of the cheek immediately swept away François's anxieties. Seeing him a prey to doubt, was Aisha trying to distract him? There was nothing unlikely about that. But why not accept this truce? He pulled close to her and kissed her forehead. Even though it had often led him astray, he had never resisted the spell of women for very long.

In the darkness, a solitary spectator applauded. His back against the low wall that surrounded the courtyard of the cloister, Colin doffed his hat low, paying tribute to the admirable way in which the wild girl of the desert had gone about taming the Parisian libertine.

*

In the refectory, the guests were talking at the tops of their voices. The prior drew his best beverage from a keg at the end of the table, generously filling a large stoneware jug, humming cheerfully as the divine nectar flowed. Federico was deep in conversation with Médard, who still disapproved of the choice of books to be taken to France and Italy. Above all, he was critical of Master Villon's *Testament*, finding it frivolous and insubstantial. He was also offended by the pompous title. There were two Testaments, the old and the new. What need was there of a third?

Federico, who was a little drunk by now, explained to him condescendingly that it was precisely Villon's flippancy that would make the greatest impression on people's minds. And on their hearts. Dante and Pindar wrote in a pure language that touched the clouds, whereas Villon addressed ordinary people face-to-face, in lively speech. His ballads did not celebrate the odyssey of gods or princes, but that of the man in the street, a hearty fellow with whom one would gladly share a drink. Therein lay their strength. Satisfied with the effects of his oratory, interspersed as they were with hiccups, Federico poured himself another generous helping as soon as Brother Paul put down the jug and invited those at the table to say grace.

30

G amliel reached the monastery early in the morning. Politely cutting short the formulas of welcome uttered by the barely sober prior, the rabbi went straight to the cellars. Brother Médard was waiting for him there, legs dangling, perched on a chest from the Indies. Rabbi Gamliel walked past the shelves with a resolute step, as if inspecting the troops. Scrolls and books stood to attention. The best trained agents could fail, make mistakes, but Cato and Averroes would not falter in the face of the enemy, nor would a noose ever be put around Homer's neck. Sea maps did not yet interest the censors. And yet the enormous distances they covered would soon make Rome tiny and insignificant. The recent auto-da-fés revealed the panic that was already gripping the clergy. But the more treatises on astronomy they burned in the public square, the more the onlookers would watch the smoke rising from the pyres. Eventually they would look up and see the stars.

Gamliel rapidly checked through the lists. The names of the greatest thinkers, the titles of the most important books, succeeded each other from line to line in a glorious inventory interspersed here and there with more lighthearted works. Nobody knew which would be better at defeating the adversary: Greek tragedies or village farces, the truth of science or the fantasy of dreams.

Gamliel bade a solemn farewell to the rows of volumes. It was in a slightly hoarse voice that he gave permission for Médard to load the wagons.

*

Colin and François sat at the long table in the refectory, talking. The only news they had of France had reached them through Brother Paul. It was not always fresh, often taking more than a month to cross the Mediterranean. Nobody knew if Louis XI's reign had survived the revolt of the barons. It was only when they got to Genoa that the book hunters would discover if they could go to Paris or if they had to give up the idea and follow Federico to Florence. If that was the case, Colin planned to run away as soon as possible and rejoin the Coquillards, wherever they were, rather than dog the Florentine's heels. Shouldn't they seize the opportunity to rob him and take revenge for the trick he had played on them? Just as François was about to reply, Colin nodded his head in the direction of the door. Gamliel was standing in the doorway. He had surely heard a good part of the conversation.

The rabbi assumed an affable smile tinged with mischief, which reminded François somewhat of Chartier's when he had entered his cell all that time ago. The bishop's aura had been accentuated by the semidarkness, his white alb illuminated by the light of his lantern. Here, it was the blinding rays of the sun that enveloped this other priest with their light, giving him the look of a prophet. But François doubted that he was bringing glad tidings. Gamliel approached and sat down. He poured a little water into a metal tumbler, took a sip then, giving François a penetrating look, told him without further ado that only Colin would be returning to France.

François leapt to his feet, his face red with anger. It was he, not Colin, who had been entrusted with the responsibility for this mission. He had to make sure personally that the cargo arrived safely. Keeping him here in the Holy Land was a scandal, tantamount to taking him hostage! Gamliel firmly rejected these outraged protests. He justified the decision by asserting that it would be inappropriate to repatriate Master Villon simultaneously with his rebellious verses, at a time when Rome would show itself most likely to pursue their author and when Louis XI, in the middle of a military conflict, would be unable to protect him. The orders of the head of the Brotherhood were categorical: Villon was staying.

Gamliel had received instructions to persuade the Frenchman to put off his departure, but was forbidden from using force to do so. Being as stubborn as a mule, Villon would not do what was expected of him if he was threatened. He had to be cajoled. Gamliel suggested amiably that François take up his pen again. In the meantime . . .

Parodying the rabbi's affable tone, François thanked him humbly, and declared himself flattered that such well-informed book hunters had found him worthy to fight shoulder to shoulder with Horace and Epicurus against stupidity and narrow-mindedness. But Epicurus and Horace were long dead. In their lifetime, nobody would have dreamt of keeping them out of the fray like this. Even as he cursed and protested, François rapidly made his accounts, less and less convinced that this extension of his stay would be as bad as he claimed. Nobody was waiting for him in Paris, apart from Chartier. There was nothing for him there but debts and problems with the law.

Colin too, beneath his angry air, felt less and less upset by the news. Rather than serving as escort to his venerable companion, he had been promoted to head of the expedition and would be in a position to deal directly with the Bishop of Paris, if not with the king himself. He was already thinking about how to take advantage of this godsend.

François continued nevertheless to chafe against the decision, declaring that Gamliel could not keep him here against his will, that it was out of the question for him to write in such conditions, that this new humiliation was the last straw. It was an insult to the crown of France!

Gamliel did not pass up the opportunity that François was

offering him on a platter, but immediately took him at his word. "The crown of France," he said, "considers this arrangement quite judicious, as it has just reiterated to Master Fust."

François could hardly believe his ears. Louis XI was in league with them! The rabbi would not allow himself to lie about something like that. In the garret in Lyon, the price had already been agreed, the deal concluded between Paris and Jerusalem. *Quid pro quo.* Villon's pen in return for Fust's services. That meant that François had never really risked the gallows! The king had pardoned him in advance. But to what end?

The Brotherhood had kept its part of the bargain. It had acquired a printing works and was now sending the texts that would feed its presses. But François could not work out what he could possibly supply in return. It couldn't have been to write rondeaus that his monarch had sent him such a long distance—or agreed that these book hunters should keep him prisoner.

He lowered his eyes and stared at the rough wood of the table. An ant was scampering along the paths traced by the veins. It ran here and there, crossing cracks and slits like a skiff braving the waves. It seized a crumb of bread, felt the rancid texture with its mandibles, then set off again at a lively pace. It seemed to be wandering at will. But it was actually working for its queen. Colin crushed the ant with his fist. François jumped, abruptly torn from his daydream. Colin had done it deliberately, to shake him.

François suddenly bent his head, but at the same time gave a thin smile that stretched the skin on his cheeks and made his face taut. Gamliel did not understand the meaning of such a grin. But Colin immediately recognized that wicked look, the look François had always had in the old days, when the whole band had gathered in the evening to prepare their latest robbery. Gamliel sensed nervously that the two Coquillards were talking to each other without saying a word. Colin, with a sardonic gleam in his eye, gently ground the corpse of the ant between his huge fingers and flicked it so that it landed at the rabbi's feet, while François, who had not moved, continued to stare at the sharp corners of the table, as if the ant were still running across it.

As Gamliel was making an effort to decipher the silent message that the two Frenchmen were slyly giving each other, Federico came into the room, as dapper as ever in his plumed hat, and brandishing a riding whip. He announced that everything was ready. The convoy would reach Acre in less than two days.

B rother Paul was scurrying in all directions, waving his censer at arm's length, filling the courtyard with an acrid odor of cinnamon and burning resin, while with the other hand, he sprinkled mules and people with holy water, muttering wishes and prayers. A windy rumble, the kind that whales made, rose from his breathless chest. Assembled in a corner, the monks watched the prior's every move, fearing that he might slip and fall on the flagstones, which were still wet with dew. Médard merely shrugged his shoulders, observing that good old Paul had made sure to clear his throat with a few morning glassfuls. In celebration of this glorious day, he even seemed to have doubled the usual dose.

Federico enhanced the ceremony in his own way, favoring those present with an even more extravagant costume than usual. He was dressed in a purple velvet shirt padded at the shoulders and elbows, the stitching camouflaged by elegant embroideries. The sleeves and collar were edged with falsely discreet pale silk flowerets. Three rows of small gold coins emphasized the bulge of the chest. They glinted in the sun and jangled in unison with each movement of the body. The handle of a knife emerged from a lizard-skin sheath hanging from a belt of Spanish leather, studded with nielloed silver. Its belligerent appearance clashed with the rest—a clear warning. The choice of these sartorial eccentricities was far from insignificant. Every detail was carefully considered so as to impress bandits and soldiers, peasants and dignitaries alike.

After a rapid inspection, Federico mounted his horse and gallantly saluted the entourage. Colin, holding his horse by the bridle, approached François. Incapable of giving voice to the mixed feelings they felt, the two men made do with forlorn smiles. Their emotion was all the more intense for being unspoken. Just as Colin turned to mount his horse, François walked abruptly away in the direction of the ramparts, from where he would watch the departure.

Once the convoy had left, the monks returned to their tasks, some to the library, some to the wine press, some to the cowsheds. The courtyard of the cloister was now deserted, apart from Gamliel, who was sitting on a bench at the foot of the bell tower, lost in thought. At his feet stretched the threatening shadow of the belfry cross, its arms spread like the wings of a bird of prey. The rabbi felt his throat tighten. He thought of the little caravan peacefully beginning its journey to the sea. Confident as it was, it was about to face a huge monster with a thousand tentacles.

The power of Rome spread over the world like the shadow of that great cross. It exercised its grip a long way from this monastery and the humble priests who lived in it, the countryside that surrounded it. No Pope had ever trodden the shepherds' paths that crisscrossed Galilee, or climbed alone, leaning on his crook, the burning hills of Judea, or descended the rocky slopes that led to the Dead Sea. In his palace of marble and porphyry, the Holy Father could follow only the lines of the illuminations in his gospel. There, fine miniatures depicted the suffering of Christ, his blood dripping in watercolor strokes tinged with vermilion. Gamliel, who had never been outside Palestine, imagined the Vatican as a huge fortress. An assault by the Brotherhood suddenly struck him as derisory. It would be crushed like the ant that had been running across the refectory table yesterday.

François and Aisha approached along the dark path that the cross drew in the sand. They noticed the rabbi's anxious expression, but their arrival seemed immediately to chase away the thoughts tormenting him. Gamliel did not know which comforted him more, Aisha's innocent smile or François's wicked grin. He told them he had to return to Safed as soon as possible. He had been summoned to appear before the *qadi* of Nazareth, of whom he had requested an interview with the intention of allaying the suspicions of the caliphate. And besides, given that the monastery might be subject to a search at any moment, it was more prudent to be far from it. François would set off tomorrow. The head of the Brotherhood had arranged a safe, isolated place for him to stay.

François, who had thought he could stay here with the monks, was taken aback. He did not even ask the name of place to which he would be conducted, or if Aisha would be going with him, especially as she was so excited, it was clear she already knew. She and the rabbi had stopped making any attempt to conceal the fact that they were in league.

In fact, Gamliel continued as if everything was normal, explaining to what extent the period was favorable for a journey. It was just before the Jewish New Year, and the roads would be filled with villagers going to the synagogue, families going to visit their relatives, artisans and workers coming to work on the preparations or to receive rewards and gifts from their employers. A young couple, she disguised as a Jewish fiancée, he as a student of the Talmud, would not attract any attention.

François was unable to suppress a sardonic little laugh. He imagined himself crossing Galilee in a skullcap and caftan, perhaps even a false beard. He saw himself blessing old women, stroking the heads of children, raising his eyes to heaven as if he were in lively conversation with the Almighty, and letting his young bride carry all their baggage. The couple would be escorted for its own safety, Gamliel made clear, but the presence of Aisha was absolutely indispensable thanks to her knowledge of the terrain. She was a child of the Atlas Mountains.

Gamliel gave an amused smile. "After all, the desert holds no secrets for her."

32

The ship moved away from the coast under full sail. The ramparts of Acre were now nothing but a grey line emphasizing the luminous ocher of the dunes surrounding the city. To the south, Mount Carmel spread its shadow over the sea. Its rounded contours gave it the appearance of a sleeping animal, while further north, steep cliffs, like wild beasts standing on their hind legs, jealously guarded access to Lebanon.

Federico and Colin stood in the prow. A westerly wind struck their faces, providing scant relief from the heat that reigned on deck. Colin was in a jovial mood, delighted to be leaving the Holy Land at last. He had never felt at ease there. Imbued with the teachings of the priests, he had expected to feel Christ's compassion, to get closer to God, or at least to find some answers. He had been up and down the roads of Galilee, traveled the length of the Jordan, and trodden the paving stones of Jerusalem, believing that they would lead somewhere. He had looked everywhere for clues. But how to find his way in that jumble of temples and ruins, of tribes and clans, of prophecies and legends? Who on earth could he ask to show him the right path in those alleys filled with ghosts, ragged children, wretched vagabonds, priests, and nomads? And what questions to ask them? And so he was leaving empty-handed. He couldn't wait to be back in his sweet France. He took the sea air deep into his lungs, as if a garrote had been removed from his throat, then turned back for a moment, pleased to see the shoreline fade and vanish in the distance.

Federico was also inhaling the air. It swelled the foremast with a healthy, alert vigor that seemed like a good omen. The vessel glided nimbly over the waves, barely swaying. He looked out to the open sea, face to the wind, eyes burning, lips stung by the sun and the salt.

33

From the height of the papal throne, Paul II listened attentively to the reading of the dispatches. The members of the College sat on the terraced benches that faced each other on either side of the council chamber. In the center of the nave, lit by a ray of sun, a young priest stood reciting the latest news in a neutral voice. He related developments in the violent fighting in Savoy, informed them of the state of health of the Bishop of Liège, described the horrible punishment inflicted on the heretics in Seville, and went through a financial report from Palermo, without any emotion disturbing his monotonous delivery. Nobody dared utter a word. The Pope did not tolerate any interruption. He never pronounced on any subject before he had heard this dull list of the day's events to the end. The young orator did not classify his announcements either by chronological order or by order of importance, content merely to read them one after the other without pause or transition. So it was between a message from the Bishop of Rouen, alarmed by the precarious situation in France, and an account of the costs of repairing the palace in Avignon, that the missive from the Archdeacon of Nazareth concerning a possible Jewish plot against Rome was presented.

A slight murmur rose from the benches of bishops and archbishops. The word "Jew," even when uttered as part of a banal communiqué, never failed to cause a certain stir. But now their eminences were confronted with another term, just as troubling and filled with mystery: "Invisible Jerusalem." But the young priest had already moved on to something else: suggestions for the menu and floral decorations of the All Saints meal.

The Holy Father seemed to make little of these accusations coming from the Holy Land. Isolated and idle, the Archdeacon of Nazareth no doubt wanted to make a good impression. Under close watch from the Mamluks, he had proved himself incapable of recruiting local spies and saboteurs with a view to a new crusade. He could not even raise the funds necessary to maintain the basilica in Bethlehem. Claiming to be bled dry by the caliphate, his flock did not pay their tithes. Did he really think he could distinguish himself by revealing a grim conspiracy, which, even if it existed, was almost certainly the work of a handful of upstarts? Rome would only give credence to such stories when it saw a fleet of Hebrew ships sailing to attack the coast of Italy, or the Jewish quarter of some city taking up arms rather than bowing and scraping.

Paul II inquired rather about the progress of the armies of the nobles opposed to Louis XI, disappointed to learn that they were making no progress at all, held back not by the regiments of the crown, but by stupid internal divisions. Charles the Bold, Jean of Bourbon and René of Anjou were disputing the throne before they had even conquered it. The legate in Avignon was warning against a victory by Louis XI, fearing that it would involve a *de facto* annexation of the Comtat. As for the French clergy, it was only to be expected that it would submit to its victorious young monarch much more willingly than to the spiritual head of the Church, who, although quite venerable, was already old and lacked a firm hand.

Since the fall of Byzantium, the influence of the Papacy had continued to decline. Only the Iberian peninsula and a few Italian principalities still saw Rome as the capital of Christendom. Paul II was increasingly isolated. By fighting the humanists with all the aggressiveness of a zealot, he had lost the respect of the Sforzas and the Medicis. His nuncios reproached him for the luxury with which he surrounded himself while at the same time, from one council or synod to the next, reducing their budgets and their privileges. Ever since the clandestine republication of the seditious writings of John Wycliffe and Jan Hus, an unhealthy wind of reform had been blowing through the German, English, Czech, and Dutch dioceses, as well as everywhere that the Inquisition did not have a grip as strong as in Italy or Spain. In Paris, Guillaume Chartier did not even reply to the injunctions ordering him to forbid the opening of new printing works within his bishopric. And now the Holy Father, in no way worried by a devilish plan of the Jews to undermine his power, was busying himself choosing the food and ornaments for the forthcoming Papal receptions.

What the cardinals did not know was that, although the Pope seemed to be paying no attention to the warnings of the Archdeacon of Nazareth, it was not out of nonchalance. Quite the contrary. He secretly maintained the hope that they would be confirmed, seeing them as an unhoped for opportunity to restore his image. The announcement of a satanic plague coming from Judea would inflame the ardor of the faithful much more than the oft-repeated accusations of anathema and ritual murder. In fighting the diabolical forces of a secret Jerusalem, Rome would present itself as the last bastion of the faith. It would again be able to unite all the Catholic kings around it.

As one of his counselors spoke of the severe measures to be taken against the reformist bishops, Paul II was thinking about the best way to spread the rumor of a Jewish conspiracy. He even thought to make the task of the conspirators easier in order for the threat to take on the required scope. Pleased with this stratagem, he dismissed the College with a brief sign of the cross. Indignant, the prelates slowly left the chamber, continuing their discussions in low voices. Their reproving murmurs buzzed through the galleries until they were lost in the distance, covered by the drafts blowing in through the large windows looking out on St. Peter's Square.

The Supreme Pontiff sat motionless, sunk in the thick cushions of his canopied chair. He sent his chamberlain to fetch the chief of the guard. The huge chamber with its marble walls stretched in front of him, empty, silent. Paul II thought about God. He imagined the Almighty, sitting up there amid the stars, gazing out at the universe. Did He feel as alone as the Pope?

A dapper-looking officer crossed the threshold with a stiff, hurried gait. He wore a ceremonial doublet and a saber whose handle was engraved with the arms of the Holy See. The chamberlain scurried after him, his nose to the ground, his back stooped. The officer stopped dead at the foot of the Papal throne and stood to attention, grotesquely frozen. With this man, Paul II did not need to bother with the mannered tone or the air of thoughtful benevolence he had to assume to address archbishops and rulers. He could speak openly, get straight to the point. In the raucous voice of an old general, he informed the officer that the Jews had just declared war on Rome.

Aisha could not hold back a derisive smile at the sight of the valiant escort accorded them by Gamliel. As thin as a piece of string and as pale as a sheet, the young man was wearing a black caftan several sizes too large for him. As for François, it struck him that if the fellow were planted in the middle of a field of barley with his arms outstretched, he would make an excellent scarecrow. But Brother Paul hastened to assure them that beneath that thin frame of a budding Talmudist was concealed one of the best-trained warriors in the Brotherhood. A descendant of the noble line of *shomerim*, the ancient guardians of the Temple, he had mastered both the secret art of Mongol boxing and the use of Moorish daggers. And, like his ancestors, he was an excellent book hunter. This last remark duly impressed François, who now saw the newcomer in a better light.

Quite moved, and with several drinks already under his belt, the prior wrapped François and Aisha in his huge arms, almost suffocating them. He muttered a short blessing before handing them over to the young mercenary, who, without saying a word, immediately began leading his protégés down into the valley. François was sorry to have to leave Brother Paul, whom he saw as his only protector in this unknown land. He had felt safe with him. But Brother Paul had refused to divulge where the Brotherhood hid the statement dictated by Jesus before he was handed over to the Romans. He preferred it to remain secret. Men were not ready to receive its message. And besides, he had said with a laugh, they wouldn't like it at all.

Standing in the doorway of the chapel, Brother Médard watched them depart, telling himself that those three would not get far. He was jealous of their youth, of their hopes. Above all, he envied them for taking the road that led to the desert. He had lived there as a hermit at the beginning of his long spiritual journey. He had crisscrossed its ravines and *wadis* for months, meditated in its caves or at the top of its plateaus, calling in vain on the Lord, his throat parched with thirst, his limbs twisted by hunger. And then, when his strength was almost gone, he had been rescued by Brother Paul, that joyful servant of God, that good soul, solid and simple, tormented by no anxieties, assailed by no doubts. When they got to the monastery, the prior had showed him the library, not without pride, and told him that he thought it a pity to look for revelations in the sand when books were overflowing with them. That was how Médard had become an archivist—and still searched for his God, wandering between the shelves in the gloom of a cellar.

Toward noon, the young Jew spoke for the first time and ordered a halt. He gently led Aisha to the shade of a row of cypresses and there handed her a goatskin, smiling with a gallant courtesy that somewhat irritated François.

"My name is Eviatar, after the dissident priest close to King David."

This brief introduction over, Eviatar lifted the ends of his caftan and nimbly climbed to the top of a tree. Perched on a branch, he scrutinized the horizon. The branch barely bent beneath his weight. He sat there perfectly motionless, sniffing the countryside. Satisfied that there was nobody prowling in the vicinity, he jumped back down, bending his knees to soften his fall like a cat. Then, in prefect Arabic, he asked Aisha if she was hungry, already pulling from his bag some oatcakes grilled in oil and thyme and spread with a paste of crushed olives.

As evening fell, the three of them reached a hillock, the top of which was strewn with heaps of stones and bricks, marking the site of a destroyed village. Eviatar advanced cautiously. Trying to avoid a thornbush, François almost fell into a pit. Eviatar pulled him back at the last moment. François looked down. The hole was a deep one, spiraling downwards as if hollowed by the twists and turns of a giant snake. Its sheer sides bristled with gnarled, clawlike roots that clung desperately to every bump in the rock in order not to tumble into the abyss. The air rushed into that cavity with a whistle, as if sucked in by the emptiness. Terrified, Aisha recoiled. François noticed suddenly that the edges of the hole were strewn with dried flowers, ossicles, amulets, and spent candles. His surprise amused Eviatar, who refrained from revealing to him what subterranean monster these offerings were intended for. He did not want to scare Aisha, who was already trembling with fear. It was only later, as they walked, that Eviatar, after making sure that she could not hear them, revealed to François the name of the mysterious place. He did not know through what misunderstanding the Hebrew Tel Megiddo, a simple town, a way station, had become, both in Arabic and in Latin, Armageddon. It was there, at the end of days, in the bloody era of Gog and Magog, that Lucifer would be defeated by the good angel. The pit into which François had almost fallen was the lair of the beast, the gate to darkness. Either that, or it was a disused sewer. François smiled, sharing his guide's skepticism. But Eviatar froze suddenly, and ordered them not to make any noise. A distant rumble came out of the darkness. It echoed in their eardrums, insistent, amplified by the peaceful silence of the meadows. François stiffened, ready to see the Horsemen of the Apocalypse loom up. Aisha stood rigid behind him, but in her case it was the *djinns* she was preparing to confront. Eviatar burst out laughing, and pointed to the buzzing hives of a beekeeper behind the bushes. François, taking the joke in good part, patted Eviatar on the shoulder. But Aisha watched the flight of the insects with suspicion. Their swarms whirled in serried ranks in the moonlight, like a host of demons.

Day after day, Aisha and François let themselves meekly be led by Eviatar, walking blindly along winding paths, climbing the hillsides, yelling like children as they ran down the steep slopes.

After many sudden changes of direction, François realized that the itinerary had not been fixed in advance. Eviatar chose their route on the spur of the moment or according to his mood, not hesitating to retrace his steps, sometimes even wasting half a day's walking in order to flee some bad omen: gazelles running away in panic, vultures circling, horse droppings. Or else he would sniff the breeze and decide to follow the pleasant scent of a vegetable garden, the rancid aroma of a grape harvest, the stench of a herd of goats. Sometimes he walked alongside a shepherd in order to discover a watering place he did not know, to buy a little milk from him, to inquire about recent movements of patrols, or quite simply to chat for a while. Of all those he met, whether they were artisans, farmers, or peddlers, however shabby they might be, he asked if there were any old parchments for sale in the area. Some raised their arms and smiled stupidly. Most could not even read. Others indicated the workshop of a tanner who salvaged hides or the recent passing of a caravan of merchants. François found Eviatar's requests somewhat comical. Yet the people showed no surprise, answering in a friendly fashion as if he had asked them where to buy fresh eggs or oranges.

The brief conversations in which François and Eviatar engaged began to weave ties of complicity between them that were hesitant at first. In spite of having to speak in an unappe-

tizing mixture of Greek, catechism Hebrew, and a smattering
of Moorish, the two men soon discovered that they shared a
similar sense of humor, salty but not sour. These feats of language greatly amused Aisha, who discovered how much
François liked to hear himself talk. For him, everything was
word, just as, for a painter, everything was color. Even the trees
spoke. Even the stones had something to say. Only Aisha kept
quiet. Her silence irritated François most of the time. Except
when he became aware of its subtle gentleness. She was one of
those muses, at once haughty and full of humility, of which the
bibles spoke.

Unless she was quite simply acting a role, as Colin had said.
If he could see François right now, Colin would be in seventh
heaven. He'd be able to tell all his cronies how his good friend
Villon had gone down into the desert, without a white donkey
or disciples, on the arms of a young girl and a little runt, one a
Saracen and the other as Jewish as you could hope to find.
François could imagine Colin surrounded by the Coquillards,
their beaming faces turned red by the fire, raising their glasses
to the health of a brilliant storyteller.

But he was quite wrong.

35

A line of cattle breeders leaving the fair to return home slowed the progress of the convoy. Fat, with pink cheeks and long thick mustaches, they led their livestock through the narrow streets, forcing the passersby to take shelter in doorways. Colin cursed. His three wagons were stuck at a crossroads. But he preferred to wait rather than go down the avenue that went past the palace of the Popes. The imposing buildings of the Papal legation terrified him.

His fears amused the men of the Brotherhood who were with him. In Avignon, even the Jews had nothing to fear from the dreaded officers of the Church. Cardinals and archbishops came here to rest, talk, and eat. No sycophant of the Inquisition or man-at-arms was lying in wait. Peddlers, street vendors, and troupes of actors circulated freely throughout the Comtat, as far as the borders of Provence. The young men from Palestine were dreading the moment when they would leave this blessed region and proceed to Paris, which Colin was so impatient to see again. Then it would be their turn to be afraid. They did not fear so much the constabulary as the bands of brigands prowling the forests, or the patrols of mercenaries pillaging farms and villages on behalf of the local landowners. From the limits of the Comtat as far as the Île-de-France stretched a barbaric, brutal land, in places just as wild as the borders of Russia or Africa.

Colin, who had done all he could to pass unnoticed, almost

fainted when his convoy at last reached the Jewish quarter. The community had arranged a welcome banquet for them in the courtyard of the great synagogue. Children laughed and danced, women bustled around huge cauldrons. The men had put on their party clothes. Set up in the open air, noisy and somewhat chaotic, this joyful reception was better suited to a wedding meal than a secret meeting.

Rabbis wrapped in their prayer shawls, well-dressed merchants, and beggars in moth-eaten caftans pressed around the young men from Canaan. They bombarded them with questions in Hebrew, questions the visitors were unable to answer. The worshippers asked for news of their families, enquired about the weather, the product of the harvest, as if the strangers they were addressing came from a nearby village. Had the harvest given a good yield? Had they finally sealed the cracks that had been letting the rain into the tomb of Rabbi Yohanan, blessed be his memory? Was the venerated Avshalom of Tiberias still alive? How old was that sage of sages? Sixty-eight? May the Almighty grant him long life! Amen!

A wrinkled old man asked Colin after the health of Rabbi Gamliel ben Sira, the *gaon* of Safed. Colin did not understand the question, which was asked in Hebrew, but recognized the name. Another Jew translated, explaining that *gaon* meant something like "genius", a title that was only given to the greatest doctors of the Law. When Colin, unimpressed by these Judaic letters of nobility, retorted that he knew perfectly well who this Gamliel was and that he had debated with him more than once, the old man prostrated himself and kissed his hands.

Meanwhile, Federico lingered in Genoa long enough to make sure that Colin had reached Avignon without incident. That at least was his pretext. He had refrained from revealing to his men that a mission of the highest importance was wait-

ing for him in this very place. It represented a crucial phase of
the operation, which would put an end to all desire for a crusade to the Holy Land. If the stratagem succeeded, the
Catholic armies would be repulsed without a single cannon
being fired. They would withdraw from the Mediterranean,
renouncing once and for all the idea of taking back Jerusalem.
But above all, they would wage war on each other.

The Brotherhood was worried about the recent expansion
in maritime activity among the Christians. Their growing
fleets, rapid and well-equipped, were a much more alarming
threat than armies arriving by land. Unlike cavalrymen, often
exhausted after long journeys and sated with the pillage carried out on the way, sea captains could get straight to the
shores of Palestine with rested troops, provisions, and holds
filled with ammunition. Not to mention the fact that arriving
by sea gave them the advantage of surprise and a mobility far
superior to any land assault. In the past, only a few ships lingered on the high seas, reaching Acre or Jaffa in a pitiful state,
forced to repair the damage and get fresh supplies before
being in any condition to mount an attack. Now, dashing
squadrons cut through the waves, confronting currents and
eddies without difficulty. What the Brotherhood dreaded more
than anything was the ardor of the Spanish, who, for a pious
vow or even at the mere whim of an admiral, would set sail
wherever they wanted. Forced to take the initiative, Jerusalem
had decided to send all these vessels somewhere else.

36

T he landscape was becoming barer, the vegetation more
stunted, the villages scarcer and more wretched, the
fields stonier. The brick houses disappeared, then those
of dried clay, then those of mud mixed with straw. All that
could be seen were a few canvas tents scattered here and there
on the sides of the hills. Even though the heat was becoming
more intense, the dry air caressed the lungs, invigorating them,
purifying them. Progress was slow now, but less painful than
before.

Eviatar and Aisha advanced with firm steps, as confidently
as if they were walking along the main street of a town. But
François dragged behind, stumbled, veered off course, like a
boat adrift. He felt a strange sensation of emptiness that
seemed to grow from day to day as he continued on his long
walk southward. The threads of his past were fraying, scrap by
scrap, clinging to the thorny shrubs lining the road. His
regrets, his hopes were flying away, borne on the wind, burned
by the sun, as if a mysterious thief were robbing him of them
one by one. François sometimes turned helplessly and peered
at the scrub in search of the brigand who was taking possession
of his soul. The birds whirling in the sky, the ibexes running
down the sunstruck slopes toward the shade, the scorpions
stumbling through the brambles had become the silent accomplices of this elusive bandit who had still not shown himself.
François could feel his hot breath taunting him, sometimes
from a distance, sometimes from close by, depending on the

wind. It penetrated his nostrils with a smell of burning. As he approached a promontory, the presence of this stealer of souls suddenly became more luminous. François sensed it in the increasingly hot and oppressive air. And now the culprit appeared all at once, on the other side of the plateau.

Eviatar and Aisha watched François, letting him discover the tide of solitude and silence overwhelming him. Seized with dizziness, he stooped and looked for the support of a rock, a bush, within the immensity. Then, little by little, he rose to his full height and confronted it. He opened his eyes wide to see his adversary's face, but nothing moved. No thief emerged to rob him.

Intoxicated by space, drunk on light, he opened his arms wide and began turning on the spot, grasping at the air with his hands as if trying to embrace the infinite. Dancing almost, he took a little step toward Eviatar and whispered to him in confidence that the place was a little lacking in taverns. And then, as if ashamed of his remark, he suddenly took off his tricorn, and bowed low to the majestic stretch of land. Eviatar looked overjoyed. He had been dreading François's hesitations. But the commander of the Brotherhood had been counting on this moment. He had said so to Gamliel, insisting on a tortuous route in order to prepare Villon, to initiate him. The recipe was infallible. First of all, a long walk to relieve the Frenchman of the futile considerations with which he was encumbered, to free him from the ghosts that haunted him. Next, a more relaxed progress that allayed his suspicions, making him more inclined to take to the open road. And then, suddenly, the abrupt collision with the desert and his new destiny.

Conscious of the trick that was being played on him, François had gladly lent himself to it. This land was finally reaching out its arms to him. Soon he would accomplish what he had come here for. Not Chartier's mission, nor the book hunters' operation, but his own exploit. This land expected nothing less of his visit, he knew. He felt at home here, in spite of all its mysteries. This was the homeland of prophets and psalmists, peasants and fallen angels, the worst despair and the craziest dreams. It had opened its doors to him, given him one of its loveliest daughters, and led him to this desert because he too was a peasant and a psalmist and, in his way, a good apostle. He could not disappoint them. Bishops and kings, emirs and rabbis, it hardly mattered. He would be able to pull the wool over their eyes. What counted now was a feat of arms that would again make him master of his own fate. A sensational poem, some incredible robbery, a fist-rate swindle? Thanks to which testament would François de Montcorbier, known as Villon, become a legend? His own, published clandestinely, or Christ's, rescued from the hands of the zealots who were keeping it hostage here?

Eviatar was pleased with the ease with which the Frenchman had passed this test. He would have liked to shake his hand. But François was already advancing with a resolute step, the first to begin the descent, impatient to enter the unknown kingdom. The sandy track down which he was running so joyfully was leading him toward a country with imprecise borders, virgin dunes, far off the beaten track.

This mysterious, bewitching world had been challenging man for thousands of years. But there was another, just as vast and wild, that man had not yet confronted. A world whose doors, as planned by the supreme head of the Brotherhood, were beginning to open just as François was crossing the threshold of this one.

37

A large bag over his shoulder, Federico was on his way to the well-to-do quarter near the harbor. Many shipowners and captains lived there in spite of the incessant noise and pestilential odors rising from the port. Federico held his nose as he approached the fisheries. With a leap here, and a detour there, he avoided the stretched nets, the heaps of dying fish, the garbage, and the seaweed, endlessly fearing to dirty the gentleman's attire he had donned for the occasion.

Genoa was the fiefdom of Francesco Sforza, granted to him by Louis XI in order to form an alliance that was as much financial as military with the duchy of Milan. Sforza was determined to extend his maritime trade well beyond the Mediterranean. Promising to supply him with the accounts and maps he needed, the Brotherhood had managed to persuade Duke Francesco to arrange a secret meeting during which Federico would hand over the maritime charts no other fleet possessed. Federico knew his visit was much awaited. The Genoese were excellent navigators but, unlike their colleagues in Oporto and Lisbon, poor cartographers. The pilots of Portuguese vessels had at their disposal meticulously prepared maps that allowed them to find their way easily in the most distant oceans. In order to compete with them, it would not be enough to steal their charts. Nor was there any point in following in their wake since, in order to take possession of a territory and install trading posts there, you had to be the first to land on it. This elementary right of precedence gave rise to a frantic race. And it was on that race that the Brotherhood was counting to launch Christian flotillas against other shores than those of Palestine. But no brave commander or bold ship-builder would undertake to sail unknown seas without first having consulted a reliable authority. Before anything else could happen, an experienced navigator, recognized and respected by all, had to be convinced. And it so happened that there was one right here, in Genoa.

Federico knocked at the door of a large building. He was welcomed by the mistress of the house, Susanna Fontanarossa, a good friend of the Sforza ladies. In the main room, the whole family was waiting in front of bowls filled with olives, grapes, and small biscuits: Domenico, the father; Giacomo, the eldest of the sons, a strapping, dark-complexioned lad aged about eighteen; and, to one side, sitting quietly, the daughters, who duly gave the dashing visitor coquettish smiles, and their younger brother, Cristoforo, a timid, reserved-looking adolescent. The usual civilities were quickly dispatched, and the mother retired, taking her daughters with her. Federico immediately opened his bag and laid out, one by one, marine charts that would have been the envy of many captains.

In Safed, Villon had surprised Gamliel entrusting a papyrus scroll to the Florentine merchant, a kind of map of the world. It was this that Federico was now handing to Domenico. This ancient drawing of the world, inspired by Ptolemy's geography, came from the library of Alexandria. But by itself, it was far from providing proof. The Brotherhood had other maps in its possession, much more recent ones, which it had acquired from the Turks during the conquest of Constantinople. These Byzantine records, compiled according to the testimonies of Phoenician, Moorish, and Indian sailors, confirmed the existence of vast unexplored lands. The chronicles of Marco Polo also referred to them. But it was the travel writings of Benjamin of Tudela, less well-known to Christian navigators, that had given the book hunters the idea of launching a treasure hunt. A practicing Jew, Tudela had not set off with the aim of exploring and conquering, but of finding the garden of Eden. In the East, he had visited fairy-tale lands, some of them wild, others a lot more advanced than his native Navarre. But he had never found paradise.

By putting together the information given by Tudela with that contained in Ptolemy's maps and the maps conserved in Byzantium, the Brotherhood had traced the chart of an El Dorado that all travelers and geographers agreed was situated on the borders of Asia, beyond the Indies and China. And then it had simply reversed the picture, transporting this wonderland to the west. It justified this conjuring trick by reference to *Critias*, *Timaeus*, and other dialogues of Plato, all of which mentioned a fabulous land, situated this time in the west and called Atlantis.

Domenico and Giacomo examined the precious documents, their deep sailors' eyes fixed on the lines and arrows crisscrossing the faded blue of the sea. The father seemed surprised by the size of the continents, almost annoyed to see them encroach on the ocean in that way. His son Giacomo found that there were far too many brown patches, as if a painter with a deranged mind had thrown them there at random. Tiny, spidery islands rubbed shoulders with huge bear paws, of which two were as large as continents. Less worried about geography, the younger son amused himself endowing these unknown or imaginary places with whimsical nicknames. Instead of being repelled, like his elders, by this disrespectful confusion that disturbed the order of the world, Cristoforo mutely applauded the jokes of this somewhat mad cartographer. By thus remolding the planet as he wished, he had made it more beautiful, more mysterious, an invitation to adventure and dream. The young man followed with his eyes these lines that led to infinity. He imagined a ship blindly following their twists and turns until it finally dropped anchor at the other end of the world, among the stars. A real ship was not made to lead from one port to another, like a wagon arriving at a way station. It had quite another destination, always the same one, which bore the sweet name "elsewhere."

Domenico Colombo politely promised Federico that he would study the maps. In fact, the Genoese did not trust these maps any more than he trusted the gossip of a ship's boy. Mariners were known to be inveterate tellers of tales. They described mountains higher than clouds, claimed to have seen monsters gobble up a whole ship with one snap of their jaws, stated that they had visited golden beaches where naked young women offered themselves fearlessly to strangers, covering them with giant flowers and amorous caresses. No serious ship-owner believed in the nonsense put about by drunken sailors.

Federico had not expected to be taken at his word. This meeting had been only a first step. The rumor of a route leading to a land of cockaigne would, however, slowly insinuate itself into the corridors of the Spanish Admiralty, onto the landing stages of Flemish ports, and into Venetian trading posts, Portuguese colonial headquarters, and French harbor-masters' offices. Whether or not they believed in such stories, the princes of Christendom would soon see them as a good excuse to raise new funds and enlarge their fleets. Anxious for their bankers to take the bait, they would take it upon themselves to make the story plausible.

Pleased with what he had achieved, Federico thanked the Colombos and took his leave. Once the stranger had left, Domenico burst out laughing. Even if these lands existed, it was out of the question to risk a ship to reach them. There was not a single port of call within sight. Giacomo agreed. He was the heir. His father's reputation with Italian shipbuilders ensured him a certain future. But Cristoforo was thinking like a younger son. When it came to birthright, he was last in line. His sisters would need good dowries to marry. The sons-in-law would join the business as associates, reducing Cristoforo's meager share even further. Dependent relatives would require expenses that his big brother would be certain to cover by drawing on the common chest. Like all younger sons of good families, Cristoforo would then have to make a difficult choice between a career in the army and entering the Church. He did not feel that he had the soul either of a soldier or of a priest. The sea was his one escape route. To the east, it belonged to his brother and all well-to-do elder brothers. All that remained to Cristoforo was the west, which nobody seemed to want.

Federico was at last able to leave this rough world of sailors and fishermen and return to the sweetness of Florence and his shop close to the Ponte Vecchio, and meditate over the grave of his dead master, Cosimo de' Medici. He was not displeased with the seed he had sown. Jerusalem had given him a whole sack full of them. This one, however, would germinate differently than the others. The Brotherhood was encouraging the Gentiles to rediscover the wisdom of the ancients, to study the discoveries of the astronomers and doctors, in the hope of guiding them toward a new world. But this seed would widen their horizons in quite another way, by offering them a New World.

38

A shepherd emerged from a *wadi* bristling with tall rushes unruffled by any breeze, driving his herd of goats toward the marshes that lined the Dead Sea, and walked, a slightly vague figure, beside the huge oily pool held prisoner by the mountains. The water, petrified into an ice floe of light and salt, barely glittered. The rays of the sun sank onto it, marbling the matte indigo of the surface for a moment before being sucked down into the depths. The reflection of a solitary cumulus skated over the water, skidding like a fly on the polished pewter of a mirror. It moved laboriously, contracted by the heat, while up above, the cloud of which it was the shadow continued on its way, gliding easily over the face of the sky. Nothing else moved. The image of the surrounding cliffs lay flat on the motionless sheet of water. Every detail was drawn on it as distinctly as on an engraver's plate. It was the real hills that seemed to shimmer, their outlines veiled by an excess of light, their slopes blurring in the heat of the rock.

Perched on a promontory, François watched the shepherd disappear into the distance, then entered the cave. It was refreshingly cool in there. Aisha was rocking back and forth on a swing hanging from heavy chains. Out of breath, François sat down on a sheepskin pouffe. The dwelling, even though meagerly furnished, was comfortable. The rough ground, leveled by pickax, was covered with a raffia mat woven from a thousand colors. A recess hidden by a canvas curtain served as a closet. Stocks of oil, medicinal balm, candle wax, almonds, dried fruits, biscuits, brandy in kegs, fresh linen, and all kinds of utensils were piled there in no particular order. A large table and two benches made up a dining room. At the far end, there was only a single bed, a large one protected by a tent-shaped tulle net. A standing writing case and two lecterns occupied the rest of the room. A few books were neatly arranged in a niche hollowed out of the rock. A big piece of wood, painted with stripes to imitate the bumps in the stone, was propped against one of the walls. It was cut in such a way as to camouflage the entrance to the cave, its outlines perfectly matching the shape of the cliff.

François had not yet decided if this residence was a prison or a refuge, a place of torment or a safe haven. Much as Eviatar might boast of the benefits of such a retreat, the strength imparted by the desert, the revelations whispered in the silence, François remained bewildered. And not very inspired. He had always written surrounded by the bustle of taverns, matched the rhythm of his verses to the stammering of the drinkers, the laughter of children, the noises of the street, the jokes exchanged by the wagoners. It was in that deafening din that he had found his words, from it that he had derived their music. Eviatar agreed about the need for noise. Nobody learned the Torah as an anchorite closed up in an ivory tower. It was in the rooms of the *yeshivot*, filled with rowdy pupils arguing over points of exegesis, bawling hymns, throwing quotations from the Talmud in each other's faces, that the word best echoed, was transmitted loud and clear. But then there came the moment of wisdom, reserved only for the masters. The moment that went beyond.

That moment was now being offered to François Villon. It was here, in this corner of the desert, that Providence had made an appointment for him, one that he had previously made every effort to postpone. True, it had done so by forcing his hand. But whatever the reason for this confrontation with

himself toward which Eviatar was urging him, François had no
intention of running away. Quite the contrary, he saw in it an
unhoped-for opportunity to regain control. Since his release
from the jails of the Châtelet, he had felt himself being shaken
from one place to another by a capricious and whimsical swell,
and he had done nothing to resist the drift. Out of a taste for
adventure, he was willing to admit. But an adventurer was only
worthy of the name if he kept going in the direction he wanted.
He did not let himself be bewitched by the unknown lands
through which he passed, nor by the beautiful strangers he met
on his route. And certainly not captured by the natives.

Eviatar raised his gourd, drank a mouthful of water, then
abruptly took his leave. He promised to return the next day at
dawn, when he would take François to see Gamliel. The rabbi,
who had come for that express purpose from Safed, should be
reaching the Dead Sea by this evening. François did not have
time to react. Eviatar was already running down the slope,
jumping from one rock to the other, hugging the ground, his
body bent to maintain balance, his right hand in front of him,
holding an invisible ramp. His shadow ran behind him, waving
over the brambles, like that of a cormorant over the waves. He
plunged into the bed of a *wadi*, reemerged for a moment, then
disappeared in the distance amid the dunes.

Setting the sky ablaze with a final glowing salvo, the sun
sank behind the plateaus, like a sentry in a hurry to leave his
post. A biting wind immediately seized the opportunity to
emerge from its lair. Crouching all day long, it had waited for
this moment to pounce on the dunes left defenseless, the
shrubs abandoned to their fate. It howled through narrow
ravines that served as its organ pipes. François watched the sky
darken. Night did not fall here as it did in Paris or Champagne.
It rose. It overflowed from the black chasm of the Dead Sea,

like a river in full spate, and spread slowly over the sand like ink on blotting paper. The stars lit up one by one, sharp and piercing. They did not shimmer timidly in the mist, or twinkle amid the treetops. Here they stretched to infinity, deployed in a huge armada.

A golden light attracted François's gaze. Crouching in front of a meager fire of twigs, of which she was fanning the flames, Aisha was roasting bean dumplings rolled in oil. She took one out, well browned, with a crackly crust, sprinkled it with thyme, and handed it to François. The feast proceeded in silence. This sudden intimacy brought about an unexpected embarrassment. Up until now, Aisha and François had teased each other beneath the watchful eye of chaperones: Moussa, Colin, Gamliel, Eviatar. Now they were faced with one another like spouses in an arranged marriage, isolated for a moment in an antechamber just before the wedding ceremony. They would spend the night together, nobody doubted that. Except them. Precisely because it was what everyone expected.

It was Aisha who rose first and, taking François's hand, led him to her bed. François hesitated for a moment. Was she following the rabbi's instructions?

Outside, the howling of the jackals mingled with the breath of the wind. The Holy Land lay there in the darkness, consenting, and the starry night accepted its offering.

When morning came, François rose, taking care not to wake Aisha. He went and sat down in front of the lectern, his back to the cave entrance. In the pale light of dawn, he carefully laid out the parchment, the inkpot, and the quill, without making any noise. And, for the first time since he had left Paris, he began to write.

39

The sun was also rising over Florence, but the sky there was cloudy, the air heavy. A short shower came out of nowhere to lash the paving stones, joyfully spattering the gaiters of the passersby as they ran to take shelter in doorways. Women laughed and shouted as they hurried to the arcades of the Via Por Santa Maria, where the shopkeepers were ready and waiting for them. If the rain lasted, they would have to buy something. On the Ponte Vecchio, pounded by the turbulent waves of the Arno, peddlers covered their goods with thick oilcloths and cursed the bad weather.

Unlike Colin, who had left in secret for Paris, Federico operated proudly and openly. Whereas the Frenchman had to take endless precautions to deceive the vigilance of the papal informers, the Italian announced his latest finds to all and sundry. It was in the very heart of Florence, on a shopping street, that he gave battle.

Since his return, Federico had grown noticeably richer. Potbellied bankers in frills and basques and powdered ladies in muslin veils were snapping up his old books, thus unwittingly spreading the boldest doctrines, the most fearless ideas, the most adventurous theories. It was a matter of who could best surprise the other by opening a drawer and displaying a mysterious essay whose provenance he could not divulge for fear of attracting the wrath of the Inquisition. These excited bibliographic conspirators leafed through compromising pages without necessarily reading them, but inevitably it was they, rather than the austere members of the faculties, who spread the revival of philosophy, from drawing room to drawing room and all the way to the antechambers of princes. And by thus defying the censors, they were gradually discovering their own power. What began as an underground current was becoming a veritable fashion. In order to be in vogue and to shine at court, burghers and nobles were now adorning their palaces with the best editions of the *Corpus Hermeticum* or the speeches of Demosthenes, much to the displeasure of their confessors.

A man with a woolen hat pulled down over his ear was walking fast between the stalls, lost in thought, heedless of the large drops dripping down his cape, wading through the pools of mud, stumbling over boundary stones, so distracted that he passed right by the place he was meant to be going. He stopped at the end of the street, turned with a surprised look on his face, then shrugged and retraced his steps.

"Master Ficino!" a clerk standing in front of a wide door called to him. "Master Ficino! It's here!"

"Yes, yes, I'm perfectly well aware of that . . . "

Marsilio Ficino was an old friend of Federico's. Both had had the same patron and mentor, Cosimo de' Medici. They were continuing his work, each in his own way. One unearthed rare manuscripts, the other translated them and wrote commentaries on them in Latin. Whenever the papal censors banned the edition of a work by Ficino, Federico arranged for it to be published clandestinely in Lyon or Frankfurt. The Brotherhood had been counting on his collaboration for a long time. It knew perfectly well that Federico's shop could not by itself modify the way the great and the good saw things. But the Academy founded by the Medicis, of which Ficino was the director, was an institution of renown which had every chance of attracting their favor. Known as far afield as Paris, Liège, and Amsterdam, it was considered just as authoritative as the Sorbonne. However, unlike the universities, it was the fiefdom not of the clergy, but of the nobility. Thanks to it, princes could defy cardinals without compromising themselves. So what if their choice of reading matter displeased the Church? Whose fault was that? Marsilio Ficino's.

The clerk relieved Master Ficino of his wet cape and admitted him to the shop. Several customers were walking hurriedly between the shelves, eager to get their hands on a rare volume before the other buyers. The richest absolutely had to be first to possess a previously unpublished work, preferably bound with taste, in a large format, and with its spine bearing a title label that could easily be seen from a distance. This was a prerequisite for gaining the admiration and approval of an important guest even before he had opened the precious copy, or rather, so that he did not need to open it at all.

Federico went from one customer to another, dispensing advice to each of them. Just as he was able to judge the quality of a manuscript at first glance, he only needed a handshake or a facial expression to sound out his prey, guess his tastes, and evaluate the chances he had of selling him a treatise on medicine rather than a psalter. Almost jostling two dapper wine merchants wearing hats that were too broad, he walked up to a nondescript man dressed all in green, stooped over a lectern. He was a regular customer, who knew what he was looking for. He was also a miser. Federico would first show him some books that were of only moderate interest to him and ask exorbitant prices for them, cutting short any attempt at bargaining. Then, as the man was about to withdraw, somewhat annoyed at having to leave empty-handed, Federico would suddenly remember a parchment behind the firewood, on Euclidean geometry, a favorite subject of this customer. The price would seem all the more reasonable for being lower than those mentioned previously for works of lesser importance. Federico would fix it according to the discount the purchaser expected. He would refrain from playing the drama of the merchant who regrets having to let go of his finest item or who, supposedly strangled by his creditors, resolves to accept an offer that he would certainly refuse in other circumstances. Federico was always firm, not very patient, and would even make a slightly disdainful pout at anyone who was not manifestly enough of a connoisseur to appreciate an object of such rarity at its true value.

As soon as he spotted Ficino's woolen hat, Federico abruptly abandoned his customers, rushed to the master, and drew him into the back room. He sat him down in a large arm-chair, placed a footrest under his legs, and poured him a full jar of brandy. His profession as book hunter had induced a some-what blasé cynicism in Federico. The reason he admired Ficino so much was that, rather than perch on the highest branch and play the peacock, he dug deep into the earth in search of the roots. In going straight for the essence, he made what was hard simple, what was confused clear, and dispensed a wisdom that was accessible to all. It was on the plain-speaking of a Villon and the intellectual honesty of a Marsilio Ficino that the Brotherhood counted to win their game. It was thanks to them that the muses of Olympus were at last conversing in the lan-guage of men. The secrets of the universe were being revealed easily, by the fireside—which, at the same time, was very lucra-tive for booksellers.

Federico held out a list of works that left Ficino speechless. A treatise by Porphyry of Tyre aiming at freeing the human soul from the excessively strict yoke of religion. A rare auto-graphed letter from Saint Augustine strongly recommending a reading of that treatise to his son Adeodatus! A manuscript by Pythagoras that claimed that the Earth did not hover motionless in the ether, but turned on its axis, afloat in a raging cosmos filled with stars burning themselves out. On the back, a few lines written by Dante stating that Pythagoras was thus confirming the existence of hell. Federico poured brandy while Ficino leafed through the minutes of the Council of Basel, where Nicholas of Cusa had demonstrated that the *Donation of Constantine*, by which the emperor was supposed to have ceded his power over Rome to the Papacy, was an outright forgery. It was now up to Master Ficino to disseminate these various theories without causing a scandal and, as a pious scholar, to reconcile them with the postulates of the faith. No frontal attack, just a discreet boost here and there, to start with.

Federico checked one last time that the volumes were in good condition, then called a clerk and ordered him to wrap them. He walked Ficino to the door of the shop. The old scholar took off his hat to say goodbye to his host, then again pulled it down over his ears. The rain had stopped. The clerk arrived, holding the precious package at arm's length, and was already rushing outside, forcing Master Ficino to gallop after him. Federico watched them scampering toward the rainbow that crowned the end of the avenue. He half expected to see them fly away on the horizon and whirl around amid steeples and towers, gaily beating their wings beyond the orange roofs of the city.

40

F rançois declaimed his verses at the top of his lungs to make sure of their sonority. His lively, almost teasing voice echoed off the walls of the cave. He wasn't displeased. The cadence was right, the melody pleasant to hear. But Aisha detected sharper, almost acerbic tones that troubled her. She was busy knotting her long black tresses at a small obsidian mirror hanging from the wall, and François could not see her face. He wondered if such a wild creature could ever be tamed. She seemed to have no allegiance except to the sun and the wind.

He was doubtless just as wild as she was. Were not the unruly verses he was reciting now, hastily composed this morning, proof of that? This journey through the Holy Land should have given rise to a splendid elegy. But all François had come up with were a few sarcastic stanzas that had no truck with lyricism. The imbroglio of schemes and intrigues, setbacks and tribulations, that had led him into the heart of the desert was not the pretext for any noble quest or painful calvary. It was a slow advance into enemy territory!

After the ballad of the hanged man, this was the ode of revenge. Whether with a knife or with rebellious verses, François had always fought head-on and paid a high price for his affronts. Now he had the opportunity to attack on the sly, to undermine the enemy's positions from the inside. It was not just a question of settling his accounts with the Church and the constabulary. Injustice did not wear only a miter or a cabasset.

But whether it hid beneath a moneylender's cap, a judge's wig, or a caliph's fez, it had the same face. And François was determined to wipe out its hateful smile.

Eviatar appeared at the entrance of the cave. He had come to find François and take him to see Gamliel, who was waiting for him not far from here, in Qumran. François quickly pocketed the draft of his ballad, went to Aisha, and tenderly kissed her. This came as no surprise to Eviatar, who was unable to hold back an amused smile. Aisha refrained from playing the prude. The sheet stained with her blood still lay on the bed. She confronted Eviatar's smile as a fulfilled woman, guessing at his fantasies, guessing too that he would hasten to announce the news to those it most concerned. After all, although Gamliel might not oppose this relationship, he feared that Aisha might fail in her task as a beautiful jailer and change sides.

The two men climbed to the top of the plateau before the morning mist rising from the salty sea caught up with them. They walked along the ridge in a northerly direction. The terrain was flat, eroded, devoid of landmarks. No shrubs, no blocks of stone. After an hour's walking, Eviatar suddenly veered right, beginning the descent at a run. The rabbi appeared when they were halfway down. He greeted François with a warm handshake, making no attempt to conceal his emotion. Behind him, a man in shepherd's garb was barring the entrance to a narrow fault in the rock. He had leathery skin and frizzy hair, but his haughty air was not that of a poor herdsman. Gamliel introduced him to François. He was the commander of the guard in Qumran, and a direct descendant of the Essenes. His clan had ruled over this domain for centuries.

The war of independence waged by the Maccabees against the Seleucid occupiers had restored sovereignty to the Hebrew people. Although chased out of the Holy Land, the Macedonians had left a deep mark on it. From a distance, they continued to exert an enormous influence over Jerusalem. Sharing the taste of the Hellenes for things of the mind, for education and ethics, the Jews were eager to absorb the teachings of Socrates and the Stoics. Some Hebrew scholars went so far as to learn Greek in order to read the precious notes brought back from Athens by the book hunters. But others were fiercely opposed to this spiritual union that linked the chosen people with a pagan civilization. Cutting themselves off from the rest of the community, the Essenes formed a dissident sect of purists and ascetics who settled in the area around the Dead Sea. Fearing that the new currents of thought spreading to Jerusalem and Safed might corrupt the Torah, they hid it here, in these caves. To this day, they were its intransigent guardians.

The false shepherd stood aside obsequiously to let Gamliel and Eviatar pass but gave the stranger who was with them a not very appealing look.

François had expected to find long corridors, their walls studded with torches. He was prepared to encounter sentries, to hear the creak of hinges, the clicking of locks. But there was nobody here. No gate separated this hiding place from the exterior. The cavity, which was not very deep, and low-ceilinged, was lit by a single oil lamp. And yet Gamliel seemed much more moved here than in Brother Médard's cellars or the lair of the secret Jerusalem. As for Eviatar, he placed two fingers on the wall then, having lifted them to his lips, recited a prayer in a low voice.

In a corner, a dozen large terra-cotta jars stood upright on the rocky ground. The rabbi hesitated for a moment, then made up his mind to reveal to François what they contained.

When the Romans burned the Temple in Jerusalem, the high priest of the Jews had appealed to the Brotherhood to save the Torah from the flames. The book hunters took the sacred scrolls and hid them in jars, which they then deposited in the caves lining the Dead Sea. The Brotherhood had received instructions not to reveal their location until the Jews regained possession of their land.

"Do you really think the Jews will come back here and reign as masters?"

"The texts buried in these jars state that very fact. Without them, Jerusalem would be only a heap of stones like any other. You've seen with your own eyes what she has become. Her destiny is not played out on battlefields or negotiated around the table. It is sealed in these writings."

The three visitors sat down cross-legged on the ground. The guard, who had remained standing, extracted a scroll from one of the terra-cotta jars and handed it to Gamliel, who cautiously unrolled it.

"This too was saved from the flames, at the request of the high priest."

Gamliel brandished the parchment. Its workmanship was primitive but François found it hard to believe how old it was. It had barely yellowed, and the text stood out clearly, in regular columns that ran parallel to the catgut seams. There was no punctuation to interrupt the continuous stream of letters.

Philo of Alexandria, Flavius Josephus, and Pliny the Elder had all mentioned the adventures of a Jewish preacher, nicknamed the "Master of Justice," who forged a new covenant with God based on repentance and humility. He reproached his brothers for their pretentious arrogance, which he claimed had little in common with the true law of Moses. His harangues greatly displeased the elders of the chosen people, the Pharisees, whom he saw as vain usurpers. Rabbis and dignitaries chased him from the Temple. Rejected by the citizens of Jerusalem, he set off to preach on the roads, in the villages, in the lairs of lepers, among the poor and the abandoned, who soon came to regard him as their savior. Pursued by the authorities, who feared a rebellion, he was forced to escape to the desert with his disciples. It was here that he continued to dispense his light. Isolated, constantly harassed, he met a cruel end at the hands of his enemies. The name of this unfortunate Messiah was Osias, the third of that name, from the line of Zadok. The document that Gamliel held in his hands was the *Manual of Discipline* compiled by his followers, the Essenes.

François raised his eyes toward the guard. The man was scornfully avoiding his gaze, unaware that he too had carried the good word, denounced the greed of the mighty, sung of the misery of the common people, and been sentenced to death. Not that he was seeking the man's approval—far from it. On the contrary, he was pleased that his ballads were declaimed in taverns or whispered in boudoirs. That was better, surely, than rotting in some jar.

Gamliel declared solemnly that this manuscript had been used to mount the most audacious operation ever conducted by Jerusalem, the one with the most far-reaching consequences. The rabbi's suddenly tense features looked red in the flickering lamplight. Eviatar poured in more oil. The flame, now golden, traveled along the wick, casting the men's shadows on the walls of the cave. Gamliel spoke in a low voice, articulating each syllable, like a teacher forcing his pupils to listen carefully.

Osias the Essene soon fell into oblivion. Fifty years after his death, in the reign of Tiberias, the procurators of Judea made the regime of Rome even harsher, plunging the country into deep poverty. The "invisible Jerusalem" decided to urge the people to passive resistance. But a clear call, spread by the men of the Brotherhood, would soon have been stifled, gatherings dispersed, the envoys arrested on the spot. It was then that the Brotherhood remembered the "Master of Justice." The plan was a simple one. The Brotherhood chose several young Jews from among those who came to Jerusalem to finish their religious education, as was then the custom. The oldest was eighteen, the youngest only twelve. The book hunters taught these adolescents the story of Osias and made them learn the *Manual of Discipline* by heart. Once they were priests, the new recruits went off across the country to arouse the crowd, gaining its sympathy from village to village, just as Osias had done.

As long as they kept to a cautious awakening of consciences, under the cover of allegories and parables, the authorities were not alarmed by these barefoot preachers. But when the young men returned to Jerusalem, they made a tragic mistake. Unable to vilify the emperor himself, they attacked the rich Jews who worked hand in hand with the oppressor, just as Osias had attacked the Pharisees of his day. The agitation that one of them caused within the capital forced the Roman guard to intervene firmly. A witness of the incident, which took place beneath his windows, was the high priest of the Temple, Annas ben Seth. He drew the young fugitive into his house. But an informer had glimpsed the agitator climbing the steps of the Temple and taking refuge in the priest's dwelling. The governor of the city, Pontius Pilate, threatened to accuse the whole Sanhedrin of complicity if the culprit was not given up immediately. After several hours, Annas had to give in—and do his best to disassociate the community from this insult to Caesar. He handed the prisoner over to the soldiers, swearing that he disapproved of his outrageous conduct. Pilate was unconvinced by this belated mark of loyalty and, to show that he was not fooled, had the words "King of the Jews" written on the cross to which the man, whom he saw as a dangerous provocateur, was tied. Sadly, most of the young men involved in this affair were arrested and executed in their turn. There were twelve of them.

François laughed and clapped his hands. The apostles, agents of the Brotherhood? It was a good joke. But Gamliel, unfazed, pointed to the walls of the cave. It was here that Jesus and John the Baptist had stayed during their time in the desert. The Essene hermits of Qumran had granted them hospitality so that they could familiarize themselves with the life and precepts of the Master of Justice. Jesus had held in his hands the scroll of parchment that now lay across Gamliel's knees.

"Think, Villon. The gospels tell the story of Christ's birth and childhood and then they suddenly lose track of him as soon as he arrives in Jerusalem, when he is still quite young. A whole period of his life remains deliberately in the dark. And none of the apostles ever betrayed the secret of it. Jesus only reappears some fifteen years later, ready to undertake his long walk across the Holy Land."

In the end, neither the Jews nor the Romans had taken much notice of this affair, thinking that Iesous the Nazarene would soon be forgotten, just like Osias the Essene. But his words took root in the mind of another young Jew, Saul of Tarsus, known as Paul, who laid the foundations for a new faith. Paul was beheaded at the foot of the Capitol. Three years later, the great revolt of the Hebrews took place. It was suppressed and the Temple destroyed by Titus's legions. But, against all expectation, a small group without weapons or shields continued to resist the tyranny, answering the call of Yeshua and obeying the precepts laid down by Paul. In spite of constant repression, the sect of the baptized spread throughout the Empire, until it fell. It was these soldiers of the faith, these first Christians, who, over time, achieved the victory over Rome that Jerusalem had been unable to obtain.

Judging that he had said enough, Gamliel gave Eviatar a discreet nudge with his elbow. The young man cleared his throat, and in a perfect French that startled François, said firmly, "The Nazarene shook Rome, Master François. With parables. Now it's your turn."

Dumbfounded, François looked around at the cave and the

mysterious jars. He was outraged to learn that Christ had been manipulated like that. He had only one idea in his head. To repair that insult! And to fool these people in his turn. Yes, he would lend himself to their game, he would be their hack, if that was what they wanted. Against Rome once again. But nobody would ever again misappropriate the holy word!

It struck him in a flash. It was the word he had come to rescue! That was the reason for his presence here. To free the word from those who had been keeping it hostage in their chapels and cellars for centuries. The scheming of the priests was just as deceitful as Rabbi Gamliel's. They were all part of the same swindle. François was jubilant. He would be able to defend the song of mankind better than anyone, just as he had always done—under the very noses of the censors and the clerics.

Two thieves were crucified on Golgotha, by the sides of the Savior. Two criminals, just like Villon. If not for the sweet Lord, then at least for those two a good peasant must take offense and show all these sanctimonious zealots what a bold Coquillard was made of.

41

A woman lay moaning amid the smoking ruins. She was struggling with an invisible demon, clawing at the air with her bloodstained fingers, her legs shaking convulsively. Around her lay corpses covered in rubble and flies. Some had been dismembered. Hanged men swung from the branches of a big oak. One of them wore a sign nailed to his chest: "Louis is my King." The village dogs were fighting over pieces of flesh. Colin and his men moved forward cautiously. The pillagers were surely not far, busy dividing the loot. Doubtless mercenaries riding up toward Burgundy to fight for the enemies of Louis XI.

Colin grabbed the woman by the back of her neck and forced her to drink. One of the muleteers went to search in the barns for food. There was not even a sack of hay left for the animals. Only the church was intact, pews and prie-dieus neatly lined up facing the altar, but brass candlesticks and silver chalices had disappeared. Little by little, grimy children emerged from the communal forest. Colin would have liked to stop them approaching. But the younger ones, more alert, were already arriving, looking for their mothers amid the ruins, knowing perfectly well that no men had survived the massacre. An agent of the Brotherhood was bending over a well. He had let down the bucket, but a dull sound had stopped its descent. A heap of bodies was blocking the bottom.

An acrid stench filled everyone's nostrils. And although most had never smelled it before, they all guessed that this

odor was the bitter stink of death. Up above their heads, sparrows were chirping gaily in the trees. In the middle of a field of
daisies, a baby donkey was grazing nonchalantly, oblivious to
the folly of men.

Colin did not feel very safe. He got back in the saddle and
curtly gave the order to set off again as soon as possible. It was
only once he reached the top of a hillock that he turned. The
village had disappeared behind a thick rampart of chestnut
and plane trees. Only the flight of crows marked the cursed
spot with a black circle in the sky.

The main road between Valence and Lyon was filled with a
rabble of cavalrymen and foot soldiers on their way to join the
forces of the league. In the rear, a swarm of beggars circled the
canteen wagons like seagulls in the wake of a ship. Colin had
planned to mingle with the peddlers who had come to sell their
goods to the soldiers: kegs of wine, grindstones, bottles of
elixir, fresh linen, boxwood rosaries, bridle decorations, playing cards, and even a few pieces of information about the
enemy's movements. But now, dreading to be searched, he
decided to take less frequented paths, at the risk of breaking
the axles of the wagons.

They would have to avoid Burgundy, the fiefdom of Charles
the Bold, in order to get to Paris. Colin hesitated to pass
through the Auvergne, whose impoverished minor lords
robbed the convoys that crossed their lands. He thought of
turning east, in the direction of Savoy, in the vague hope of
meeting one of the detachments sent by the Sforzas to help
Louis XI. In any case, there was no question of going through
Lyon. Colin had not expected to find his homeland so torn
apart. He was distraught. But it was in the confident tones of
a general that he gave the order to turn off and head for the
mountains.

Among the young men from Jerusalem, laughter had given way to a confused silence. They were not unfamiliar with violence and war. Each had lost at least one of his family in this kind of massacre, whether it was a close relative from Samaria or a distant cousin in the Jewish quarter of some city. It was not so much the heaps of corpses that troubled them as the strange feeling of guilt, or shame, whose horror slyly undermined those it spared.

The swaying of the wagons cradled the travelers, gradually calming their rancor. The luxuriance of the countryside dazzled them. All that greenery! All those rivers! Willows caressed the waters, filtering the current through their fingertips, like dreamers sitting on the bank. The undergrowth was carpeted with moss and bracken. The chestnut trees collapsed beneath the weight of their foliage. The cornfields waved in the wind. By the end of summer, even Galilee seemed unpleasant. And the Jordan, lined with crimson brambles, was no wider than a stream, whereas here the earth itself was damp. It stuck to your feet instead of burning your soles. But as soon as it started to drizzle, the young men complained. And after an hour of gray skies, they all longed for the sun.

The noise of clanking rose from the valley. The mules reared and neighed. Horses answered them from a distance, still hidden by the edge of the plateau. The mules' hooves struck the stones, sending them rolling down the slope. Out of breath from the climb, they snorted through their nostrils. Raucous voices urged them on. Then, all at once, a squadron appeared, blocking the horizon. These weren't the king's troops. Their crudely embroidered banner, creased and dirty, bore the arms of some obscure local baron.

Colin looked in vain for a path by which to escape, bushes to hide in. It was too late. The soldiers were already surrounding the convoy. Without dismounting, their commander inspected the crates, springing the lids with a single stroke of his sword. Colin's men held themselves ready to leap on the adversary. One of the muleteers jumped to the ground and ran off into the forest. He collapsed after a few yards, pierced by an arrow.

The commander seemed puzzled. What were all these books doing here? Colin approached, held out his hand, and told him how pleased he was to encounter these men in uniform rather than brigands. The other man did not reply. Colin explained that this cargo was intended for the bishopric of Dijon, but he had no documents on him to prove it. The officer did not seem convinced. He looked at the sturdy, somewhat dark complexioned young men sitting on the benches of the wagons. They did not look either like novices or inoffensive carters, nor did they lower their eyes when he stared at them.

Sensing the mayhem that was about to ensue, Colin hastened to point out that he was an excellent purveyor of bibles and missals, and declared himself ready to offer his services to any pious knight anxious to adorn his chapel with the best sacred texts. Irritated by so much talk, the officer pushed Colin away. He thought for a moment, then gave the order to confiscate the shipment.

In one bound, the young warriors of the Brotherhood threw themselves on the soldiers with the fury of wildcats, yelling, hitting, their daggers slicing through flesh. The officer fell to the ground, his throat cut. But his men continued to fight hard. None ran away. Colin found such bravery surprising. The reason soon became apparent to him. As he was gradually retreating toward the bushes, a second detachment appeared, much larger than the first, and immediately joined in the fight. Blades cut through the air, blood spurted. One of the wagons was overturned. Dozens of books were strewn in the mud, trampled by men and beasts. The skirmish was brief and without mercy. After a few minutes, the din of weapons faded, giving way to the muffled groans of the wounded. A young Jew lay among the torn books, his dead eyes staring at a page of Plato's *Protagoras*. A mule grazed on the scattered sheets of a treatise on astronomy. A surgeon began bandaging the wounds of the soldiers with pieces of parchment and paper.

The sun was still high in the sky. Crows were gathering on the branches, waiting patiently for the survivors to leave the battlefield and abandon to them the pieces of flesh strewn over the grass. Huddled beneath a stone, a toad croaked, annoyed at the commotion that had disturbed the peace of its domain. Some way below, under the cover of the foliage, his back stooped, Colin hurtled down the slope as fast as his legs would carry him.

42

A scorpion buried its eggs in the sand then scuttled away, its pincers in the air. Aisha stood aside to let it run by. She was walking along the white bank, not far from the place where Lot's wife, turning back toward Sodom, had been turned into a pillar of salt. No wind was blowing. The stones were boiling in the sun. The shadow of a sparrow hawk striped the surface of the water. Everything here took place against a background of silence. Aisha knew how much François hated this dead calm. This morning, he had gamely sung her a poem, but his voice had been hoarse with melancholy. It was the voice of a caged bird. He needed the din of the crowd, the noises of the street, the incessant fanfare of swearing and laughter. Would he also turn back in the end, like Lot's wife?

And if he did, how could Aisha blame him? François had crossed the immensity of the dunes without complaint, letting their kisses moisten his lips. Would she have been capable of following him blindly through the grimy outskirts of a big city? Sooner or later, her master of wind and sand would catch up with her. She would be too hungry for light. And for freedom, just like François.

Up there, in the cave, François and Eviatar were bent over a lectern. Eviatar was translating a text by Luke. François could hardly believe his ears. Even though he had never set foot outside the Holy Land, the youth spoke wonderful French. He had learned it from the monks. Since his earliest years, he had been studying the language with the sole aim of deepening his understanding of the Torah. Like many, François was unaware that the Hebrew Bible was strewn with commentaries in good old French. For several centuries, Jews throughout the world, whether they were from Spain or Russia, Constantinople or Chandernagore, had based their reading of the Bible on the interpretation by Rashi, a rabbi from Troyes. Whenever he had not found a Hebrew word allowing him to express a nuance of the sacred text with enough precision, this son of the Champagne region had gladly turned to the subtleties of the French language. It was the better to grasp the master's thought that Eviatar had been eager to extend his knowledge of the language in which the rabbi had expressed himself with so much eloquence and accuracy, just as a learned man learns Greek the better to read Aristotle. And so it was not for his martial skills that Eviatar had been chosen to accompany François to the desert, but in order to be his translator and secretary, assisting him in the mission the Brotherhood would entrust to him.

The friendship between the two men, born out of the long road they had traveled together, was consolidated as they studied. Eviatar continued to guide François, drawing him by the hand along new paths. For these commentaries on the Bible were as tortuous as *wadis*. And, like them, they seemed to lead nowhere. They twisted and turned, tirelessly digging deep into the arid rock of the Law. The controversies of the sages were as difficult to follow as the tracks of gazelles amid the rocky ground, their questions as thorny as cactus needles. The sweet fruit of wisdom could only be plucked after many scratches, plunging your hand ever deeper into the branches. François was not accustomed to these winding ravines. He came from the green meadows of Picardy, from the valleys of Touraine, where there was always a steeple on the horizon, where shrines

and the statues of saints reassured the lost traveler. He amused
Eviatar by revealing to him the secrets of other sages—auc-
tioneers, poachers, hunters of wood pigeons—who also had
things to say. Eviatar and François were struggling now with a
text by Luke, wearing out the soles of their shoes, scraping the
gravel, strangely united. Both of them, the Jew and the gentile,
expected much more of their God than help and mercy. They
called him to account. François was surprised nevertheless by
the young Talmudist's choice.

Of all the apostles, Luke was the one who had said most
about women. As a physician, he was better informed about
them than his contemporaries. Even though he had no doubt
at all that Mary had been a virgin, he did not accord this a great
deal of importance. For him, it was not the act of procreation,
however miraculous, that made the mother of Christ glorious.
It was her role as counselor and guide, and not as vestal. "Mary
treasured all these things, and pondered them in her heart."

These "things" were doubts, questions the defenders of the
dogma forbade themselves from asking. It was with an audacious commentary on the writings of Luke, a fake that François
would compose himself, that the Brotherhood hoped to spur
those in England, in Prague, and in the Palatinate who were
trying to reform the Church. Jerusalem saw the Hussites of
Bohemia and the prelates of Oxford as much more reliable
allies than the humanists. Their doctrines were not at odds
with the Law of Moses. That was why these fervent Christians
were as harassed and persecuted as the Jews by the Inquisition.

The Brotherhood could have asked one of its own scholars
to produce a perfectly acceptable pastiche. But its commander
considered that only a born Christian, also a victim of the
power of the priests, would be able to speak to the men who
were currently fighting the tyranny of the Papacy. That was
why had therefore long searched for a suitable voice among

recalcitrant monks, dissident priests, and mystics of all kinds. He would never have thought that a Parisian bishop would have handed him one on a platter—and with the tacit agreement of the King of France, to boot.

François was reluctant to dip his pen in a font and get it damaged for the sake of a theological dispute that didn't concern him in the least. Especially not for the benefit of those who were keeping him prisoner. Nevertheless, after giving it much thought, he had decided that this might be an opportunity to be seized. The opportunity to settle a few scores while gaining the trust of his jailers. After all, wasn't Jerusalem the patron he had always dreamt of? A discreet protector who did not demand that he submit, but on the contrary, that he be as insubordinate as possible.

François bent and, his nose close to the page, started to scribble a few notes. "'My soul doth magnify the Lord,' says Luke." François scratched the paper with his alert handwriting. He knew that these first lines would be conveyed to the head of the Brotherhood. "'He hath put down the mighty from their seat, and hath exalted the humble.'" Eviatar craned his neck, eager to read the commentary. He did not see the grin spreading slowly across François's face. Exiled against his will in a distant land, François was rotting in a cave, under guard. And yet he had never felt so free.

"For Luke also says: 'Can the blind lead the blind? Shall they not both fall into the ditch?'"

43

T heir tasks completed, the clerks had lowered the shop front and returned to the bosoms of their families. Federico, already in his dressing gown, lit two tallow candles and sat down at his desk. For a long time he dipped his quill in the inkpot, unable to make up his mind to take it out, as if he feared using it.

Guillaume Chartier, was furious and had informed him of the fact through the Medicis. The promised books had never arrived. The Bishop of Paris threated to incarcerate Fust and his son-in-law in the Châtelet, regretted having dealt with the Jews, and was speaking of reprisals, even of a crusade. The Brotherhood would have to mount a new expedition as soon as possible. But gathering the volumes required would take time.

Federico had had no news of the convoy dispatched to the court of France. The last to have seen it was a Jew from Valencia, more than a month ago. Since then, no message, apart from a carrier pigeon that had returned to the fold without any note attached to its claw, only a ring indicating that it was one of those supplied to the young book hunters who had set off with Colin. No agent had found a trace of the small detachment. It was as if men and wagons had been swallowed by quicksand.

Federico had waited for a whole month to go by before declaring the mission a failure. Now he could no longer procrastinate. Just as he was at last placing the tip of his quill on the paper, he heard a slight scratching at the shutter of the shop. He tightened the belt of his robe and went to open up.

There in front of him stood a stooped old man in a black caftan holding out his hand, demanding alms. Federico threw him a coin and made to slam the door. But the door was violently thrown back and a fist sliced through the air. Narrowly avoiding it, Federico struck his assailant on the throat with the edge of his hand. The man staggered, choked by the pain. Just as Federico was about to hit him in the groin, three figures appeared, brandishing clubs. Hit on the temple, Federico collapsed. Covered with a canvas sheet, gagged and bound, he felt himself being abruptly lifted by four pairs of arms and transported through the streets like an old eiderdown.

When he recovered consciousness, he was sitting in the middle of a spacious drawing room. His hands were tied behind his back by a chain that held his wrists. Two guards stood on either side of him. Facing him, a short man gave him a bittersweet smile. He had a pale but rather affable face, and was looking at Federico with amused curiosity. When he stood up, Federico realized that it was pointless asking questions. His host was wearing a white tunic with wide sleeves and, on the chest, the scarlet cross of the Inquisition.

Federico quickly examined the room out of the corner of his eye, looking for a way to escape. The doors and windows were bolted. He could dash forward and knock over the two candelabra standing on the massive table that separated him from the prelate. But his gaze suddenly stopped. In a corner, a shadow had just moved. It slowly approached the light. A huge strapping man appeared, dressed in rags, his cheeks covered with a filthy beard, his forehead hidden beneath a moth-eaten hood, pulled down as far as his eyebrows. The light of the candles was briefly reflected in his shadowed eyes, which avoided looking at the prisoner. The man had come and stood beside the Inquisitor and was now whispering a few words in his ear, indicating Federico with his finger. The old man nodded and gave him a buckskin purse. The informer gave a bow and nimbly pocketed his reward. He went around the table to get to the exit. Federico did not even deign to watch him go, even though he had recognized the big brute.

Head bowed, Colin hurtled down the stairs and rushed outside. He started running at top speed through the deserted streets. He had finally had his revenge. It was now the Florentine's turn to learn what prison was like.

44

Aisha was sad. François was neglecting her, absorbed in his reading for nights on end, composing homilies and fake commentaries all day long, his pen between his teeth. He would wink at her tenderly from time to time, and when he took her, just before dawn, it was with passion, but then he would lie down beside her, exhausted, without a caress, without saying anything. This silence weighed on her. Mute priestess of the desert that she was, she suddenly needed words, soft words. But she hesitated to be the first to speak. For if François's silence upset her so much, it was not because she doubted his love. It was because she knew that he was hiding something from her. And in addition, he had started drinking again.

Aisha had the feeling she had failed in her mission. She was to have been the rope that kept François tied. With Colin gone, she should have become his confidante. That was what Gamliel had been counting on anyway. In return for her services, he had promised to set her free. The fact was, she was as much of a hostage here as François. But he had never been a slave. So why was he working so hard and so unflinchingly for the Brotherhood?

Every Monday, a messenger took away the drafts. He would return the following Monday, out of breath from riding, with Gamliel's comments and corrections, the passages to be refined or rewritten. The rabbi crossed out words, deleted passages, scrawled over the pages, and François grumbled, his nostrils flaring. He had always spoken frankly, always said what he had on his mind. But Gamliel was trying to teach him the magic of what was not said, the power of insinuation, the secret sword thrusts of rhetoric. François was trying hard to learn how to use them, because it was with their own weapons that he hoped to vanquish his enemies. Those here, and those in Rome and Paris, all the zealots and schemers who thought they could make him bow down before them. So, in his writings against dogma, he now refrained from asserting anything specific, giving the censors nothing to grab hold of. He sowed doubt, implied, made conjectures, retracted them, attempted a brief attack then again beat a retreat, leaving the reader puzzled, dissatisfied, but forever shaken in his most deeply held convictions. A doubt sowed on the wind bears more seed in men's minds than a truth dug in the ground. That at least was what Gamliel believed—and what he should be left to believe.

Whatever Jerusalem and the Medicis might think, it was the poets who would bring about change, not the scholars and the metaphysicians. The humanists were merely popes of a new kind, pontificating just as much, just as eager as the clergy to obtain faculty chairs and incomes for life. Master Villon could not say if the times to come would be better or worse, just that they would be lacking in shadowy corners in which to take shelter from the excess of light, and therefore lacking in poetry. No rosy future would bring salvation other than the one it was enough to grasp right now.

So if he wanted to save poetry, it was now that he must act.

Aisha put a platter of almonds and dried fruits down on the table. A thin ray of sunlight penetrated the cave. Eviatar was nervously pacing up and down. The Frenchman was drunk again. He had emptied two gourds of date wine. Eviatar brusquely pulled a half-empty jar from François's hands, tipping over the platter of fruit. François leapt to his feet, his face red with anger, forcing Eviatar to take a step back. As if by magic, a knife appeared in the young man's hand. Eviatar did not carry this weapon in a sheath but at the top of his sleeve, just inside the elbow. All he had to do was shake his forearm for it to slide down to his wrist. François knew well the piercing glare his rival now threw at him. He had seen that gleam in the eyes of more than one adversary. After all this dissecting of ancient texts and old parchments with him, he had forgotten that this studious young man was an accomplished warrior, always on the alert. The whistle of air brushed against his cheek. The knife came to rest in a hanging gourd. A stream of fermented nectar immediately gushed out and dripped down the wall. François turned. The gourd was bleeding like a gutted rabbit. Aisha, who had feared the worst, laughed nervously and applauded. François had drunk enough for today.

Eviatar sat down, a calm smile on his lips. He was delighted that François had finally lost his temper. It was not pernicious commentaries on the Gospels or nicely written pamphlets that the book hunters hoped to obtain from Villon by keeping him so conspicuously on a leash. They expected him to champ at the bit, to defy them. Unlike Fust or Chartier, Ficino or Gamliel, Villon had no ties. He was the only one who could play the game as an irregular. Sooner or later, he would strike out on his own. The head of the Brotherhood was counting on his impetuous nature, certain that, when the moment came, Villon would release an arrow that could come from no other bow than his own. A solitary arrow that Rome could not trace back to its origins as easily as a mass volley from Florence or Jerusalem.

Eviatar feared that this stratagem might blow up in the faces of those who had devised it. Above all, although he found it hard to admit this, he felt pity for this poor fellow whom everyone was manipulating for their own ends. If he disappointed, nobody would come to his rescue. And as for Aisha, what would become of her once her services were no longer needed?

The sound of footsteps cut these questions short. Eviatar ran to the cave entrance. The Essene shepherd from Qumran was clambering up the slope with the help of his crook. As soon as he reached the threshold, he began talking and gesticulating excitedly. Eviatar translated, informing François of Federico's arrest. He added that the news had taken more than three weeks to arrive, brought in relays by carrier pigeon. Federico may already have succumbed to the torture.

François found it hard to imagine the dapper merchant chained to some horrible instrument of torture. He would surely find a way out.

"That rascal has more than one trick up his sleeve. And he's a damn good liar."

Eviatar repeated François's words to the Essene, thinking they might calm him. But the shepherd responded curtly, throwing a stern glance at François. Eviatar turned pale. He was so disconcerted that he could not immediately translate. When he spoke at last, he himself seemed incredulous. The guardian of Qumran knew Federico well. He had often given him shelter. He came here to study the Greek, Hebrew, and Aramaic texts hidden in the surrounding caves. Every morning, he got up for prayer, wearing a large shawl and phylacteries, then went to purify himself in the *wadis* that lined the Dead Sea, as ordered by the Holy Torah.

45

B ent over his desk, his nose almost touching the paper, a scribe transcribed each of the questions asked by the inquisitors. Ignoring the tortured man's screams, he scribbled a little cross to note that no reply had been forthcoming. Three priests were present at the interrogation, observing the prisoner's reactions with a resigned air: they were going to have to be patient. After each cry or contortion, they conferred briefly in low voices, then signaled to the torturer whether he should inflict more pain or observe a pause.

Federico was tied to a rough wooden chair. Facing him, in full sight, a panoply of pliers, mallets, needles glittered in the torchlight. Hot coals were burning inside an iron cauldron supported by a tripod. The torturer moved slowly. He heated a pair of pincers until they were white-hot, calmly contemplating the dancing flame that caressed the metal. When he took them out, they were steaming. He brandished them for a moment in the air as if he were undecided, then, taking his time, examined the different parts of the body. Each of the limbs he looked at in turn was already burning with anguish. Then for a long time he trailed the pincers over his victim's skin, without touching it completely, moving from the thighs toward the chest, then, all at once, closed the instrument over the right nipple and squeezed tightly, without moving or batting an eyelid, his eyes aimed vaguely at the far end of the cell. The flesh immediately melted with a great hiss. Galvanized by the pain, Federico began shaking compulsively. A hot current ran through his veins. His brain was about to explode. In spite of the terrifying smell of burning flesh, he could smell the stronger stench of alcohol emanating from his torturer's toothless mouth, the only sign that the man was even human. Even in the throes of torment, his body arched, his head thrown back, Federico tried to stay fixed on the brute, to look into his glassy eyes and curl his lips in a kind of complicit smile, as if both of them were on the same side. The torturer gently released his grip then disappeared from his field of vision. He returned with a bucket and planted himself in front of Federico, awaiting further instructions. After a moment, a jet of icy water struck the prisoner's face to stop him fainting. Federico knew that the sufferings he was enduring at present were only a prelude. He tried to draw strength from every spasm of his muscles, to find courage in the most secret crannies of his soul.

One of the inquisitors stood up. He was holding a thick volume, which he leafed through distractedly as he approached. Reaching the wooden chair, he slammed the book shut and showed it to his colleagues, by the light of the cauldron, then to Federico. The binding bore the Medici coat of arms surrounded by a motto in Hebrew. The gilding on the arms shone in the middle of the cover. Its familiar glitter comforted him, and he clung to it like a drowning man to a piece of flotsam. The monk spat on the emblem. As Federico was laboriously getting his breath back, he heard a metallic sound. A bar ending in a stamp in the shape of a cross was being dipped in the coals.

46

Archbishop Angelo reached out his hand so that his visitor could kiss the huge sapphire he wore on his finger, then languidly put his arm back on the embroidered cushion that lay on the armrest. Having muttered the appropriate blessing, he inquired after the health of Pietro de' Medici, expressing surprise that he should have sent his son rather than handling such an important matter in person. Lorenzo professed some feeble excuses, explaining that, following the death of Francesco Sforza, his father had to ensure the rapid transmission of powers in order to safeguard the interests of the two families, the Sforzas and the Medicis, especially as regarded the maritime trade in Genoa, the factories in Milan, and the various trading posts they ran together.

The archbishop invited the young lord to sit closer. Holding his wrists with a somewhat embarrassing softness, he politely asked for news from Florence. Lorenzo answered patiently. It was not for him to bring the conversation around to the reason for his being here in Rome, nor to withdraw his arm from the prelate's affectionate grip. Taking the young man by the elbow, Angelo drew him toward the library, where Lorenzo was afraid he might make more urgent advances. But as soon as they entered the book-lined room, the archbishop pointed to a work placed in open view on a pedestal table. Lorenzo immediately recognized the gilded arms of his family and the kabbalistic signs surrounding it. The book definitely came from his grandfather's private collection. Ever since his youngest years, he had seen Cosimo de' Medici lovingly classifying his books. But he was unaware of the significance of that emblem. It was the archbishop who now explained it to him. Only volumes coming from a Florentine bookseller named Federico Castaldi bore that undoubtedly strange mark. And all of them had been strictly forbidden by the Vatican.

In its clemency, and out of respect for the memory of Cosimo, the Council would have turned a blind eye to this indiscretion. Unfortunately, the Inquisition had just uncovered a serious conspiracy being fomented by the Jews against Christendom. Federico Castaldi had been arrested and was being tortured at this very moment. The inquisitors suspected him of being in the pay of a mysterious brotherhood based in Jerusalem. There was a strong possibility that his confession would implicate the Medicis in this sordid business. Especially as their famous protégé, Marsilio Ficino, regularly obtained his supplies from this Federico. Many of the works he had acquired from him bore the famous coat of arms combined with the Hebrew motto of the sworn enemies of Rome. It went without saying that the repercussions of a trial would oblige the Church to take up a position and show firmness in applying the verdict. Ficino would risk the stake, and his accomplices, excommunication.

Lorenzo tried to keep calm, merely knitting his brows. But it was obvious that he was nervous, which led Monsignor Angelo to soften his tone. In order not to tarnish the noble name of the Medicis, he suggested handing the prisoner over to the Florentine authorities so that they themselves could continue the interrogation and assume publicly the defense of the faith. This proof of allegiance was indispensable if they hoped to persuade the inquisitors not to arrest Ficino, thus avoiding the embarrassment his imprisonment would cause his distinguished patrons.

Lorenzo refused to be intimidated by this barely concealed threat. He knew that the archbishop was expecting to be remunerated for his intercession. A large donation would suffice. But the Vatican also had to be compensated. Only too happy to have the Medicis by the throat, the Pope would be implacable in his demands. Indeed, Angelo now announced that His Holiness would not be content with a cash ransom. It so happened that the Jews had long had possession of a document whose rightful place, according to the Holy Father, was in Rome. It contained the minutes of the interview between Jesus and the high priest of the Temple before the latter handed him over to Pontius Pilate. Christ had used the few hours he spent with Annas to dictate a plea intended to prove the rest of the Jewish community innocent. By assuming full responsibility for his actions, he had saved his people from terrible reprisals. But, in addition to this confession, Jesus had dictated to Annas his last wishes, a kind of testament that was none other than Christ's final message to his human brothers.

Crusaders and Templars had tried several times to lay their hands on this text, searching Jerusalem from top to bottom, taking hostages, threatening to set the Jewish quarters on fire. In vain. The Church had even considered handing back some of the sacred ornaments of the Temple, brought to Rome by Titus to celebrate his triumph over the Hebrew revolt. But, up until now, the Vatican had not known with whom to negotiate. Scattered to the winds, divided up into a swarm of different communities, the Jews had no king and no ministers. But now the opportunity had presented itself to negotiate with a group that was able to make decisions. The book hunters of Palestine, since they were attacking Rome, could clearly be considered the opposing side with which to begin possible talks. And above all, they had ambassadors of renown, the Medicis, through whom the two parties could negotiate.

Lorenzo doubted that Jerusalem would agree to pay such a

high price to get its eminent allies out of trouble. After all, the Medicis were sufficiently powerful to look after themselves. Relations between Rome and Florence had always been uneasy, sometimes tense, but never openly hostile. Lorenzo wondered therefore why the archbishop was choosing to play such a card. Was it because the Holy See suddenly felt strong enough to go on the offensive? Or else so threatened that it had to resort to blackmail?

The young man knelt and promised to return promptly with an answer. The archbishop kissed him fervently on the forehead by way of farewell.

Escorted by two novices, Lorenzo walked down the long corridor that led out of the basilica. He thought of Federico, and prayed that he would hold out. He had always sensed that there existed some kind of private complicity between his grandfather and this Federico. While quite young, sitting quietly in a corner of the great library, he had often been present at their long conversations. Whenever they looked at books, the two men almost forgot his presence. Cosimo, usually so authoritarian, would speak in a soft, almost childish voice, express joy at the sight of each binding, wonder at each stroke of calligraphy, declaim aloud passages from *The Iliad* or Aesop's *Fables*, describe spellbound the details of an engraving. He knew that his grandson was watching and listening, but he pretended to be unaware of the fact. He wanted to communicate his passion to Lorenzo without imposing it on him, inviting him tacitly to come and join him in this wonderful world of ink and paper. Sometimes, Cosimo and Federico would lower their voices and whisper secretively, their expressions suddenly serious. Federico's visits were always surrounded with mystery, with magic. He would disappear for months on end, and the announcement of his return would delight Cosimo, who would leave all his other business to receive the bookseller and whisper solemnly in his grandson's ear, "He's just back from the Holy Land!"

Once outside, Lorenzo peered at the buildings lining the great square. In which one did the Inquisition have its torture chambers? He listened carefully. The chirping of sparrows echoed off the walls, horses' hooves struck the cobbles, and the bells of St. Peter's pealed out, drowning the cries of the tortured.

T he dim light of the oil lamps barely lit the cave. The Essene shepherd remained in the entrance, nervous, turning sometimes to peer into the darkness. Inside, Gamliel and Eviatar were sitting at the little table that served as a desk. François stood, wondering if he should kneel or even prostrate himself. He was shaking with emotion. Aisha was sitting on the ground, struck dumb without being quite sure why. She could simply feel the intensity of the moment. And François's panic.

It was Eviatar who opened the iron box and took out the precious manuscript. Unsure how to handle it with the required solemnity, he held it at arm's length like an offering. Gamliel untied the reed cord surrounding the parchment. He was content with a brief examination, then tied the cord again without saying a word. Eviatar immediately put the scroll back in the box, relieved at having passed the test.

"We'll have to wrap it in dry cloths, crumpled and not too clean, in order not to arouse curiosity."

François was astounded. Gamliel had not even given him the chance to touch the manuscript. François gazed at the box, dismayed to see such a relic treated like a common package. And above all to learn that it was going to be used as a bargaining counter.

"That's a high price to pay for your friendship with the Medicis."

"It's a moral commitment, Master François. And a way of

gaining time. The manuscript will take more than three weeks to reach Italy by sea. In the meantime, we—"

"In the meantime, surrendering it is a dangerous admission on your part."

"But it is also proof of our strength. The Church has always dreaded Annas's minutes being made public before it was able to study their contents."

"Well, now, it knows who has them. Perhaps even where they are!" François's features tensed in an exasperated grimace. "Such a profanation will justify a call for a crusade. Or reprisals against the Jews. The last words of Christ cannot be the object of a deal, or the stakes in a trial of strength."

"Unless they again save our people from the anger of Rome."

François fell silent. A tear ran down his cheek. Was the Savior to be crucified a second time? And was he, François, another Judas?

Gamliel wrapped the box in the cloths prepared by Eviatar. The fringes of the material were frayed. Everything was clumsily held in place with hemp string. The package was innocuous enough not to arouse the suspicions of the customs officers or the envy of the sailors. Monks dressed in the habit of their order would undertake the journey, without an escort. The rabbi said he had chosen excellent candidates, reliable emissaries who spoke several languages and, although having a humble demeanor, would know how to conduct themselves in society, men with enough self-assurance to defy both the tricks of brigands and the traps of the Papal court.

François knew that several monks from the monastery spoke fluent Italian, as well as the ecclesiastical Latin current in the Holy See. Unlike Paul, who was a simple country priest, most came from good families. Among them were younger sons of the nobility, sons of merchants, ruined burghers. All the same, he was surprised that the Brotherhood should entrust such a mission to Christian monks, rather than to its book hunters, who were better trained and certainly more loyal to the cause.

Gamliel whispered the names of the emissaries in Eviatar's ear.

The young man's reaction was immediate. "Does the commander of the Brotherhood approve this choice?"

"Absolutely."

This laconic reply brooked no discussion. Eviatar nonetheless sensed a hint of unease in the rabbi's voice.

Gamliel regretted having to lie. But how to admit that he was in no position to obtain his chief's agreement? The latter would no doubt never have allowed him to play for such high stakes. Let alone use Gentiles to do so. Nevertheless, Gamliel had no choice. Nobody must know that the commander of the Brotherhood was currently rotting in the jails of the Inquisition.

His presence in Italy was indispensable. A figure of the stature of Cosimo de' Medici would never agree to deal with an underling. And he fully expected the general from Jerusalem to lead the operation in person and aid him on the ground, first in Italy, then in France.

"Have you any other questions?"

Eviatar made him up his mind. He handed the wrapped package to the rabbi. As soon as Gamliel had left the cave, François fell to the ground and crossed himself twenty times. Feeling helpless, he imagined these monks from Galilee, with their tonsures, their sandals still filthy from their long journey, prostrating themselves in front of the Pope and his cardinals, extracting the Testament of Christ from an old bag. Aisha had never seen François like this, on his knees with his hands joined in prayer. She turned to Eviatar, who did not seem surprised by such fervor. He had never doubted that, under the cover of his great quarrel with heaven, Villon had private conversations with the angels and their Lord—if only to pester them. Aisha did not know if Eviatar, standing there frozen, was also praying at that moment. Impossible to say. The Jews prayed on their feet.

François stood up and walked to the entrance of the cave. In the distance, against a background of the silvery shimmer of the Dead Sea, he made out the figure of Gamliel advancing amid the stones with a confident step, moving through a beam of moonlight, his package under his arm.

48

Drowning in cushions, the archbishop spoke in a honeyed voice, weighing each word, feigning indecisiveness. Lorenzo sat on a pouffe, clearly impatient. He was not disposed to bother overmuch with the customary niceties or to discuss conditions. The archbishop's hesitations irritated him. The Medicis had been sufficiently generous to be able to expect a quick end to this regrettable business. After all, the last words of the Lord certainly did not lend themselves to backstage maneuvers! But Angelo would not let go. He was afraid of being duped by these crafty Florentines. Pietro de' Medici was much too clever to pay such a high price for a promise that the Pope would probably never keep. The only concrete favor he was certain of obtaining was the freeing of Federico. In itself, that hardly justified such generosity.

Of course, the Brotherhood was demanding that the Pope commit himself to mounting no further crusades. If the Vatican did not honor this clause, the text of the precious document would be made public. Dozens of booksellers were holding themselves in readiness to spread it. But how did Lorenzo plan to prove that the Brotherhood would not carry out its threat anyway? Could he vouch for them? That was why the archbishop was continuing to be difficult. But things were becoming urgent. Federico was refusing to swallow a single drop of water, and spat out everything his jailers stuffed down his throat. The archbishop feared losing badly if the prisoner took his own life. He had already tried several times.

Lorenzo swore on the Holy Bible, with unconcealed emotion and obvious sincerity, that the Medicis had no interest in cheating. To do so would run the risk of public opprobrium, which the Pope would be only too happy to stir up. Just like the Holy Father, Lorenzo's father was not in favor of an open conflict from which neither the Vatican nor Florence would emerge unscathed. He much preferred to keep to this discreet and amicable arrangement.

Such candor touched Angelo, who demanded nonetheless to know what guarantees of authenticity those scoundrels in Judea intended to provide the Church's experts. The most eminent scholars in Christendom would have to examine the manuscript before Rome could finalize the exchange. Lorenzo reassured Angelo on this point. Annas's notes had been handed over to pious servants of God who dreaded their disclosure as much as the Pope, monks from the Holy Land who had assumed responsibility for bringing them. They were doubtless already sailing for Genoa.

Tired of the archbishop's incessant questions, Lorenzo stood up, threw a purse full of crowns on the episcopal divan, and abruptly left the room. Angelo quickly counted the gold coins, sniggering as he did so. These diplomatic negotiations were completely superfluous. In reality, the Pope's orders left no room for maneuver. Obtain the precious manuscript at all costs. Promise the Jews what they wanted. They certainly wouldn't be taking it with them to paradise.

The sun was setting. A last ray of light set the lace curtains ablaze, flooding the room with patches of red that slowly climbed the walls and faded on the ceiling. The archbishop sent for his secretary. It was by candlelight that he dictated a short letter informing the Holy Father of the outcome of his conversation with Lorenzo. Having dispatched it, he wrote a request for an investigation into the status of the Jews of Spain, who seemed to be doing remarkably well.

49

Two monks hurtled down the alleyways leading to the harbor. One, tall and slender, walked with his neck craned, while the other, who was shorter, huddled beneath his hood. They scurried between the stalls of fish, the barrels of oil, the crates of dates, ignoring the whores who teased them by crying "Bless me, my father," pulling on the brown material of their habits, and asking them what they were hiding under there, much to the amusement of the provosts and sailors walking along the seawall. Angrily, the first monk suddenly grabbed a clerk who was laughing uproariously.

"Are you baptized, my son?"

Without waiting for an answer, he threw the unfortunate fellow in the water, amid the garbage that floated on the waves, then rose to his full height as if to say, "Does anybody else want a turn?" His companion tightened the strap of his bag, fearing a brawl. But sea dogs and mercenaries, usually not very respectful of the skullcap, responded with reverence. The big monk's resolute air discouraged any threatening moves. This humble servant of God didn't need sermons to convince people.

Brother Martin continued on his way in a dignified manner. Brother Benoît hurried after him, waddling somewhat as if his side hurt. Wedged at the bottom of his canvas bag, the precious box kept shaking about and knocking against him. His rope sandals skidded on the cobbles made shiny by dirt. The hemp of his habit scraped his skin. Why run like this? The ship would not set sail for several hours. It had barely started loading. Bundles lay heaped on the ground, in the shade of the pulleys. A sailor was greasing the helm. Another was dozing in the shade of the foremast. More alert, the first mate stood at the top of the gangway. The monks hailed him loudly and slipped him a few coins to ensure that he would take good care of them during the crossing.

Brother Benoît felt slightly dizzy when, after he had been pushed onboard by Martin, the ground fell away beneath his feet, pulled like a carpet by the indolent movements of the sea. Sadly, he turned to look back at the hills of Galilee. He had not had time to bid them farewell as he would have liked. It had all happened in a rush, a whirlwind of preparations and last-minute instructions, giving him no opportunity to put his thoughts in order. Should he be grateful for the honor the Brotherhood was doing him? The trust shown him by the rabbi of Safed? Or else feel sorry at being the unfortunate person chosen to hand over the Savior's words to the bigwigs and schemers of the Vatican, whom he had always despised? Before leaving, he had knelt in the courtyard of the cloister for Brother Paul to bless him. Overcome with emotion, the prior had hugged him in his big arms and whispered, low enough for Gamliel not to hear him, "Don't forget! You are the envoy of God. Not of the rabbi . . . "

But it wasn't the Lord that Benoît was thinking about as he tried one last time to glimpse the ridge line vanishing into the heat haze. Martin knew that perfectly well. But he said nothing, also gazing at the horizon, thinking of the domes in St. Peter's Square and how terrified he would be, finding himself alone among the cardinals and nuncios who were waiting for him so anxiously. But wasn't this what he had always wanted? This test? This confrontation?

Several sailors approached, respectfully took their hats off, and asked for a blessing for the journey. The two monks made signs of the cross over their bare foreheads and muttered a few pater nosters.

When the sailors had gone back to work, Martin turned suddenly to his companion with an embarrassed look on his face. "I have a confession to make, my dear Benoît."

Benoît, worried at hearing Martin stammer like this, lowered his hood and looked at the young monk apprehensively. The other remained on his guard, as if ready to dodge a fist.

"I'm listening, Martin."

"It's . . . It's about Aisha."

Brother Martin did not know how to announce the news. He made sure that nobody could hear them. "She isn't being kept as a hostage, Master François. It's because of her condition . . . "

Brother Martin hesitated. François grabbed his arm.

"Speak, Eviatar."

"She's expecting a child."

50

M aster Ficino stood by the window, bathed in the gentle light of the Florentine autumn, watching patiently as, below, the pilgrims washed their feet at the fountain in the patio. Birds were dancing on the coping, pecking at the crumbs of rancid oatcake that the two travelers had just dropped as they turned out the pockets of their habits. A student brought fresh linen and canvas slippers, then picked up the worn sandals with a frankly disgusted air that made the strangers smile. The younger of the two monks gaily sprinkled himself with cold water. His companion stood back slightly for fear of being splattered, moistening just his fingers. During all this time, he did not let go of his bag, moving it from one shoulder to the other, holding the strap between his teeth when he wanted to have his hands free. This one must be Brother Benoît, Ficino told himself. He had been expecting someone more imposing, with a sterner demeanor. But the book hunters' emissary could easily pass for a simpleton. He had a smile that was amiable enough, although a touch stupid and slightly askew. Nonetheless, Ficino refrained from judging Brother Benoît by his appearance. He had been told that beneath this somewhat disarming exterior was concealed a fine soul and a great scholar. In any case, Ficino could not help but admire the courage demonstrated by anyone who would agree to carry out such a perilous mission.

While the student led the visitors to the kitchens to eat and drink, Ficino cleared his work table of the manuscripts cluttering it, straightened his chair, and dusted off his sleeves, as if he were about to receive a visit from some eminent people.

When Benoît and Martin appeared at last in the doorway, he stood up to greet them. The two monks stood there open-mouthed, ignoring their host's formulas of welcome. Their wide-open eyes traveled along rows of books with spotless bindings, wandered amid scrolls of parchment tied with ribbon, and came to rest here and there on scientific and medical instruments. There were as many rarities here as in Brother Médard's cellar, but no locks or bars. Stepladders and lecterns were an invitation to nose around and freely consult any work without an ill-tempered dwarf barring the way with his club. This was the famous Platonic Academy, founded by Cosimo, to be used by any curious mind in search of knowledge.

Behind Ficino's desk, several books lay faceup. All bore the Medici coat of arms surrounded by a motto in Hebrew. Ficino let his guests stand there stunned for a moment, then addressed Benoît, assuming that the novice who was with him was an assistant, unaware that the tall, pale-cheeked fellow was there to keep the other in check.

"You know Master Federico, I presume."

"I have only met him three times. An excellent book-seller . . . "

"And a great friend."

"A cunning fellow, anyway. I'm surprised he was so easily caught."

Ficino, somewhat chilled by this remark, cut short the pleasantries. "May I?"

The monk handed over his bag, heaving a sigh of relief as he freed his neck from the strap. Throughout the journey, he had not once let the precious package out of his reach, endlessly touching it, opening and closing it, wedging it beneath his head while he slept, gripping it with both hands as he walked. Liberated from this burden, he collapsed with exhaustion on a chair. Accumulated fatigue seized his limbs.

Ficino untangled the cloths and string, then opened the iron box and carefully took out the manuscript. As director of the Platonic Academy, he had examined a great many extremely rare books, restored valuable volumes acquired by Cosimo, studied originals from the times of Plato, Horace, and Virgil, translated treatises dating from the era of Ptolemy, but he could never have imagined holding a sacred text like this in his hands. He read the first lines apprehensively. They were indeed minutes. Each paragraph began with the words "I say," "I ask," or "Yeshua answers," "Yeshua says." The document was signed by Annas. At the bottom, it bore the high priest's seal. The wax was cracked and blackened like dried blood. A shudder ran through Ficino's body. Next to the seal, there was another signature, traced in a confident hand, in Hebrew. That of Annas's interlocutor.

Overcoming his agitation, Master Ficino resumed his reading. He read out loud, slowly, in a drone, punctuating each sentence with an admiring sway of the head, breaking off at times as if dazzled by too bright a light. There was such wisdom here, such humanity, such enlightenment. Everything that needed to be said had been said, in a few words, and for all time.

"What's written right here? My eyes betray me."

"I'm sorry, master. I can't read Aramaic."

"You haven't read these minutes, then?"

"My opinion is of little importance."

Ficino was somewhat surprised by this admission. And by this lack of curiosity. Eviatar, too, had always been astonished that François had never asked to know the contents of the holy document he had in his keeping. It was as if he were afraid, as if reading it would have been not an act of faith, but a sacrilege. But François had been adamant. He did not want to know anything of the last words of Jesus.

It was already far into the night by the time Ficino finished reading Annas's minutes. He found the parchment in remarkably good condition, too much so in fact. The Pope's scholars were likely to be suspicious of such a state of preservation. Lit by a lantern, Ficino bent over his large desk. He lightly scratched the hide with a bone rasp, puffed on the fine shavings to blow them away, and sprinkled the marks left by the rasp with a fine grey ash-like powder. Eviatar watched his slightest gestures, holding the sheets well stretched, fearing that the old scholar's trembling hands might waver. Craning his neck to see better, he read and reread the sacred text while Ficino worked. The language was perfect, if a little cold, the handwriting elegant and confident. It was that of a high priest. But it was the words of Christ that overwhelmed him, simple, almost ordinary words. They troubled him all the more in that a Jew was not supposed to trust them. Let alone succumb to them. As for Ficino, he was unable to conceal his emotion, and had to force himself to hold back his tears for fear that they might fall on the holy manuscript.

At dawn, he at last put it away, placing it in a splendid casket that he then wrapped in a piece of purple velvet with golden fringes. No more old cloths or iron boxes. But still the same bag, eaten away by sea salt and yellowed by the dust of the roads, in order not to attract attention. The old master thanked the novice who had assisted him during the night.

"Are you ready to do your duty, Brother Martin?"

"It is too late to turn back."

"Then all we can do is pray."

The two men knelt. Ficino turned to Brother Benoît to invite him to join them in this moment of meditation. But the good monk was asleep, snoring like an old cat, arms dangling, lips curled in a blissful smile. He was dreaming of a child who would soon be born in a godforsaken corner of Palestine, a bastard he might never see if his plan failed.

By now the sun had appeared over the line of roofs, tinging the slates with a coppery light, gilding the domes with its fiery halo, striking the glittering pavement as if beating it on an anvil. After that night filled with shadow and mystery, Eviatar and François felt reinvigorated. The glorious weather immediately chased away all doubts and anxieties.

The envoys from the Holy Land donned their patched habits and rope sandals. François carefully wedged the package with pieces of coarse parchment, hardened by time, crumpled and rolled into balls, so that the casket, in being shaken about, should not hurt his loins. Eviatar wondered where François had found these scraps of hide with their faded ink, which gave off a disgusting smell of mildew, At least they were unlikely to attract pickpockets.

Master Ficino walked his guests to the doors of the Academy. The student from the day before appeared, as haughty as ever, looking the monks up and down scornfully.

"Conduct these good souls to the palace. The duke's men are waiting for them there to take them to Rome."

The pilgrims resumed their journey. François walked behind Eviatar and the guide, his head up, admiring the flower-filled balconies, the statues embedded in the house fronts, the frescoes adorning the pediments. He strolled like a carefree pedestrian, his bag over his shoulder. After a few steps, he stopped. A shriveled piece of parchment was sticking out of the bag. He stuffed it back in with his hand, making the dried-up material crack. Occupied thus in arranging old pieces of hide that swelled the canvas of his bag, he looked like a beggar adjusting his rags. Ficino watched him from a distance, somewhat put off by these pranks. But it was the sardonic smile that Brother Benoît gave him before disappearing around the corner of the street that completely shook his confidence.

Paul II swept majestically across the hall. The cardinals bowed as he passed, the movement of their cassocks forming a purple wave through which his white alb cut like a sail. The Holy Father followed the line of the carpet that led to the dais. Archbishop Angelo stood to one side of the nave, leaning on a pillar. From there, he could see only the tip of the Pope's miter rising above the skullcaps. He craned his neck to look toward the far end of the basilica, where the benches reserved for important guest were located. As a sign of his disapproval, Pietro de' Medici was not there. After all, the Pope had forced his hand. Once again, he was represented by his son, Lorenzo the Magnificent, who was subtler and more diplomatic. Lorenzo was dressed in a glittering doublet, its gold and silver brocade gleaming in the light from the stained-glass windows. He sat with his back straight and his head high, defying the austerity of the place with his ardent beauty, the insolent richness of his attire, the flashy rings, the huge plumed hat placed in full sight on the armrest of a prie-dieu. The two monks who had come with him were sitting behind him, their figures somehow blurred, timid, retiring, askew, as if they were merely the shadow of the dapper young lord. A patched-up bag lay across the knees of one of them. It was still stuffed with the pages that had served as wrapping. Their yellowed, crumpled ends stuck out from the flap, as hard as pigskin, dotted with mold, their sheen diminished by the years. The poor monk was constantly trying to push them back into his bag as if he were ashamed of such a pitiful package. But the recalcitrant leather kept unfolding, embarrassing him even more. Angelo looked at him pensively. His sandals were dusty, the material of his habit dulled by the sun. And yet there was a luminous, almost arrogant quality in his gaze. He might be the only real man of God here.

A casket adorned with precious stones lay on the Papal throne, its glitter forming a limpid prism. The Pope slowly climbed the steps, hiding now the halo of the emeralds and rock crystals. He took the key handed to him by his secretary then knelt and inserted it in the lock. All present prostrated themselves. He carefully opened the lid, murmured a blessing then, suddenly seeing the faded letters, crossed himself and burst into tears. The silence was so absolute that it was as if the voice of the Lord was rising from the casket. The Holy Father kissed the sacred manuscript with his fingertip, not daring to take it in his hand. The parchment was crumbly. The Vatican archivists had recommended that it not be exposed to the light. One of them began reading the Latin translation that had been made of it by the experts.

Jesus knows that he will soon die. He makes no attempt to conceal his terror. Annas tries to comfort him, assuring him that his sacrifice will not be in vain. But Jesus refuses to be consoled. He is in no way resigned to his fate. Is he not being killed to stop him from speaking, because his confessions disturb Jerusalem as much as Caesar? The Jews are wrong to believe that his execution will assuage the anger of the Romans. Many others will perish, like him. The temple will be destroyed, says Jesus. And Rome will fall.

The interpreter broke off his reading abruptly. Paul II stood up, announcing sternly that the revelations that followed related to future times and that it was not appropriate to divulge then too soon. Spread prematurely, Christ's last message would be misunderstood by the faithful. Worse still, it would be distorted by the enemies of the faith. The assembled nuncios and legates muttered in frustration and disappointment, but the Holy Father was already closing the casket back up. He gave the key back to his secretary and let a majordomo quickly remove the fabled text to the cellars. That very evening, soldiers of the Vatican guard would round up all the scholars who had had access to Annas's notes and put them to the sword.

"Write this. There is a beginning and there is an end. The temple will be destroyed. And Rome will fall. In the last resort, God will die with man . . . "

"You blaspheme!"

"What father would want to survive his child?"

I ask the accused to retract, but to no avail. He remains insistent.

"Write this. There is a before and there is an after. Everything begins and everything ends when the first inno-cent dies. And God dies with him. It is you who blaspheme by denying him that death, that sorrow."

"What kind of Jew are you to talk thus?"

Sitting by the fire, Paul II reread the Nazarene's statement one last time, his diatribe against priests and Caesars alike, his predictions of the atrocities that would be committed in his name, his rejection of any special treatment, any burial, his farewell letter to Mary. When you came down to it, Christ's reproaches were as harmful to the rabbis as to the priests. The Brotherhood had never had any intention of spreading them. This was simply a settling of accounts between Rome and Jerusalem, which concerned nobody else. The freeing of one of their people was a mere pretext. The book hunters had just been waiting for the convenient moment. And now the times were favorable to them. An insidious wind was blowing through Christendom. That was why they were throwing themselves blindly into the battle at the sides of those they thought they could win over to their wretched cause, in Paris, Florence, and Amsterdam—people who would betray them at the earliest opportunity. They had become much too sure of themselves. Here was the proof. By communicating Annas's minutes, the Brotherhood was doing a lot more than challenging the Papacy. It was showing its strength, convinced that it had gained its first victory. But it was the Church that would win the war against the Jews and the humanists. Louis XI and the Medicis would sing a different tune when they saw their allies sentenced to burn at the stake.

Paul II thanked the Lord for having entrusted the defense of the faith to him and for having at last restored Christ's last words to whom they most concerned. He would show himself equal to the task. He summoned his secretary and immediately dictated his instructions to the Inquisition, ordering a hardening of the censorship with regard to heretics and the suppression of the Jews, wherever they were, followed by an appeal to the Catholic kings to support him in his struggle against all these abominable attacks from the enemies of God. All his doubts were gone. He knew now that he had been chosen by Providence to protect the Savior's message from the folly of men. They were not yet ready to receive so much light. He, Paul II, would be their guide. The Vatican would now keep the truth in its cellars, under seal, until the day of Revelation.

If the infidels in Palestine had not grasped the deep meaning of the Nazarene's words, it was because they had not read them as believers, as followers. Annas had been mistaken. Christ had not blasphemed. God did indeed bleed with the blood of man and weep with his tears. "He dies," as Jesus had said so eloquently, in spite of the high priest's outraged protests. Those who rejected this teaching of Our Lord were therefore denying the suffering of God. Well, they would now have to be taught that suffering.

52

I see neither title nor signature."

"Nevertheless, this is the manuscript of the *Testament*."

"A worthless testament, basically."

"Worthless?"

"Villon isn't dead, as far as I know!"

Fust refrained from responding. He himself had no idea what had become of the poet. Chartier gave back the bundle of pages. He was firmly opposed to the publication of Master François's ballads. There were already enough copies in circulation. Sadly, Fust put the collection back in a drawer.

The two men bent over the desk laden with books. Chartier was quite inflexible. He quickly sorted through the volumes, rejecting most of the works proposed. Not that Fust was intimidated by the bishop's threatening looks. After all, Louis XI, satisfied with the first editions produced in Paris, continued to protect the printers. He was even sponsoring two faculties devoted to humanistic studies, one in Valencia, the other in Bourges, since the Sorbonne was still firmly opposed to accommodating such centers of intellectual debauchery. It was hardly surprising that Chartier was in such bad humor. He knew that many university scholars visited the booksellers in secret. So it hardly mattered if he allowed or banned this or that publication. It would get to them one way or another anyway. Guillaume Chartier remembered having shown Villon a truncated edition of Plato's *Republic*, badly bound, full of mistakes, which was then being sold clandestinely. Right there in his cell, two steps from the gallows, Villon had immediately grasped the significance of such a text. As it happened, the king had become so enamored of the idea of *res publica*, or "commonwealth," that he was trying to take it up on his own account. It was for him that Marsilio Ficino had just translated into French Nicolas of Cusa's notes putting forward the principle of a government "by the people and for the people." Louis XI was so delighted, he had asserted that he had found the recent works submitted by the book hunters for the approval of the crown "truly fine." Ever since he had said that, courtiers and scholars alike had started talking about "fine writing" and "fine arts." Curiously, nobody ever spoke of "fine science."

As the bishop pushed the rejected volumes—treatises by Lucretius, Neapolitan madrigals, maps of the heavenly vault, amorous tales—to the end of the table, Fust meekly piled them willy-nilly at the bottom of a crate.

When Guillaume Chartier finally left, Fust collapsed on his chair. He opened the drawer of his desk, took out Villon's *Testament*, and read a few lines at random. Whores and noble ladies, bandits and notaries, lords and laborers, some touching, some grotesque, paraded through the stanzas, all more concerned with love and good food than with knowing if the earth was flat, round or quadrangular.

For Villon was not only the herald of a new age. He was the pallbearer of this one. He drew a tender line under an era that was dying. But he refused to die with it. He had vanished, leaving priests and men-at-arms, ambitious kings and corrupt bishops in the lurch, bequeathing his legend, his melody, to whoever might want it. To the men of tomorrow, he had addressed no fine speech or proclamation, just a gentle wink.

53

The rain rattled deafeningly on the slate roof and the shutters banged. The howling of the north wind was trying to get in through the chimney, but by the time it reached the hearth, choked by the smoke and the soot, it emitted only a dull moan. Tuscan peasants in rags and Florentine burghers wrapped in their cloaks sat huddled on the benches. An icy cold lashed their cheeks whenever the door of the inn burst open. The candles flickered, threatening to go out. A tall strapping man appeared in the doorway. He was so big, and made all the bigger by his thick leather cape, that he took up the whole doorframe, barring the wind from entering. He peered into the gloom, looking the drinkers up and down, as if he were searching for someone. The innkeeper was about to reprimand him, but changed his mind when the brute turned toward him. His grimacing smile, lost amid the cuts and scars that crisscrossed his face, had all the seduction of an open wound. So it was with a keen sense of relief that the innkeeper saw the rogue at last close the door and go straight to the far end of the room.

A hooded monk was sitting in a corner, holding a bowl of hot cider in his cracked hands to warm them. He did not move when the giant shadow of the man in the cape loomed on the wall.

"Brother Benoît?"

The monk nodded.

The ogre immediately sat down and poured himself a drink. "What news do you bring from Galilee?"

The monk's only response was to raise his bowl, take a decent swig of cider, then wipe his lips with his sleeve. The hood left the features of his face obscured. Only his chin protruded. His lips, though, could vaguely be made out in the red glow from the hearth. They were slightly twisted, the corners lifted toward the cheeks in a disconcerting grin. "Hello, Colin," he said at last.

Colin lost his balance, his bench fell backwards, and he ended up lying full-length on the filthy flagstones of the tavern, much to the amusement of the customers. Colin stood up again, groaning, ready to strike those who were mocking him, but then he merely threw them a scornful glance, turned his back on them, threw himself on François, and gave him an almighty hug. The audience looked on speechless, unable to decide if the monster was going to devour the prey he was crushing in his arms or if the monk would brandish his wooden cross and repulse this attack with a quick "*Vade retro, Satanas!*"

Colin at last relaxed his embrace and quietly sat down again, his cheeks red with emotion. Disappointed, the gallery lost all interest. The two men decided nevertheless to speak in low voices, leaning toward each other across the table.

"You're looking well for a priest," Colin said

"The book hunters have taken good care of me."

François was amused to see the lines of bewilderment that furrowed his old companion's brow. Whenever Colin thought hard about something, his features became twisted and his veins stood out, as if he were lifting a tree trunk.

"You made yourself the accomplice of those unbelievers!"

"To each his own treachery . . ."

"That's rich, coming from you!" Colin replied, offended. After his convoy had been ambushed and he had escaped by a miracle, he had hurried to Italy to inform Federico and claim the payment that was due to him. In order not to die of starvation, he had committed a few thefts on the way, and had been caught by the constabulary not far from Parma. It was to save his skin that he had denounced the bookseller. He had merely paid the Florentine back in his own coin.

"Whereas you set about getting him released. And at what a price! By selling off the words of our Lord Christ!"

François shrugged. He knocked back what remained in his tankard, avoiding his friend's angry glare. After a moment, he even seemed to forget his presence, and sat lost in thought, gazing at the reflections of the fire dancing on the wall. Outraged, Colin grunted and stood up, throwing a couple of coins on the table for his cider. François held him back by his sleeve. He held out his bag, the flap open.

Colin, still standing, took the bag and felt the weight of it. There were no crowns or ingots in it. He fingered the outside of it with an expert hand—the hand of an experienced brigand.

He distrusted François's tricks. Head thrown back, holding the thing at arm's length, he gently moved the canvas sides apart. All he could see was a package rolled up into a ball. Making up his mind, he took the package out, turned it in every direction, then peeled it like an onion, throwing off one by one the crumpled scraps that surrounded it. All he found in it was a hunk of dry bread. Annoyed, he abruptly thrust his hand back into the bag, touched the rough bottom with his fingernails, even looked for a secret pocket, while François bent down to pick up the fragments that had fallen to the floor. Suddenly he brandished a whole bundle of them.

"These are the words of Jesus."

The dim lighting in the tavern made the pages look even more pitiful. The faded ink and soiled parchment gave them an ashen hue. The letters were barely visible amid the folds in the hide and the patches of mold. There were no illuminations, not even any margins, just spidery scribbles covering almost the whole page. Colin wondered if François was making fun of him That would have been sacrilege.

"The Pope doesn't have the Savior's last wishes in his palace. What he has is quite another testament."

"The testament of a thief like you?"

"Who better to recount the concerns of a man condemned to death?"

"And of a saint?"

François proceeded to tell how Colin how he had spent time in the desert, how he had slowly been initiated, how he had familiarized himself with the scriptures of Qumran, and how he had produced parodies and imitations, corrected by Gamliel and translated by Eviatar. Nobody had suspected how opportune these pranks and stylistic exercises would prove to be—not even François, who had only agreed to take part in the game while waiting for an opportunity to play the winning hand and escape the clutches of the Brotherhood.

"Yes, it was necessary to get out of a tight spot. But not like you."

"How, then?"

"By fooling everyone."

Colin looked at the shriveled pieces of parchment. He wondered why the Lord had been unable to escape punishment while the criminal opposite him claimed to have successfully led Rome, Jerusalem, and even Satan by the nose. The answer no doubt lay in those yellowed pages, thrown willy-nilly on the table of the inn. There they were, between two wretched thieves, just like Jesus on his cross.

"What does Christ say?"

"I have no idea. I can't read Aramaic."

That took Colin's breath away. François hadn't even read the testament of Jesus. He had simply composed his own pastiche of it. Colin scratched his beard. François surely couldn't have concocted, all by himself, an imitation that could fool the doctors of the faith so totally. To commit such an act of treachery, he would have needed the help of a mentor versed in the Holy Scriptures, assisted by a translator capable of putting his Parisian troubadour's language into old Aramaic, as well as a skilful copyist, not to mention skillful forgers able to imitate the right ink, and so on. In other words, a whole team of pen pushers and Bible punchers!

François let Colin ponder like this for a while before deigning to enlighten him. "Do you remember Brother Paul?"

Colin nodded. François explained to him how, as soon as he returned to the monastery, he had persuaded the prior to help him save Jesus's confession from the hands of the inquisitors. But also from the book hunters. He had presented him with quite another testament, the *Ballad of a crucified man,* which he had composed in secret in the desert. Paul, who had read and studied Annas's minutes, had suggested a few changes and corrections to François, and then Brother Médard and his monks had immediately set to work. François had delayed his departure for Acre by pretending to be sick. For three days, Aisha had made him teas from wild flowers that induced fever. She had believed that François was using this subterfuge to stay with her a while longer. François had asked that she be allowed to come on the journey, disguised as a gypsy, but Gamliel had been firmly opposed to the idea. It was only once he was at sea that he learned the real reason for this refusal. The pregnant Aisha had feared that François did not want a child. She had not even seen fit to tell him the news. What if, once he had regained his freedom, François decided never to return to the Holy Land?

"That girl really has brought you nothing but bad luck. And now she's burdening you with a bastard."

It was a slap in the face, but François refrained from responding. Colin was a lout, who knew nothing of the affairs of the heart. So how could he understand that it was "that girl" who had set him on the path he was currently following? Preserving the words of Jesus Christ was of no interest to her, she had made that quite clear. She was a Berber. On the other hand, she had seen it as a way for François to save his own soul. And his own *Testament*. For it wasn't so much the Nazarene's words that mattered, it was the poetry that emanated from them, the emotion they inspired over and above the words themselves. And it was the same with Villon's song. It was the sound of both these singular voices that had to be preserved at all costs because they were the song of mankind.

Aisha had nurtured François with her silences, her caresses, never burdening him with idle chatter, in the same way as she respected the breath of the wind. François, though, had owed it to himself to act in a more decisive manner, armed with his pen and his incorrigible nerve, but not only that. He had first of all to walk in the footsteps of Christ, from Galilee to the desert, from Nazareth to Jerusalem. Constructing his own legend as he went, just as Jesus, that other rebel, that other dreamer, had done from village to village. As a woman, Aisha had foreseen "all these things," and had simply wanted to be there, by François's side, just as Mary Magdalen had wanted to be with Jesus in his ordeal. She would never have forgiven herself for standing in his way, robbing him of his destiny.

Colin, who did not care about his own destiny, or that of his fellow men, did not give a hoot for whatever fate had in store for him. He was as fatalistic as a mule pulling a plow. So what was the point of bothering him with these explanations? On the other hand, he could appreciate a good trick. So François told him how, having arrived in Florence, he had switched the manuscripts, under the noses of Gamliel's spy Eviatar and of old Marsilio Ficino, who had been eager to free his friend Federico as soon as possible.

Colin found it hard to believe that François could have fooled the Brotherhood so easily. There was nothing to prove that these pages were not just as fake as the pastiche he had composed with such ardor. François had not even taken the trouble to read them, or to verify their authenticity.

Had he pretended to believe the words of Brother Paul and Gamliel? Why would he have lent himself to such a game? And what about Ficino and the Papal experts? Had they all played this same game at the expense of the Savior?

François, in no way troubled by such doubts, stroked the pieces of parchment with a veneration that disconcerted Colin.

"I have no idea what the Lord recorded here. Whether these scraps really contain what Christ said or not, I have vowed that His word will never again be distorted by zealots, whether they are Catholics, Jews, or Saracens. Nor will they ever usurp His name for their own ends."

Colin grimaced, but François was enjoying himself.

"The Vatican has calculated things with a discernment that does it honor. Now the Pope won't get any nasty surprises concerning the content of Christ's last words. By placing its seal on my pastiche, the Church has protected itself wonderfully. Any other version that its enemies would try to make public will immediately be taken for dubious. Including the real one."

"Which is still kept by the book hunters!"

"Or else by me, at the bottom of this bag. You see, it would have been in Jerusalem's interest to have the Pope read it. Most of what Jesus says in it was either censored or even dictated by Annas to exonerate the Jews in the eyes of Rome. But if the Brotherhood gave me a fake after all, or a version that had been cut to serve its purposes, it must now be keeping the existence of the original secret."

Colin was still not convinced. He gave the bag back to François. "Real or fake, Jerusalem must surely have a copy."

"Yes. But, real or fake, it couldn't use this text twice."

"Except to discredit yours."

"But mine suits everyone better than the truth."

François and Colin both laughed out loud. They poured themselves more cider and drank each other's health, just as they had in another tavern, in Lyon, not so long ago.

"Nobody will dare admit such an outrage . . . "

"After all Christ can't contradict himself . . . "

"Nor can eminent popes and wise rabbis get things so wrong . . . "

"Especially not Chartier, who commissioned you." Colin's face clouded over and he thought for a moment. "You're just as caught as they are, François. You'll never be able to give the game away . . . "

"They know that perfectly well. That's why I'm sure these are the genuine minutes."

"In that case, the Jews have played a nasty trick on you. It won't be them the Pope's men will be hunting down, it'll be you."

"And all Christians who take Jesus at his word and challenge dogma."

Colin put down his tankard. He looked at his companion with a suddenly severe air, pointing at the canvas bag lying on the bench. He now saw the old pieces of parchment in a new light. With reverence.

"What are you going to do with them?"

54

The doctor put his black felt hat back on. The cone was so long and pointed that it almost touched the branches of the chandeliers. Sprawling on the divan in the library, Lorenzo half expected to see that witch's hat rip the cobwebs hanging from the crystal pendants or even touch the candles and catch fire. Heedless of the danger, and full of his own knowledge, the doctor assumed a self-important air and began pouring out an interminable flood of obscure terms, in Latin and sometimes in Greek, which did not augur well. He aimed his verdict at the rows of books, as if they were a circle of scholarly colleagues. It was only when the young aristocrat, sated with medical jargon, untied his purse irritably that the doctor at last consented to speak clearly. The patient presented many scars, bruises, and bumps as well as being alarmingly thin. A good meal, preferably a leg of lamb, would be sure to perk him up. And bleeding him would free him of the bilious humors from which people who had been subjected to torture usually suffered. Reassured, Lorenzo clicked his fingers. A footman immediately escorted the quack to the doors of the palace.

A young monk, invisible until then, emerged from an alcove adorned with the bust of Cosimo that separated the shelves of old books, Roman or Hellenic, from the modern ones, Italian or French. He asked permission to pay the convalescent a visit. Lorenzo consented with a magnanimous gesture of the arm. The novice hurried upstairs.

As soon as the monk entered the room, Federico threw back the sheets covering him. He managed to sit up, support-ing himself on the eiderdowns, fearing that the monk was about to administer the extreme unction of the Gentiles. But Eviatar immediately threw back his hood and addressed him in Hebrew. The young man was unaware that the survivor of the Vatican jails was his commander in chief. All he knew was that this man was a Jew just like him, as the Essene shepherd in Qumran had revealed. Relieved, Federico invited his visitor to sit down at the foot of the bed. Eviatar, shocked by the book-seller's pitiful state, did not dare ply him with questions. It was the patient who took the initiative, with a strangely amused smile. He easily guessed the identity of this tall, thin, pale-faced youth so poorly disguised as a monk.

"And what of your friend Villon? How is he?"

Federico clearly did not expect a reply. He even claimed to know where Master François was at this moment. Not far from here, in a low tavern in the poor part of town, with Colin.

It was the Brotherhood that had insisted on that impromptu reunion. It had only been necessary to announce to Colin, who had been hiding in the court of miracles in Aix, that a monk by the name of Benoît was waiting for him there with news from Galilee and an urgent message from Villon for Louis XI.

A simple written report by Fust on the success of the oper-ation would not content the king. Colin would be a more con-vincing witness. He would have seen the precious document with his own eyes, and would also know that François was alive and well. As the bearer of such good tidings, Colin would has-ten to get back to Paris where the announcement of such a glo-rious feat would ensure him a fine reward.

All of this duly impressed Eviatar. But what glorious feat was the bookseller referring to?

"You failed in your mission, Eviatar."

The young man gave a start. How did the bookseller know

his name? Ignoring Eviatar's surprise, Federico revealed the
trick François had played. It was Ficino who had realized the
dodge and informed the Medicis. François had given him a
document that was in far too good a condition, one he must
have reworked in haste. It had then occurred to Ficino that the
Brotherhood, not wanting to let go of Annas's minutes, was
counting on him to refine the forgery that Brother Benoît and
Brother Martin were bringing from Galilee. He was right:
Jerusalem had been perfectly well aware that Master Villon
would steal the original and replace it with a pastiche of his
own. At the monastery, Gamliel had let him go ahead, ordering Brother Paul to participate.

The venerable rabbi had doubted the legitimacy of the
negotiations that had been set in motion to bring Villon to the
Holy Land. He was now forced to admit how clear-sighted his
superior had been. As soon as he had learned of the existence
of this poet of the suburbs, "neither completely mad, not completely wise," then read the manuscript of his ballads brought
from Paris by a zealous book hunter, the head of the
Brotherhood had sensed the undeniable asset this inveterate
rebel would mean sooner or later for the success of the operation.

Many relevant texts had been gathered, those of the Roman
orators for the Medicis, those of the Sophists of Athens for the
guidance of King Louis, but they were merely the gunpowder.
What had still been lacking was the spark that would set it
alight. All these fine texts had been holding themselves in
readiness to enter the arena against dogma. The printers
deployed on the ground had simply been waiting for a signal
to step up to the firing line. It was Villon who had given this
signal. It was he who found, between two glasses of wine or
marc, the watchwords, the right tone, the emotions that would
set in motion that awakening of souls on which the
Brotherhood was counting to go into action. That was what

Cato and Virgil, Lucretius and Demosthenes had lacked, a living language that roused burghers and monarchs, solid citizens and students alike. It had only remained for the Brotherhood to season that talent with a sharper spice and a few reliable herbs—Palestine, the desert, a woman of the dunes—and let it simmer.

Eviatar was surprised by the expertise displayed by the bookseller. And by his self-assurance. The dapper Florentine he had embodied had completely disappeared, as if flown away. This bedridden man, stripped of his extravagant attire, his body covered in wounds and blisters, was nevertheless just as radiant as the Federico of the old days. But in another way. Firmer, more imposing. So much so that Eviatar hesitated to pursue the conversation without being given permission. There was one last question, though, that he was itching to ask. How was it that Villon could move about freely with his bag over his shoulder and the precious manuscript rolled up with his linen and his traveling things?

As if he had read his thoughts, the convalescent leaned toward him. Coughing, squeezed between pillows, he informed him that the Brotherhood had unfortunately never possessed the original of Annas's minutes. The high priest had hidden that in one of the seven branches of the sacred candelabra, the menorah, which Titus had carried to Rome in triumph after the destruction of the Temple.

What Villon was carrying in his bag was merely the hasty transcript of a scribe, censored by the rabbis of the Sanhedrin and intended to persuade Pontius Pilate to spare the Jewish community the reprisals with which he had threatened it. But however truncated, they were the words of Jesus Christ.

Only Villon could reconstruct the message of the Savior that so many had sought to distort. An agitator and visionary like the Nazarene, he had been able to hear the very voice that everyone wanted to stifle. He had perceived the suffering that voice expressed on behalf of all men. He had felt it in his guts. Not as a believer, nor as a scholar, but as a poet and a brother.

"Villon will return to the Holy Land. You can be sure of that. You will stay here to assist me."

Eviatar was surprised by the confidence with which this was said. Wasn't Villon unpredictable? He could just as easily set off for Paris with Colin. Or at least flee somewhere other than Palestine.

All Federico said was, "He left his tricorn there."

55

The rain had stopped just before dawn. Colin and François had slept on benches, nursing their ciders. Helped by the stable boys, the innkeeper threw them out, threatening to summon the constabulary. He only refrained out of respect for François's habit.

Still half asleep, Colin could barely grumble. His head and guts hurt too much. François, who felt more cheerful, warmed his limbs in the first rays of the sun. It was a glorious day. The cobbles smelled good, freshly washed by the shower and brushed by the wind. The road, dotted with puddles, stretched between the last hovels that clung to the walls of the city. Colin, who hated farewells, strode northward, toward the duchy of Milan, and then France. Let the damned poet go wherever he liked, he'd brought him enough bad luck!

His footprints were already fading in the mud.

The fair had been set up on the banks of the Arno, near an old bridge. Men and animals waded through the sludge. Squares of straw marked the positions of the booths. An old priest was blessing customers for a duck's leg or a sausage, stuffing his alms in a bag sewed from a rough ecclesiastical badge. Near the stage where the traveling acrobats would perform, a book peddler was arranging his meager merchandise on a wooden tray hung around his neck by two leather straps. On one side of the tray, the shop. Two or three soiled missals, a pious engraving, a few ex-votos with blessings for the home, for good health, for mercy, to be hung on the door or over the stove. On the other side, the office. The paraphernalia of a public letter-writer, consisting of a box of pens, a salt cellar to dry the ink, and a few sheets of vellum. The man was young but looked as if he knew his business. He first solicited a local dignitary and sold him the engraving for a good price. In between writing a request from a tenant farmer to his lord and a will for a bankrupt cloth merchant, he disposed of his ex-votos to passing women, hailing only the fattest, or the oldest, with honeyed words and sly smiles. He praised the exceptional calligraphy of one of his missals to a pork butcher who couldn't even read. With a discreet sign of the finger, he called over an onlooker who had been observing him disdainfully and, almost in secret, took out a small bound volume he never showed anyone. Grumbling about how hard times were, almost weeping, he sold it off cheaply to this great connoisseur.

François waited patiently for the young man to fill his coffers. He watched him pocket his earnings, one by one, and tried to calculate how much they came to. It wasn't until the end of the day that he approached, greeted him amiably in polished schoolboy Latin, and handed him a manuscript filled with crossings-out. The young man looked through the text, in a detached way at first, then appearing more intrigued. From time to time, his face lit up with delight at a good rhyme, a clever turn of phrase. The story was amusing, and the title as convoluted as you could wish: *In which is recounted the ill fortune of Master François, born of the many difficulties he had with Mother Justice, the Holy Father, and good King Louis, as well as with priests, rabbis, Moors and Mongols, all put into rondeaus according to the taste of Paris and dedicated to the gentle Jesus, who truly saved him.*

With a friendly smile, the merchant handed back the manuscript and began to pack up, ready to leave.

François caught him by the sleeve. "I'd like a little for it. Just enough to get to the nearest port."

The peddler rubbed his chin. The takings had been good today. You had to eat, though, find lodgings, buy paper and ink. There wasn't much left after that. True, the text hadn't been lacking in quality. But he could only resell it to a merchant from the rich part of town or an informed connoisseur. He suggested a sum at random. François frowned and made a timid counter-offer. The peddler scoffed. That was far too much. He was ready to make a bit of an effort, but no more than that. This expense was totally unplanned. He wasn't even sure he could make a profit on it. At least not in the short term. He took out a handful of coins, counted quickly, put part back in his pocket, and showed the rest in the palm of his hand. François accepted, with a contrite air, but then tried to extort a few more pennies. He'd had enough of wearing this moth-eaten habit. He needed fresh clothes. Or rather, a new disguise.

"I also have this."

François searched in his bag and took out a bundle of shriv-eled pages. The peddler inspected the parchment with an expert eye. The surface was dry and covered in illegible scrib-bles. If you scraped it well and then dipped it in oil, it might regain its texture. The material was thick enough. Cut up and stuck to wooden boards, it would make an excellent leather for binding. The scraps could be used as straps to tie around the covers to keep the book straight and properly closed. But in the state it was in, it wasn't worth more than half a sou. François hurriedly pocketed the coin, as if the peddler had paid him in gold crowns. The young man threw his purchase into his sack, along with the old papers and pots of ink. François watched him until he disappeared in the distance, taking with him the last wishes of Christ. The testament of Jesus was in good hands. The peddler was as much the heir to it as anybody. The Savior didn't need a certificate from a notary. Beyond all words, wasn't it from His legend that all men drew their own?

François touched the coin in his pocket. Half a sou. It wasn't much and it was a lot, to save the Word. And give it back its freedom.

Just before nightfall, François went into a secondhand clothes shop and chose some new garments. As he walked up and down the shop in the gathering dark, he noticed a crate full of old canes and blunt sticks near the door. He rummaged through it blindly and took out a long rough club. He handed his half a sou to the shopkeeper, who did not even thank him.

Outside, it had started raining again. François gazed up for a moment at the few stars visible through the drizzle, then, with his bag secured over his shoulder, set off along the road that led to the sea.

Note

Villon's ballads were printed for the first time in 1489 by Pierre Levet, Paris, under the title *Le Grand Testament Villon et le Petit*. This edition is unfortunately incomplete, as are all subsequent ones. Villon's manuscript has never been found.

About the Author

Raphaël Jerusalmy was born in Mont-martre, France in 1954. After receiving diplomas from the Ecole Normale Supérieure and the Sorbonne, he worked with Israeli military intelligence. He currently sells antique books in Tel Aviv.